'You can be too ~~honest~~ for your own good, Emm~~a.~~'

'That is a ridiculous st~~atement.~~'

'Ridiculous, is it?' Lytham frowned. 'Or have I mistaken your intentions? Can it be that you approve of Mrs Flynn's behaviour? That you see nothing wrong in her becoming that man's mistress? Perhaps you hope that one of his dubious friends will show an interest in you?'

'How dare you?' Emma lost her temper. 'Please leave. I do not think we have anything further to say to one another.'

'Do you not?' Lytham towered above her, anger sparking out of him, driven beyond reason by her apparent calm. 'Then let me tell you this, Emma. I am perfectly willing to offer you *carte blanche*, and I am far richer than Lindisfarne or any of his cronies. Think carefully before you make your choice.'

Anne Herries lives in Cambridge but spends part of the winter in Spain, where she and her husband stay in a pretty resort nestled amid the hills that run from Malaga to Gibraltar. Gazing over a sparkling blue ocean, watching the sunbeams dance like silver confetti on the restless waves, Anne loves to dream up her stories of laughter, tears and romantic lovers.

Recent titles by the same author:

THE ABDUCTED BRIDE
CAPTIVE OF THE HAREM
THE SHEIKH

and in the Regency series
The Steepwood Scandal:

LORD RAVENSDEN'S MARRIAGE
COUNTERFEIT EARL

A DAMNABLE ROGUE

Anne Herries

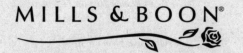

First published in Great Britain 2003
Harlequin Mills & Boon Limited,
Eton House, 18-24 Paradise Road, Richmond, Surrey TW9 1SR

© Anne Herries 2003

ISBN 0 263 83945 1

Set in Times Roman 10½ on 11¾ pt.
04-0104-86681

Printed and bound in Spain
by Litografia Rosés S.A., Barcelona

A DAMNABLE ROGUE

Chapter One

'I cannot tell you how sorry I was…' Sir William Heathstone looked at the young woman standing so silently before him. In truth she was not so very young, being less than two months from her twenty-seventh birthday and therefore unlikely to marry. In the light of events this past year, she had a bleak future before her. 'As you know, Emma, your father was my lifelong friend…'

His tone and sympathetic expression made Emma's eyes smart with tears. The shocking manner of her father's tragic death had stunned her, and her mother's near collapse on hearing the dreadful news had given her no chance to grieve. For the past eleven months she had devoted herself to the care of her mother and the estate, which left little time for thinking about her own life.

Nor was there time for tears now. The future must be decided before Sir William and Lady Heathstone left for their long winter holiday in the warmer climes of Italy.

'It is because of that friendship and your kindness that I have dared to ask so much,' Emma Sommerton replied with quiet dignity. 'If Mama is forced to spend the winter alone at the house I think she may sink into a decline and die.'

Her clear eyes were deeply expressive, carrying as they did
a look of appeal, which touched the older man's heart.

'If it had not been for that damnable rogue!' he exclaimed with a flash of temper. 'He led Sir Thomas into a
trap, my dear…taunted him the way he does all his victims,
from what I've been told.'

'I have heard that the Marquis of Lytham is scrupulous
in matters of play,' Emma said, managing to control the
rage she felt inside against the man who had ruined all their
lives. 'Papa's lawyers assure me that he was warned not to
put up his whole estate to the marquis that night, but ignored all advice. And the marquis has been considerate in
the matter of claiming his rights, you know. His lawyers
assured us that we must continue here as if nothing had
happened and that he would not trouble us until our year
of mourning had passed. He has been as good as his word,
for we have heard nothing from him. We were told we
might apply to the lawyers if we needed anything, but of
course we have not. Mama has her own small income and
we have managed on that.'

'Oh, I am not saying there was any question of anything
underhand,' Sir William said frowning. 'Just that Lytham
managed to get underneath your father's skin, driving him
to do something that I am convinced he would not otherwise—'

'Please, sir,' Emma said, blinking hard against the sting
of tears. 'It does no good to speak of these things. Papa
was foolish to gamble, but he chose to do so that night
with…' she choked back a sob '…disastrous consequences.'

'I never realised Thomas was so desperate,' Sir William
said, looking distressed. 'He must have known I would
have helped him.'

'I dare say he was too proud to ask,' Emma replied.

'Besides, it seems there was nothing of any consequence left.' She lifted her head proudly. She was not pretty by the standards of the day, her thick hair dark brown and drawn back in a sleek style that made her look older than her years, but her eyes were extremely fine, a wide clear grey, and her mouth was attractive, especially when she smiled. 'Which brings me to my request. Will Lady Heathstone take Mama with her to Italy? I know it is a great deal to ask…'

'Stuff and nonsense!' Sir William said stoutly. 'It was our intention to ask you both to come and live with us when Lytham takes over the estate. Your mama and Lady Heathstone have always dealt well together, and we shall all put our heads together in the matter of your future, my dear.'

'I thank you for your kindness,' Emma said and smiled. It was a smile of rare sweetness and made Sir William catch his breath for a moment. Had his own sons not already been married he would have welcomed Emma as a daughter-in-law, for she would surely make some worthy gentleman a good wife. He knew of one or two widowers who were comfortable enough with regards to money, and he might see what could be done to help the gel towards a suitable match. 'But all I ask is that Mama shall be taken out of herself this winter. As for myself…' She drew a deep breath. 'I have found myself a position as a companion.'

'A companion? No!' Sir William was outraged. 'You a companion—that is impossible, my dear. Most unsuitable, Emma. I am sure your mama would never allow it.'

'I am afraid poor Mama has no choice but to allow it,' Emma replied. 'As you know, Papa quarrelled with his family some years ago, and Mama has none living. There is no one to whom we could apply for help other than you, Sir William—and although I am grateful for your offer of a home, I believe it would not be right. I am young and perfectly capable of earning my living, and as long as I know that Mama is well…'

'I must beg you to reconsider.'

Emma shook her head as she saw the anxious look he gave her. 'I assure you I shall be quite content, sir—which I should not be if I were a burden on you and dear Lady Heathstone. Not that you would consider me such, I know that, but—'

'It would not sit comfortably with your pride?' Sir William was thoughtful. Emma Sommerton was a woman of independent spirit, and perhaps it was as well for her to be allowed a little freedom for once in her life. She had not taken in her season for some reason, and after that her mother's delicate health had kept Emma tied to her apron strings. Perhaps it would be a good thing for Lady Sommerton to learn to do without her daughter, and it might give Emma a chance to live her own life. Who knew what might happen then? Emma was not pretty, but there was something attractive about her. It might be that she would catch the attention of some worthy gentleman, a man in his later years perhaps who would appreciate her qualities. 'Then I shall not interfere with your plans, my dear—but you will give me your promise that, if you are ever in need of help, you will come to me?'

'Who else would I turn to?' Emma said and took the hand he offered her. 'You have always been as a kind uncle to me, sir—and Lady Heathstone is a good friend to Mama. I shall be able to leave her with a quiet mind now.'

'Then you must do as you wish, Emma. When do you take up your position?'

'At the beginning of next month,' Emma replied. 'I shall then be almost at the end of my mourning and can go into company without fear of giving offence. The position is with a lady who has recently come from Ireland. Her name is Mrs Bridget Flynn and she is a widow.'

When Emma had spoken of becoming a companion, Sir William had imagined it would be to a lady of quality, and to discover that she was planning to work for an Irish woman of no particular family shocked him.

'But you cannot!' he exclaimed. 'She sounds… common.'

'I know her to be extremely wealthy,' Emma said, a little amused by his expression. 'Her husband was a distant cousin of the Earl of Lindisfarne, and a favourite with the earl apparently. She herself comes from a good family, though gentry, not aristocracy, and the earl is sponsoring her in society.'

'Lindisfarne? I have heard the name, though I know nothing of the man. This all sounds a little dubious.' Sir William was still doubtful, his heavy brows lowered as he looked at her for some minutes. He was a worthy man of broad stature, and kind, though perhaps not the most imaginative of fellows. 'Are you perfectly sure this is what you want to do, Emma?'

'Yes, perfectly,' Emma replied, crossing her fingers behind her back. She had not told her generous friend the whole story and hoped he would not learn of the true nature of Mrs Flynn's relationship with the earl. 'I—I knew Bridget a little when I was younger. We attended Mrs Ratcliffe's school together. Bridget's parents were in India, her father was a colonel in the British army, and she was left at the school for a year before she went out to join them. I think that was where she met her husband, who was a major before he was killed.'

'And she returned to Ireland after her husband was killed.' Sir William nodded. One of his own sons had served with Wellesley in India some years previously, and a widow of a British major naturally assumed more respectability in his eyes. 'She is to spend some time in London? And she will be sponsored by Lindisfarne?'

'Yes.' Emma crossed her fingers once more. 'Bridget is a year younger than I am, sir. I believe the earl hopes that she will find happiness again.'

'Yes, she is young to be a widow,' Sir William agreed. He was not sure why he felt that Emma was not telling him the whole truth, for he could not see why she should lie to him. However, at the age of six and twenty she was at liberty to do whatsoever she pleased with her own life, and, since he was not her legal guardian, he could not gainsay her. 'Then I shall not question you further, for you have made up your mind on this. Yet I ask you to remember your promise to come to me if you are ever in trouble.'

'You have been kindness itself, sir.'

'Then I shall take my leave of you,' he replied and held out his hand. She gave him hers and he pressed it warmly. 'We shall call for your mother on Monday next—and you leave a few days later for London. Will you be comfortable here alone for that time, Emma?'

'I shall not be alone,' Emma replied. 'I have received instructions from the marquis's lawyers that all the servants are to be retained, and that I am to await his coming at the beginning of next month.' A flash of temper showed in her eyes. 'When he will presumably wish to be shown whatever treasures the house contains. I am afraid he will be sadly disappointed. Papa had sold off most of the silver and pictures before he threw away the estate.'

'So you will have Mrs Monty with you—that will be a comfort to you, Emma.'

'And Nanny—at least until I leave here,' Emma said. 'Poor Nanny has talked of retiring to live with her brother for years, and at long last she may do so. I shall be sad to see her leave, but pleased that she will not have the trouble of looking after us in future.'

Sir William thought privately that in recent years it was Emma who had cared devotedly for Nanny as well as her mother, rather than the other way around.

'Well, I must wish you happiness, my dear. And now I must go.'

Emma went to the door with him, pausing as he climbed into his carriage and was driven away, then sighed as she turned back to the house. That was her first hurdle over, now for Mama…

Her expression was determined as she went upstairs to her mother's boudoir, for she knew that Lady Sommerton would resist being sent off to Italy with her kind friends. She had been insisting on staying to meet the marquis, and was prepared to throw herself on his mercy in the hope of retaining her own home. Emma, however, was not. Nor was she willing to allow her mama to debase herself to that…that monster!

What had Sir William called him? Ah, yes—a damnable rogue! Indeed, he must have been a rogue to provoke Sir Thomas to gamble away his entire estate. Not that there had been so very much to gamble, Emma admitted privately, for she better than most knew that her dearest papa had been worried to death about various debts. He had, she knew, been contemplating the sale of yet another stretch of land by the river, and it would have gone on that way until they had nothing left.

Why must men throw their fortunes away at the gaming tables? It was a mystery to Emma, and although she did not entirely blame her father's gambling for their troubles—there had also been unwise investments—she believed it was a curse.

She put her distressing thoughts away, smiling as she

went into her mother's room to find her lying on a daybed, a kerchief soaked in lavender pressed to her forehead.

'Are you feeling any better, dearest?'

'A little.' Lady Sommerton raised her head. 'I am sorry to be such a trouble to you.'

'You could never be that, Mama,' Emma said and meant it sincerely. Her decision to give up all thought of marriage to look after her mother had not been entirely the fault of a disappointment in love. She had been happy at home with her parents, despite their faults, of which she was perfectly aware, and she had long ago made up her mind that she would never make a marriage of convenience. 'I have some wonderful news for you, dearest. Sir William was just here. He and Lady Heathstone have begged for the favour of your company on their travels this year.'

'No...no, I could not possibly leave,' Lady Sommerton replied. 'I must be here to greet the Marquis of Lytham when he arrives. Besides, there is Tom. Supposing he should come home?'

'That is unlikely, Mama,' Emma said. 'If Tom had wanted to come home he might have done so at any time these past months. He must surely have heard of Papa's accident.'

'My poor boy is dead,' Lady Sommerton declared dramatically, pressing a hand to her breast. 'I know that he would have come to me if he could.'

Emma wondered if that might be the case. Her brother had disappeared three years earlier after a terrible row with his father and they had not heard from him since. Like his father before him, he had a temper when roused. It was quite possible that he had done something foolish, which had resulted in his death.

'I am sure that is not the case,' she told her mother, despite her own fears. 'Please do not distress yourself, dearest. It may be that Tom has gone abroad to take service in the army. You know he always wanted to be an officer.'

'If his father had only bought him his commission,' Lady Sommerton said with a sigh as a tear rolled down one cheek. 'But he would not and now I have neither son nor husband—and that wretched man will take my home away from me unless I am here to throw myself on his mercy. He will want to see everything. I must be here to greet him, Emma.'

'Not at all, Mama,' Emma replied serenely. 'I shall do all that is necessary myself.'

'That would not be proper, Emma.'

'I shall keep Mrs Monty with me,' Emma said. 'And I also have dear Nanny. It will be perfectly proper. Besides, I am hardly a green girl in the first flush of youth, am I?'

Lady Sommerton looked at her doubtfully. 'No, and of course I have perfect trust in your good sense, Emma…but I still think I should be here with you. We must take the greatest care not to alienate him, my dear. He might decide to let us stay here if I ask him.'

'Supposing he refuses your request, Mama—would you not find that embarrassing? Besides, there is the rest of the winter to consider. You know that I am pledged to Mrs Flynn and you will be here alone.'

'But I cannot live with Sir William and Lady Heathstone for the rest of my life…' Lady Sommerton choked back a sob. 'If only your papa had not quarrelled with Tom.'

'There is nothing Tom could have done to prevent this,' Emma said. She too had often wished that Sir Thomas had not disowned his only son after their violent quarrel, for it was only after their breach that his gambling had become much worse. 'It is useless to upset yourself, Mama.'

'But why has Tom not been in touch with us if he is alive?'

'I do not know, but he must have his reasons,' Emma said as she had a thousand times before. 'Do not fret so, dearest.'

'I do not know what is to become of us when Lytham turns us out,' Lady Sommerton said and dabbed at her eyes.

'Sir William and Lady Heathstone have offered you a home for as long as you need it, Mama,' Emma said, trying not to see the tears in her mother's eyes. 'It really is the best thing for you. Even if Lytham were to allow you to stay here, you could not manage on your income. This house is far too expensive to run. But if you accept Sir William's offer, you can afford to buy your own clothes and make your hosts the occasional little gift. Otherwise, you will have to manage with what I can give you, which will be very little.'

'Oh, no, I do not wish to be a burden to you,' Lady Sommerton said instantly. 'You have already given up too much for my sake.'

'I have given up nothing, Mama,' Emma said and smiled oddly. 'You know very well that I did not take in the drawing rooms of London.'

'I have never understood that,' Lady Sommerton said. 'I remember thinking that one or two of your suitors would definitely come up to scratch.'

Emma reflected that they might well have done so given the slightest encouragement but, in the throes of first love for a man who was not the man she'd imagined him, she had positively discouraged the more worthy gentlemen who might have offered for her. Her father had suffered some reverses at the card table that season, which had meant that she had never again had a chance of another season, something she did not particularly repine.

'Are you sure this is what you want?' Lady Sommerton looked at her daughter. 'I am aware that Mrs Flynn was a friend when you were at school, but what will she be like as an employer? Have you thought of that, Emma? People often change when they go up in the world, and if she is to be sponsored by her husband's relative…'

'Oh, I think I shall be quite happy with Mrs Flynn,' Emma replied. 'She is very eager for me to go to her, and though she means to pay me a wage, she says I am to think of myself as her guest.'

'Then I suppose I must let you go to her.' Lady Sommerton pressed her lavender-scented kerchief to her head. 'There is nothing else for it, Emma.'

'No, Mama.'

Had things been different, Tom might have managed to save something from the ruin of their estate, but as it was there was no hope—either of saving the estate or of his returning.

There was nothing else for either of them to do. Sir Thomas's folly, followed by his tragic death, had left them little choice but to accept the generosity of their friends.

'I don't see why you have to go down there yourself.' Tobias Edgerton looked at Lytham with a lift of his brows as they sat in the marquis's library sharing a bottle of exceedingly fine claret. 'Why don't you send Stephen Antrium to look it over for you? He is a good fellow and does well by your own place. The Sommerton estate is bound to be in a ramshackle way, stands to reason… Sir Thomas wouldn't have been so desperate otherwise.'

'I fully expect to find it will be more of a burden than a pleasure,' Alexander Lynston, Marquis of Lytham, said to his friend. 'But what else can I do? The son is missing and we must presume him dead, for otherwise he would surely have come forward this past year. I know there was some scandal concerning him, but nothing was ever proved and

I fully expected him to demand his rights of me, which is one reason I have waited so long before doing anything. There *is* a widow and a daughter—of the spinster type, I am told. They have been left destitute and their minds must be set at rest. My lawyers told them to apply for funds if they were in need, but they have not done so and I cannot think how they have managed all this time. It was not my intention to leave them in poverty.'

'Damn it all, Alex, you weren't to blame for what happened to Sommerton. Why should you take on the responsibility of two women who are not related to you? You told the fool to call it a night—'

'In such a way that he practically threw his estate on to the table,' Lytham replied. His handsome face belied the nature of the man, which could at times be Machiavellian, his eyes just now as black as the midnight sky and just as mysterious. He smiled at the younger man, of whom he was fond in his own careless manner. 'The devil was in me that night, Toby. Sommerton was a fool, but I did not imagine he would deliberately walk in front of a speeding carriage and horses the next day. The only mercy was that he died instantly and did not linger—but it was so unnecessary! Had he kept his appointment with my man of business as I requested, all would have been well.'

'You could not have known he was that desperate,' Toby said. 'Besides, you won fair and square—pay and be paid, that's my motto. His estate was forfeit. A man should not gamble if he cannot afford to pay.'

Lytham smiled inwardly. It was easy for the young man to speak of such things; the only son of a wealthy father, he had never known what it was to want. Toby's fair good looks and blue eyes won him friends easily, and he had never experienced the loneliness that can haunt a man possessed by fear.

Lytham had understood the look in Sir Thomas's eyes that night, and knew that a part of his recklessness had come from his desire to punish, to seek revenge. It was because of Lytham's brother that he had cast his son out, and the suffering was there in his eyes. It must have cost him much pain, though he had held it within, where it had festered and clung like a limpet, bursting out of him in uncontrollable hatred the night he found himself so deeply in debt to Lytham that he could never pay him. He had wanted to best Lytham at any cost, and in pitting his wits against him had lost everything.

'I do not want his damned estate,' Lytham replied on a note of irritation. 'Nor do I want the trouble of running down to some village in the back of beyond.'

'Steady on, old chap, come from Cambridgeshire myself. Ain't that bad…some pretty villages, and the city has some damned fine buildings.'

'Cambridge is well enough, but this wretched estate is off the beaten track—out near somewhere called Ely, I understand.'

'Been there once,' Toby supplied helpfully. 'Got a cathedral—built in Ethelreda's time.'

'Good grief! Are you turning into a bluestocking?'

Toby blanched at the suggestion. 'Not me, Alex—please! Just a bit of information I picked up along the way.'

'Well, spare me your lectures,' Lytham replied, his amazingly dark eyes bright with mischief. He flicked back a lock of almost black hair that was too long for fashion, and might have given him the look of a poet had his features not been too strong, too masculine. He looked, rather, what indeed he was, the last surviving scion of a noble family who had descended into debauchery and decay, squandering much of their fortune on their merry way to hell. 'You disappoint me, Toby. I quite thought you had nothing in your head but horses and clothes.'

The Honourable Tobias Edgerton was known for his elegance, which far outshone that of his careless friend. Somehow, however, it was always the marquis who commanded attention whenever they were together.

'Bamming me,' Toby said mournfully. 'Might have known—thought you meant it for a moment. Suppose you know all about the place anyway. Ain't much you don't know, Lytham.'

He looked ruefully at his friend. Lytham could be a devil when he had the bit between his teeth, but he was also the best of men when you really knew him. His rather satanic good looks were universally admired, and he was spoiled by adoring mamas and their hopeful daughters alike; his ready wit and undeniable charm won him many friends in high places. The Regent always made a beeline for Lytham whenever they met in company, although the marquis was not one of his intimate cronies—through choice.

'Trouble is you ain't one to let on what you're thinking.'

Toby studied his friend thoughtfully. Bit of a dark horse, Lytham! He was in his mid thirties, having escaped the matrimonial market when younger by virtue of having been forced to supplement his living in the army.

'It comes of necessity,' Lytham said, a reflective expression in his eyes. 'I never expected to inherit the title— wouldn't have if Father had had his way.' He frowned as he thought of the circumstances that had brought him into line. His two elder brothers had died, Henry from a putrid infection of the lungs and John Lynston from a fall from his horse. John was said to have been drunk at the time, a normal state of affairs, and riding recklessly. His sudden death had precipitated Alexander's hasty return from the army for the tenth marquis had not long survived the demise of his favourite son.

'Father and my brothers had done their best to ruin the family estate, as you know. Needed my wits about me to manage when Father cut me off and I learned to keep my own counsel.'

'Well, you've turned the estate round these past three years. My father says you've one of the best heads for managing your affairs that he's come across, but he thinks you're a mystery—can't see why myself.'

'You put up with my moods, Toby,' Lytham said. 'Not everyone is blessed with your good nature.'

A wry smile touched his mouth as he reflected on his life. He supposed others must find him an uneasy companion at times, for he was prone to moods. He thought of them as his devils; they rode on his shoulder, prompting him to do or say things he often wished unsaid.

'My father, for one, thought I was a rogue and a wastrel. Our quarrel was never resolved.' There was a slightly bitter taste in his mouth as he remembered his father's words as he cast him off.

'My hope is that I shall never see you alive again. You are no son of mine!'

Alex had always been aware of his father's dislike, even as a child. He supposed he ought to find an ironic pleasure that it was he who had eventually inherited the estate and rescued it from ruin, but that would have been a meaningless triumph. His life was empty in many ways, his heart untouched by love. He had had his share of mistresses over the years, young and beautiful women who had offered their favours, but none of them had ever meant more than a fleeting pleasure to him.

'Lady Rotherham and her daughters seem to find you fascinating,' Toby teased recklessly. 'And I can think of a few more who wouldn't say no to becoming the new Lady Lytham!' Toby knew that, since Lytham's return from the army, both aspiring mamas and women of another kind had relentlessly pursued him.

'Or to my reputed fortune,' Lytham replied, an odd expression in his eyes. 'You know, of course, that Rotherham is facing ruin if he can't marry those girls off to a fortune?'

'Well, I'd heard a tale,' Toby said. 'But you always seem to get to the bottom of these things, Alex. I'm damned if I know how you do it.'

'Your faith in my powers of omnipotence is flattering, Toby—but I fear you are sadly wrong. Had I, for instance, been privy to that fool Sommerton's state of mind, I might have prevented a tragedy.'

'Well, that's different, desperate men do desperate things,' Toby said. 'What are your intentions? Planning to let the girl and widow stay on?'

'As my dependants?' Lytham gave him a withering smile. 'Now what gave you such a foolish idea? I shall naturally turn them out into the snow.'

'Ain't snowing,' Toby observed, knowing that his friend hated to be thought generous. 'Ain't likely to for months.'

'In that case I shall have to wait for my wicked pleasures—or I might pack them off to keep Aunt Agatha company. She is always complaining that Lytham Hall is like an empty barn. A widow and a spinster daughter should be just the thing to keep her busy.'

'Get her out of your hair for a while?' Toby grinned. Lady Agatha was the best of her family and the only one who had ever had a kind word for Alexander, which was perhaps why he cared for her opinion. A redoubtable lady of seventy years with hair as red as a hot poker—and only a fool would suggest it was a wig in her hearing!—she had a sharp sense of humour and an even sharper tongue. 'I pity the poor widow.'

'Then you waste your pity,' Lytham remarked, carelessly flicking at a speck of dust on the sleeve of his immaculate blue cloth coat. He was dressed in casual fashion in riding breeches and a simple white shirt and neckcloth, but his boots were of the finest leather and polished until they reflected his valet's face; he had a natural air of style and authority that made him the envy of lesser dandies. 'Agatha will mother them both. It is the best solution to the problem. I have been considering whether or not to keep the estate, but I think a quick sale—and a trust fund for mother and daughter...' A look of relief came to the midnight eyes as he made his decision. 'Yes, that should be sufficient.'

'Your lawyers could arrange that,' Toby suggested. 'Save you the bother of a troublesome journey.'

'I think it would be best coming from me.' Lytham finished his wine. 'I had intended to wait until the end of the week, but I think I'll go down tomorrow. Get the business settled before I visit my aunt.'

'Come with you if you like,' Toby offered nobly.

'My gratitude for your friendship is always boundless,' Lytham drawled, his mouth lifting in what others would see as a sneer but was actually self-mockery. 'But I fear your absence at this time might hinder your attempts to secure the beautiful Miss Dawlish. No, Toby. Stay and win yourself an heiress if you can.'

'Don't care for her fortune,' Toby said. 'Inherit one myself one day. Trouble is, not sure Lucy really cares for me—enough to marry me, anyway.'

'My advice is to be persistent.' Lytham smiled oddly. 'The heiress has a bevy of suitors, but half of them are interested only in her fortune. If she is as wise as she is beautiful, I believe Lucy Dawlish will soon begin to sift the dross from the gold.'

'Can't call Devenish dross,' Toby said gloomily. 'Still, she might notice me eventually, I suppose.'

Being an exceptionally observant man, Lytham believed the elusive heiress had already noticed his friend. Although not in line for an earldom as were some of Miss Dawlish's suitors, he was undeniably a very eligible *parti,* besides being good humoured and easy going. Lytham thought the heiress would have to be stupid to take Devenish instead of Toby. However, he was not in the habit of paying his friend compliments and kept his thoughts to himself.

At any other time he would have been glad of Toby's company on what was certain to be a tedious errand, but it might prove embarrassing if he was as unwelcome a guest to the Sommerton family as he fully expected.

'Don't forget to take your shawl, Emma,' Nanny said as her former charge, now become friend and comforter, prepared to leave the house. 'It is nearly October and the weather can turn nasty of a sudden.'

At that moment they were enjoying what was often termed an 'Indian' summer and the afternoon was both warm and sunny. However, Emma draped the shawl over her arm to oblige Nanny before she went out.

It was two days since Lady Sommerton had departed for the Hall with four large trunks full of her personal possessions, one or two of which might reasonably have been called part of the estate. Since no one had bothered to take an inventory in the months since Sir Thomas's death, there was no need to worry that Lady Sommerton might be accused of theft. However, Emma had been scrupulous in packing her own trunks. She would in any case be unable to take as much as her mama, and had decided to dispose of some of her unwanted clothes.

She imagined that the Reverend Thorn's wife, Mary, might know of a few deserving cases in the village and surrounding cottages, and it was to discuss the matter and take leave of her friend that she had ventured out this afternoon.

The walk to the Vicarage was pleasant on a warm, dry afternoon and Emma took the shortcut, avoiding the village by going across the fields. For once she had not bothered to put up her heavy dark hair into the usual coronet of plaits, and it hung loosely on her shoulders. She felt a release of the tension that had hung over her these past weeks and even sang a few bars of a popular melody as she walked.

Mary Thorn was as delighted to see her as Emma had known she would be. She was taken into a pretty parlour, given tea and cakes and thanked for the offer of the clothes.

'You know we can always find a use for them, Emma—but are you sure you won't need them?'

'Mrs Flynn has told me not to bring too much as she intends to buy clothes for herself and me,' Emma said. 'Besides, I had three new gowns last year and they are quite adequate. If my evening dress is too shabby, Mrs Flynn will no doubt provide something.'

'Your future employer sounds very generous.' Mary Thorn looked at her curiously. 'How did she know you were in need of a position?'

'She heard that Papa had died,' Emma replied, a break in her voice. 'And since she needed a respectable woman to keep her company, she wrote to ask if I would go to her.'

In fact, Bridget Flynn had written a long and revealing

letter, begging Emma to stay with her. She had a most urgent need of female companionship, and had perhaps confided more than was wise in the letter to her old school-friend.

The earl has agreed to sponsor me in society, Emma, Bridget had written. *But he vows he loves me and I believe he is determined to make me his mistress. I find him fascinating for my part, but I am determined not to succumb. It is marriage or nothing...except that he makes me feel so very delicious...*

'Was that not the most fortunate thing!' Mary Thorn was thrilled by Emma's good luck. 'I hope you will enjoy yourself, dearest Emma—but should you have reason to leave Mrs Flynn, you know you may always come here for a visit. The vicar would be happy to see you.'

Emma thanked her. She felt that her true fortune lay in having friends like Sir William and Mary Thorn, and she felt a little guilty at deceiving them. They would both have been utterly shocked had they guessed that her future employer had confessed to being on the verge of becoming the Earl of Lindisfarne's mistress.

Emma was not sure what would happen if Bridget did give way to the earl's persuasion. He was obviously a great temptation to her, but since the earl was unmarried there was no real reason why he could not offer her marriage. However, Emma had heard a whisper that he was a notorious rake, who had had a string of mistresses.

She was thoughtful as she began her walk home. The sky had clouded over and she realised that Nanny's advice had been sound as she hugged her shawl about her. She would undoubtedly have been wiser to look elsewhere for employment, since she could not afford the loss of reputation that she might suffer if there were to be a scandal.

Yet her life had been so quiet of late and she felt that this might be her last chance of having a little fun…a little excitement.

As she entered the house, Emma noticed the hat and fashionable travelling cape in the hall. She was surprised as most of her father's friends had already called to pay their respects to her mother and she was not expecting company.

Indeed, the house was looking sadly neglected, for many of the little items that had made it a home had gone with Lady Sommerton, and the whole impression was rather more shabby than usual. Emma had fetched a few bits and pieces from the attic to fill up the empty spaces, and the Chinese vase in the corner with an arrangement of dried flowers did not look too bad if you did not look at the crack, which she had turned into the wall. Not that it mattered, for nothing could disguise the fact that the house had not been refurbished in an age.

About to enter the small back parlour, which was the room she and her mother had most used these past weeks, she heard Nanny laugh.

'You are the veriest rogue, sir! None of your flummery, now… Ah, here's Miss Emma back from her visit.' Nanny greeted her with a smile of welcome. 'Now here's a surprise, my love. The Marquis of Lytham come to see us a few days early…'

Emma had been studying the rather large gentleman who was standing before the fireplace, wineglass in hand, apparently completely at home in the parlour he seemed to make smaller by his very presence. Her first thought had been that he was remarkably good looking, but as his dark, challenging eyes turned to survey her she felt a surge of anger. How dare he look at her in that way? She was aware that her hair was windblown and her cheeks pink from the

cold, and wished that she had gone upstairs to tidy herself
before meeting her guest.

'My lord,' she said, head up, eyes flashing with unconscious pride, 'we had not anticipated your coming until the
weekend...' When she had confidently expected to be on
her way to London and beyond his reach.

'I believed too long had passed with no word from me,'
Lytham replied, hard gaze narrowing as he read her hostility. 'I am sorry to have missed Lady Sommerton, and glad
that I have managed to catch you before you left for London.'

'Indeed?' Emma's tone was cool, her manner dismissive.
'I cannot imagine why, sir. Your lawyers have made all
clear. I fear the estate may not be what you hope.'

'Since I hope for nothing, that matters little,' he replied,
as cool as she now. 'However, I dare say something may
be salvaged.'

'Nanny—would you arrange some tea, please?'

Emma waited until her nurse had left the room before
rounding on him. 'You may do as you please with your
own property, my lord. I shall make arrangements to leave
first thing in the morning.'

'You will do no such thing,' Lytham said in a tone that
brooked no denial. 'If it offends you to have me beneath
your roof, I can stay at the inn.'

'You will find that uncomfortable.' She was angry and
her words were perhaps too harsh, too hasty. 'Why was it
necessary to come earlier than planned? We might have
avoided any unpleasantness.'

'I made it clear that you and Lady Sommerton were to
remain here as my guests. I ought perhaps to have come
sooner, but I did not wish to intrude on your grief—and
was uncertain what to do for the best.'

'There was no need for you to concern yourself. We have made our own arrangements.'

'Your mother's visit to Italy with friends is perfectly acceptable,' Lytham said. 'But I cannot allow you to continue with this foolish idea of becoming a companion to a woman whose situation in life is below your own.'

'*You* cannot allow…' Emma was indignant. 'I beg your pardon, my lord. I was not aware that you had become my guardian. I am almost seven and twenty, and even Papa would not have spoken to me in these terms.'

Damn it, but there was fire in those eyes! Lytham was surprised and amused to discover that he had been so misled as to the nature of Sommerton's daughter. He had been told she was a confirmed spinster and well past her last prayers, but that was clearly not the case. She was not pretty like the enchanting Lucy Dawlish, but she was certainly a woman of spirit.

'I spoke as a gentleman, as a man of honour…' He saw the disbelief in her face and smiled inwardly. The little firebrand was not above showing her contempt. 'Believe me, Miss Sommerton, I had no desire to win your father's estate in that card game. I suspect it will be more trouble to dispose of than it is worth…' In saying that he was not speaking only of financial matters, but Emma was not to know that she herself was destined to be the cause of more bother than her father's debts.

'You intend to sell, then?'

'I do not imagine you could afford to continue living here if I offered you the opportunity? And, since there has been no word from your brother, I think I have little choice.'

Emma looked into his eyes and then away as her heart caught, stopping for a moment and then pounding wildly for some unaccountable reason.

'I imagine you know our circumstances as well as we do, sir.'

'Yes. I have been into your father's affairs thoroughly, Miss Sommerton, and I believe what he did was a desperate act. Had he held the winning hand, he might have been able to stave off ruin for a time—for there was a considerable amount on the table that night.'

Emma's face was pale as she stood before him, hands clasped in front, to stop them trembling. 'I am aware of Papa's debts. Will the sale of the estate cover them?'

'I believe with some small attention to detail it may do a little more—there may be a small sum…' For some reason Lytham was reluctant to inform her of his intentions to invest that money on her and her mother's behalf.

'Not equal to what my father would have won, though?'

'No, not that much.' Not by a half or a quarter, but he would never tell her that.

'Then he cheated you…'

'Sir Thomas was desperate. A desperate man may do many things.'

He had not denied it! Emma was silent. She was mortified and thought guiltily of the small treasures her mother had taken with her; nothing had been of great value, but still…she ought not to have removed things like the enamel and ormolu gilt clock from the drawing room or the best silver tea service.

'I am sorry my father deceived you.'

'You have no need to be. I accepted the bet, knowing the estate could be worth little. I should have refused to do so, of course. Perhaps then—'

'He would still be alive?' She read the answer in his eyes. 'Yet he would have continued until there was nothing left. After the quarrel with Tom, it seemed that nothing else would content him but to gamble it all away.'

'I am afraid it is often the way with unlucky gamblers. Please accept my condolences for your loss, Miss Sommerton,' he said, his eyes dwelling intently on her face as he watched her struggle for control. He saw anger, grief and despair register and then fade into resignation. 'I feel in part responsible for what happened—and it is therefore my intention to offer you…' He paused uncertainly. He had meant to offer a home, but she was too proud to accept charity from him. 'The post of companion to my aunt. She is a wonderful old lady, but needs young company about her. Aunt Agatha would like you, Miss Sommerton—and I believe that you might like her.'

Emma was surprised. She had the oddest notion that he had intended to say something entirely different.

'That is considerate of you, my lord—but unnecessary, as you must already have realised. I have a very comfortable position to go to. Mrs Flynn is an old friend, and I have promised to join her at the house she has taken in London.'

'An odd time to visit London,' he said. 'The season is over. You will find there is very little going on at the moment.'

'I believe Mrs Flynn has her own reasons for visiting at this time. Besides, I think she means to retire to the country after a while—or perhaps to Bath. Her plans are not quite formed yet.'

'I see…' Lytham gave her an enigmatic look. 'Will you not change your mind? I believe my Aunt Agatha would be a more suitable person for you to know than this Mrs Flynn would.'

'How can you say that since you know nothing of Mrs Flynn?' Emma's hostility towards him had waned, but now it came flooding back. How dare he presume to dictate to her? 'I thank you for your consideration, my lord—but I can manage for myself.'

'Can you?' He seemed doubtful. 'I take leave to wonder.'

'What does that mean, sir?'

'For goodness sake, call me Lytham,' he burst out. 'I have not come here as your enemy, Miss Sommerton.'

Emma's answer to that was forestalled by Nanny's arrival with a maid bearing a tea tray. She beamed at them innocently, clearly having taken to the marquis at first sight.

'Here we are, then,' she said. 'Isn't this nice, Emma dear? It's always pleasant to have a gentleman in the house. Shall you pour?'

'Please excuse me,' Lytham said. 'I must forgo your kind offer to stay the night, Miss Sommerton. I have pressing business elsewhere.'

Emma caught the mocking tone of his voice, but he had her at a disadvantage. She knew that she had been less than polite, especially if he had come all this way to offer her and her mother help.

'Oh, must you go?' Nanny said in the slight pause that followed. 'Surely you will stay one night, sir? He would be very welcome, would he not, Emma?'

'Yes, of course,' she said stiffly. 'It is too far to return to town this evening, my lord—and the inns are not always reliable.'

She saw a gleam in his eyes and knew she had fallen into his trap, but what choice had he given her? He had been sure Nanny would react exactly as she had.

'Then of course I shall stay. I am delighted to accept your hospitality, Miss Sommerton.'

'My lord...' She raised her head, receiving a little shock as she looked into those devastating eyes and saw the imp of mischief that resided there. 'I shall leave you to your tea while I speak to Cook about dinner.'

'Oh, there is not the least need,' Nanny said innocently. 'Cook has been planning dinner ever since his lordship arrived. That is why you must not even consider leaving, sir. She would be most upset.'

'We cannot have Cook upset,' Lytham said, somehow managing to look almost as innocent as his new-found admirer. 'Especially if she is a good cook!'

Emma saw that he was laughing inside. She raised her head, giving him a reproving glare. Did he imagine she was to be won over so easily...even though it had been seldom that she had discovered a similar sense of humour to her own in a man?

Sir William was right about the Marquis of Lytham after all. He was a damnable rogue!

Chapter Two

There was to be no escape for Emma until much later that evening, apart from the half an hour it took her to change for dinner. After tea, the marquis had asked to be shown the house, which Emma had felt obliged to do herself. He had made encouraging noises about it being an attractive property, and possibly more valuable than he'd thought, and had spoken of staying until the end of the week so that he could ride over the estate with Sir Thomas's bailiff.

'I am inclined to think that something may yet be accomplished here, Miss Sommerton. It would be a pity to dispose of a substantial property too hastily. I shall have to think seriously before I decide. Had your mama still been here, I might have suggested you both remain in residence, for a while at least.'

'Mama needs company and the sunshine of Italy will be good for her,' Emma replied. She had decided to retreat behind a mask of cool dignity. His arrival earlier had taken her by surprise and she had been betrayed into a shocking display of temper, but now she was in control. Her hair was wound into its usual coronet of plaits and it was a different Miss Sommerton who dined with the marquis that evening. Lytham was intrigued by the change, both in her appearance and her manner. Who did she imagine she was fooling by this calm, spinsterish behaviour? He might have been deceived for a while had he not seen the real Emma, but it was too late for pretence. Intrigued and amused, he discovered that what he had thought would be an awkward visit was actually proving enjoyable. He had been growing bored of late in town, and this was just what he had needed to divert him.

'You must, of course, do just as you please,' Emma told him when he announced his intention of staying on. 'But Nanny is due to leave the day after tomorrow and I shall bring my own journey forward by one day. It would not be proper for me to be alone with you in this house, my lord.'

'No, I dare say it would not,' he agreed, the light of mischief lurking in his eyes had she dared to look. She was a challenging minx, and worthy of the contest. He was going to enjoy this tussle of wills. 'But I believe Nanny might delay her journey by one day if I asked her—and then, you know, we might travel together. I am sure you would find my carriage comfortable, Miss Sommerton.' He smiled across the table at Nanny, who was dining with them at Emma's insistence, and she immediately agreed that it would be no trouble at all to delay her journey.

'For you know Sir William has put his gig at my disposal, Emma—and you were to have travelled on the Mail coach because you feared it would be too expensive to travel by post chaise, dearest. Think how much more comfortable it will be to travel in his lordship's carriage. It is excessively good of you, sir, and I am sure Emma is most grateful.'

Inside, Emma was fuming, but she could only accept her defeat and agree that it would be more comfortable to travel in the marquis's carriage than by public coach. She had felt it necessary to save what little money she had, and had not been looking forward to the journey. However, she was not pleased by the way she had been persuaded to agree, but her attention was diverted by the marquis's next words.

'You shall not go anywhere in a gig, Nanny,' Lytham said and earned Emma's instant approval. 'I am sure you would find it more comfortable to travel by chaise—and you will allow me the privilege of paying your expenses.'

'But it is merely a distance of ten miles, sir.'

'Which you may as well travel in comfort. Indeed, I insist and shall be hurt if you refuse me,' Lytham said and was rewarded by a beaming look from his elderly devotee.

There was no doubt that the marquis could be a charmer when he chose, thought Emma. However, she had no fault to find with this latest evidence of his generosity. The expense was nothing to a man of his fortune, of course, but it was nevertheless a kind thought.

Without her realising it, Emma's manner towards the marquis had thawed slightly, and before she knew what was happening he had refused a solitary glass of port in favour of taking tea with her and Nanny in the parlour. His manner was exactly what it ought to be, gentlemanly and courteous, and his stories of what was happening in town were vastly entertaining. It was only when the longcase clock in hall struck ten that she was aware of time passing.

'I must bid you goodnight, sir,' she said as the clock finished striking. She stood up, signalling her intention to retire. 'We have kept poor Nanny from her bed long enough. I fear we have not been used to late hours here.'

'Forgive me...' Lytham sprang to his feet. 'Goodnight, Miss Sommerton...Nanny...'

'You must stay and take a glass of brandy,' Emma said. 'I believe you may find my father's cellar tolerable—what is left of it.'

He inclined his head, a flicker of amusement back in his eyes. Miss Sommerton was most definitely a challenge, and of all things Alexander Lytham enjoyed pitting his wits against a worthy opponent.

She was determined on taking up this post as a companion, and it seemed nothing would change her mind. There was really no reason why she should not do as she had planned, but he would use every effort to deter her. He had no charge to level at this Mrs Flynn, and yet his instincts told him something was not quite as it should be.

Miss Sommerton had looked a little odd once or twice when she mentioned her future employer. Now why should that be? Lytham could not decide, but that inner sense that had always directed him was seldom far out. It was telling him now that he would regret it if he simply abandoned Emma Sommerton to her fate.

Alone in her room a little later, Emma took the unusual step of locking the door both to her dressing room and her bedchamber. She did not imagine that the marquis would wander in his sleep, but it was best to be careful.

She suspected that he was a man used to having his own way. However, he was undoubtedly a gentleman and she was not really afraid that he would seek to abuse her hospitality. No, she was just being prudent.

She undressed, donning a plain white, much-washed nightgown and her shabby old dressing robe. Then, having brushed her hair until it shone and fell in gentle waves to her shoulders, she went to stand at the window and look down at the garden. The moon had shed its soft light across a swathe of lawn, shrubs and trees, turning them to a curious silver. She felt a pang of regret as she remembered that she would soon be leaving it for good. Yet there was no point in repining and she was looking forward to a change in the slow pace of her life.

What was that? She stiffened as she saw something moving...a man's shadow in the shrubbery? Had the marquis gone out for a walk in the gardens? It seemed the most logical explanation, and yet the shadowy figure had seemed too slight for the man she had dined with earlier, and its movements had appeared slightly furtive.

For a moment Emma was tempted to go in search of the elusive figure, but then she remembered that she was scarcely dressed for such an excursion. Besides, she could not be sure that she really had seen something out there. It might have been a trick of the light—a cloud falling across the moon, perhaps?

Going over to her bed, Emma slipped between cool sheets. It felt strange to think that she was sharing her home with a man she had only met that afternoon—a man she ought to hate and despise.

She had believed that she hated him for what he had done, but during the evening she had discovered that she could not do so. She hated and despised what he stood for—this careless society that allowed the ruin of a man's life, and his family, on the turn of a card. Gambling was surely an abominable practice and ought to be banned. And yet...perhaps it was only her father's own weak character that was at fault?

Emma decided that she did not entirely dislike the marquis, but she certainly did not trust him. No, indeed she did not! There was something hidden...something that went much deeper than the charming manner he had shown them over dinner. Yes...something hidden. She felt that he was a man of secrets, a man with a past.

It could not matter to her what kind of a man he was! She was forced to accept his company for the next few days, but once they reached London they would each go their own way. She would never need to see him again unless she wished.

Feeling vaguely restless, Emma reached over to blow out her candle. It had been a long day and she was feeling tired.

'Goodbye, Nanny. You must write to me once you are settled.'

Emma felt the sting of tears as she kissed her nurse's soft cheek. She had been prepared for this parting, but it was still difficult now that it had come. She was, after all, being torn from all that she held dear—home, friends, and family. Nanny had been almost a second mother to her and she knew that she would miss her sorely.

After Nanny had been seen safely on her way, it was time for Emma to take her seat in the marquis's comfortable carriage. It looked new and she thought the springing would be better than on her father's old coach, which had been most uncomfortable. Despite its smart appearance and the obvious quality of his horses, she noticed that it did not carry his coat of arms on the side panels. Most men of his importance would have had their family crest emblazoned on the sides, but Lytham had chosen not to. She wondered why, then forgot it as she saw that inside it was every bit as comfortable as she had expected, with cushions and a travelling rug to keep her warm.

Lytham was travelling with her and had insisted that one of the more responsible maids should accompany them for the sake of propriety.

'It would be too exhausting for you to travel the whole distance in one day,' he had insisted. 'We shall stay overnight at a good posting inn, and you will need the assistance of a maid.'

Emma had tried to protest that such consideration was

not necessary. Indeed, she would have preferred to complete her journey in the shortest possible time, but she was given no say in the matter.

'There is still time for you to change your mind,' Lytham said, pausing with his foot on the step. 'Give the word and I shall take you to my aunt instead.'

'I believe I have made my wishes clear, sir,' Emma said, her eyes sparking at him. 'Indeed, I think I have done so several times these past two days.'

'Then I shall ask no more,' Lytham promised and gave the order to move off as he climbed into the carriage.

'Thank you.'

Lily, the young maid travelling with them, was overawed by the marquis's presence, and had scarcely uttered a word since accompanying Emma from the house. She looked frightened to death at the thought of leaving familiar surroundings, and even a reassuring smile from her mistress did not take the anxious look from her eyes.

Emma leaned back against the squabs. It was an exceedingly comfortable conveyance, much better than Sir Thomas's antiquated travelling carriage. She closed her eyes with a little sigh, hoping that the marquis would take that as a sign that she did not wish for conversation. He immediately followed suit, crossing his long legs and, when Emma dared to peep, gave every appearance of intending to sleep throughout the whole journey. This had the desired effect of making Emma open her own eyes and begin to look about her at the countryside through which they passed.

Sitting with her back to the horses, Lily had shrunk back into her corner and was looking fixedly out of the window. From the tension in her manner, she was apparently expecting disaster to strike them at any moment.

* * *

'And so…' Lytham said when they had been travelling in silence for some half an hour or more. 'Does Mrs Flynn hope to entertain much? As I believe I have told you before, I think you will find London thin of company just now.'

His sudden question startled Emma, for she had been dreaming, but she recovered quickly, meeting his eyes, only to look away again almost at once.

'I believe Mrs Flynn seeks to purchase a new wardrobe,' Emma replied. 'And then we may go elsewhere for the winter months. It has not yet been decided.'

Lytham nodded, his eyes narrowing intently. She appeared so cool and calm, completely in control of her emotions, but he suspected it was a pose and that the real Emma was lurking behind the façade she showed to the world. He would swear there was something Miss Sommerton was hiding, but it was clear that she would not be drawn.

'You will keep me in touch with your movements, Miss Sommerton?'

'Oh—why?' Emma arched her brows. 'I really see no reason—'

Whatever she had meant to say was brought to an abrupt ending because the carriage came to a sudden halt and she was thrown across the space between them into the marquis's arms. She gave a startled cry, looking up into his eyes in alarm, but he merely smiled reassuringly, his strong grip saving her from falling to the floor. Lily screamed once, but hung on to the tassel hanging from the corner of the carriage and retained her seat.

'Are you all right, miss?' she asked after a moment, looking shaken and nervous.

'Yes, thank you,' Emma replied and straightened her bonnet. 'Are you?'

'Yes, miss…I think so…'

From outside Emma could hear shouting and some

curses from the coachman and groom, and then, as the marquis gently righted her on the seat opposite him, an anxious face appeared at the window.

'Beggin' your pardon, my lord. I hope neither you nor the young ladies were harmed?'

'I think not,' replied Lytham with a sharp look at Emma, who nodded to indicate that she was merely shocked. 'But it was most unfortunate—what caused the incident?'

'There is a fallen tree across the road, my lord. I think we can clear it, but it will take time.'

Lytham's groom opened the door for him and he got out to view the situation himself. It was actually only a large branch, but it had blocked the narrow road, which wound between dense woods on either side, and had given his driver no choice but to pull the horses to an abrupt halt.

'I think the three of us should be able to clear this,' Lytham said, and took off his coat, tossing it inside the carriage, where it lay on the floor until Lily retrieved it, folding it neatly on the seat beside her.

Emma glanced out of the window and saw that the three men were tugging the heavy branch, which looked like the whole top part of a large elm, to the side of the road. One of the horses was moving restively, and Emma thought it wise to get down in case the nervous animal, which had already been unsettled by the sudden halt, should make a sudden lunge.

'I think I shall get down,' she said to Lily. 'You stay here for the moment.'

'Yes, miss—but be careful…' Lily hesitated as if wishing to say more, but held her tongue.

'Yes, of course.'

Emma descended from the carriage and went to stand at the horse's head, reaching up to pat it reassuringly. She actually had her hands on the harness when the shot rang out, and she felt the immediate pull of the frightened horse. Instinctively, she braced herself for the jerk she knew would come as the horse tried to bolt, and felt herself almost lifted off her feet by its wild plunge.

'Whoa there, old fellow,' she said in a voice of command. 'Steady…steady, boy…'

Her calm voice and the fact that she was already at the horse's head when it was frightened probably saved it plunging blindly into the men ahead and dragging the carriage and other horses with it. The men had stopped pulling at the fallen branch and were staring down at someone lying on the ground. For some minutes, Emma was too busy calming the horses to see what had happened, but then, as the groom came hurrying to take over from her, she gave a cry of distress as she saw for herself what had happened.

The marquis had been shot! He was back on his feet as she began to run towards him, but he was clasping his shoulder and she could see the crimson staining his shirt.

'Oh, my lord,' Emma cried in distress. 'Are you badly hurt? What happened—did you see who shot at you?'

Lytham grimaced and took his hand away from his shoulder for a moment to look at the powder-burned hole in his shirt.

'I think it is a flesh wound only,' he said. 'I saw nothing for my attention was all on our task, but whoever it was must have taken a pot-shot from somewhere in the trees.'

'The shot came from behind us,' the driver said. 'I felt the wind as it whistled past me, my lord. Whoever did it must have been hidden in those trees as you said, sir.'

'He must have been waiting there…'

Emma had taken a small penknife from her reticule and approached him purposefully. 'May I slit your shirt and look at the wound, sir?' she asked. 'I think some attempt should be made to staunch the blood for it will be a while before we can reach a doctor.'

'You should return to the carriage,' Lytham said. 'That rogue may still be lurking in the woods.'

'I shall be pleased to do so if you come with me,' Emma said. 'Your men can finish clearing the road. Besides, I doubt a poacher would remain long once he had so misfired as to hit you.'

'A poacher?' Lytham frowned, then nodded. 'Yes, perhaps it might have been. I dare say there are small deer in these woods, and certainly a few rabbits.' A smile flickered in his eyes as he looked at her. 'You are remarkably calm, Miss Sommerton. Most young ladies of my acquaintance would be screaming or lying prostrate on the ground from a faint.'

'It was not I who was shot at,' she replied, her lips curving in response to his expression. 'And I do not think you need another incident of that nature. Please come inside the carriage, sir, and let me see what I can do to stop that bleeding.'

'I am in your hands, Miss Sommerton.'

Emma allowed the groom to hand her into the carriage, and then watched as Lytham followed. Her heart was thumping madly and she was not in the least calm, but she had no intention of letting him guess it. He was also putting on a mask, for she suspected that he was in some pain, but was refusing to let it show.

Once he was seated, she knelt on the seat at his side and slit the shirt, taking the large kerchief he offered her to gently wipe away the blood oozing from the wound. Since she could see only a shallow gash across the skin and there did not seem to be a hole in his shoulder, where the ball might have entered, she decided that it was as he had said, merely a flesh wound. He had been fortunate, it seemed, which relieved her mind.

Lily watched with huge rounded eyes, clearly too upset by what had occurred to offer assistance to her mistress. Naturally a timid girl, she sniffed into her kerchief a couple of times, as if overcome by the terrible things that had happened.

'I think we might use your neckcloth to bind the wound,' Emma said. 'If you would permit me?'

'Please feel free to do whatever you wish with me,' Lytham said mockingly. 'I am entirely at your mercy, Miss Sommerton.'

'I shall be as gentle with you as I can,' she promised and began to deftly unravel the folds of his white cravat, which she then used to pad and bind his arm, fastening the tatters of his shirt around his shoulder with a pin when she had finished. 'There…that should hold until we reach an inn,' she told him with satisfaction. 'I fear I have nothing to give you for the pain…unless you happen to have some brandy amongst your luggage?'

'You are an amazing woman,' Lytham said. 'Do you always carry emergency supplies with you?'

Emma smiled and shook her head at his mockery. 'I have often found a penknife useful, my lord—and what respectable woman would go anywhere without a few pins or a needle and thread?'

'No, indeed,' he replied. 'That would be shockingly bad form, would it not?'

'Shockingly,' Emma agreed, a smile quivering at the edges of her mouth. 'I suggest that if you have no brandy amongst your things, you should close your eyes for a moment.' She glanced out of the window as she heard the groom shout something. 'I believe we are almost ready to move off. I shall tell the driver to take us to the nearest inn.' She leaned out of the door and beckoned to the man, giving him the required direction, then sat back. The marquis had taken her advice and was leaning his head back against the squabs, his eyes closed. 'There, now, we shall soon find somewhere comfortable where you may rest for a while.'

Lytham opened his eyes and looked at her. 'My intention in escorting you was to take care of you, Miss Sommerton. It appears the roles have been reversed.'

'It was nothing,' she assured him. 'Yours is not the first wound I have bound, my lord.'

'Indeed? You interest me, tell me more.'

'You have not forgotten that I have a younger brother?' She could tell from his expression that he was interested in learning more. 'As a child Tom was always in trouble. Once he stuck a pitchfork through his leg and it was I who stanched the bleeding and bound the wound.'

'And where is your brother now, Miss Sommerton?' Lytham asked with a slight frown. 'I had hoped that we might hear from him before this. He is, after all, the heir to your father's estate.'

'I wish I might tell you,' Emma replied. 'As for being the heir…Papa cut him off without a penny years ago. My brother was always in trouble, but he did something unforgivable, and Papa would not have his name spoken in his presence. Mama was broken-hearted, but even she agreed that Tom had gone too far.'

Lytham tensed, waiting for her to go on, but she did not. He was well aware of the reasons for Tom Sommerton's quarrel with his father, but he was not sure how much she knew of it.

'May I ask what this terrible sin was?'

Emma bit her lip. 'I am not perfectly sure, for I was

never allowed to hear the whole story—but as I understand it, my brother was accused of cheating at the card table.'

So she did not know it all; well, he would not be the one to tell her, though he knew she might learn of it from others. Her brother had been suspected of causing the accident that had killed Lord John Lynston, Lytham's own brother. He was said to have been having an affair with John's wife, something that was suspected but not known generally, though Aunt Agatha had told him it was true.

'That is a serious crime,' Lytham agreed. 'But I would not have thought it enough for a father to disown his son.' He probed gently, for it was important to know just how much she either knew or suspected. She must blame him for her father's untimely death, but did she also lay her brother's disgrace at his family's door?

'I believe there was more,' Emma said with a frown. 'Mama whispered to me that a friend of the man who accused Tom of cheating said that Tom had insulted his wife, and I believe he took a horse whip to him. A few days after that the man who whipped him was thrown from his horse and died of his injuries…and Papa…' Emma faltered. 'Papa believed that Tom might have been involved in the accident, but I am sure that, whatever else Tom might have done, he would not have caused another man's death.'

Lytham frowned as she stopped speaking.

'Do you know the name of this gentleman?'

'No, my lord. I only know that Mama became ill after my father and brother quarrelled, and my brother stormed from the house, vowing never to return.'

'I see. And you have not heard from him to this day?' Lytham's gaze narrowed. It seemed that she was in ignorance of the facts, which he had not known himself until this past year when he had asked his lawyers to investigate the estate. It was his agent, Stephen Antrium, who had told him the full facts of the case.

'We have heard nothing in almost three years,' Emma said. 'My brother is three years my junior, my lord, and I have missed him for we were very close as children.'

'It was unfortunate for the family,' Lytham said. 'Tell me, would you accept your brother if he tried to contact you?'

'Yes, of course,' she replied, head lifting proudly. 'I do not for one moment believe that Tom had anything to do with the death of that man. He may have flirted with a married woman—my brother was a flirt by all accounts—and he may possibly have cheated at cards, though I cannot think it, but he would never murder anyone.'

'You seem very confident that he would not have stooped to murder?'

'I do not believe my brother is capable of such infamy, sir.'

'Would you be happy for me to make certain inquiries concerning his whereabouts? I have not done so thus far, for I imagined he might come to me.' He had expected Tom Sommerton to demand his rights of him, but it had not happened. Why? Was he afraid that Lytham might press charges against him? Or was there another more sinister reason for his silence?

'But why should you want to help Tom?' She blushed as she looked at him, finding his intent gaze unsettling. 'Surely my family has caused you enough trouble, sir?'

'At the moment my most pressing problem is to get you to use my name,' he said, lips quirking. 'Would you prefer to call me Alex as my friends do?'

'Certainly not,' Emma said at once. 'I should not dream of being so presumptuous, Lord Lytham.'

'Lytham...' he murmured and grimaced as he felt the

pain in his shoulder. 'You know, I think I shall take your advice and try to rest for a few moments.'

'Of course. I shall be as quiet as a mouse.'

He smiled as if he doubted it, but she was as good as her word. He put his head back and closed his eyes, but sleep did not come for his mind was far too busy.

He had been told that his elder brother John had been involved in an unpleasant scandal shortly before the accident that had killed him—something involving a young man he insisted had insulted his wife. There had been an ugly brawl, and John had had to be restrained, pulled off the man before he beat him to death. Yet until the fateful night when Sir Thomas Sommerton had gambled away his estate, he had not bothered to go into details.

John had been a brute and a selfish hedonist; it was little wonder that his wife had sought comfort elsewhere. Yet Lytham could well believe that his brother might have been jealous of his beautiful wife, and would have done whatever he thought necessary to rid himself of a rival. It might prove fruitful if he were to seek an interview with Maria, though he was not sure that his brother's wife would confide in him. Why should she? Nearly three years had passed since her husband died, and no doubt she wanted only to forget all the distress it had caused her.

Stephen Antrium had said that there was no doubt the accident was purely that, the result of John's recklessness, but supposing there had been more? Supposing the rumours had been true and Tom Sommerton had been in some way responsible?

Lytham did not believe the pot-shot taken at him from the trees had been a poacher misfiring, but as far as he knew he had no particular enemies. Unless… A young man disowned by his father, perhaps because of an injustice, and now his inheritance stolen from him at the gambling tables by the brother of the man who had ruined him—sufficient cause for an attempt at murder? He wondered. It might be if Tom Sommerton was desperate enough—and yet Lytham was not convinced.

Who else would like to see him dead? Lytham reviewed the possible candidates in his mind... Who had he upset recently? He was often lucky at the card table, but few men were so foolish as to throw their estates into the pot, and most could afford to lose what he won from them. He had stolen the occasional mistress from beneath the nose of a rival, but such things were usually taken in good part.

Who would benefit from his death? There were some distant cousins in the north, but he had never met them to his knowledge and could not think that they would go to such lengths to inherit his estate. Especially as he believed they were quite wealthy themselves.

It seemed, then, that Tom Sommerton had the most reason to wish for his death.

Emma was relieved when they reached the inn after some twenty or so minutes more on the road. Although the marquis was able to descend from the carriage without assistance, she had observed that he looked pale and she knew that the wound had opened again when he moved, for there was a fresh bloodstain on his shirt.

The innkeeper was quick to bustle round and organise rooms for them both, and a doctor was immediately sent for. Emma was left sitting alone in the parlour, Lily having gone off with their hostess on some errand of her own, when the doctor came in to tell her that he had finished attending the marquis.

'His lordship asked me to tell you that he would be remaining in his room for a few hours,' he said. 'I have repaired the damage, Miss Sommerton, and given him something to ease the pain. Providing that he does not take a fever, he should be well enough to continue his journey tomorrow.'

'Thank you,' Emma said feeling relieved. 'Shall you be calling again, sir?'

'Not unless you send for me, Miss Sommerton—which you may do if you have cause for concern.'

'We shall see how we go on,' she replied and thanked him once more.

Emma felt at a loss after he had gone. It was far too early for her to think of nuncheon, for she had eaten only an hour or so before they set out on their journey, and she was restless. Since she could hardly go up to visit the marquis in his bedchamber, she decided to go out for a walk.

'You should take care, miss,' the innkeeper advised as he saw her about to leave his house. 'There are some bad people about these days—and you don't want to get yourself shot like his lordship.'

Emma thanked him for his advice, and said that she did not intend to stray too far from the inn, but she had not taken more than a few steps before Lily came flying after her.

'Oh, miss,' she said breathlessly. 'I saw you from the upstairs landing and came to warn you.'

'To warn me of what?' Emma said, a little amused by Lily's expression. 'I shall not wander as far as the woods. I am not so foolish after what happened to the marquis.'

'I didn't like to say, miss…not with the marquis there…'

'To say what?'

'I saw someone following the carriage, miss…almost from the time we left home.'

'You saw someone following?' An icy prickle ran down Emma's spine as she stared at the girl. 'Do you mean a man on horseback?'

Lily nodded, her cheeks pink. 'He kept some distance behind as if he didn't want to be noticed, and then he disappeared into the trees when we got to the woods.'

'You mean he could have ridden ahead and...' Emma was shocked. 'But that would be a deliberate act, Lily... almost planned.'

'Yes, miss.' She bit her lip. 'I was too upset to think proper at the time. I should have mentioned it, shouldn't I?'

'Don't worry,' Emma said as she saw the girl's awkward look. 'I shall tell the marquis later—and it wasn't your fault. No one could have dreamed something like that would happen. Besides, it may have been an accident.'

'Yes, miss.' Lily hesitated. 'It's just that there have been tales of a highwayman...a local man...'

'That is the first I've heard of it,' Emma said and frowned as she saw that Lily was looking hard at the ground. 'What do you mean—a local man?'

'I'm sure I don't know, miss.'

'Yes, you do.' Emma took hold of her arm. 'What have you heard in the servants' hall, Lily? What is it you don't want to tell me?'

'There have been half a dozen robberies on the London road,' Lily said. 'They say he knows the area too well to get caught, although there have been attempts to trap him.'

'And what else do they say?'

Lily's cheeks were bright red as her mistress gave her an impatient little shake. 'Cook said it was all nonsense, but others said as it was Master Tom.'

'Are you saying that my brother has become a highwayman?'

Lily hung her head. It was obvious from her manner that she had heard the tale, and that she believed it.

'And you think it may have been him following us?'

Emma saw the truth in the other girl's eyes. 'But why would Tom shoot at the marquis?'

Lily was silent and Emma frowned. Surely it was nonsense? Why would her brother try to kill the Marquis of Lytham?

Oh, no! Surely he could not be out for revenge for what had happened to their father? The thought was so shocking that Emma felt sick. Tom would never deliberately try to murder someone—would he?

She remembered the quarrel between her father and brother. She had heard them shouting at each other in the library. Tom had bitterly denied his involvement in the crimes his father had accused him of and then he had stormed from the house. At the time she had not attempted to stop him, for she had imagined he would return when tempers had cooled, but he had not. She and her mother had deeply regretted the breach, and Emma suspected that her father had also come to wish he had not banished his only son, that he had brooded over it and his unhappiness had led to the increasing recklessness in his gambling.

She had thought Tom might come home after her father's death, had half-expected to see him at the funeral, but there had been no sign of him, and she had given up hope as the weeks and then months passed.

A memory stirred in the back of her mind. She had seen someone in the gardens outside her bedchamber on the night that the marquis had first come to the house.

Had that been Tom? Had he been watching the house, waiting for his opportunity?

Such an idea was very distressing to Emma, and she dismissed the thought almost immediately. Why should Tom have skulked in the bushes like that when he might have come into the house? Had he had something to say to Lytham, surely he could have said it face to face? The

brother she remembered would certainly have done so—
but had he changed? Had she ever really known him?

'You are to say nothing of this to the marquis,' she told
Lily. 'I shall tell him you think someone may have been
following us—but I want none of this foolishness over
highwaymen, or that there is a tale about my brother. It is
all gossip and I will not have it—do you understand me?'

'Yes, miss,' Lily said. 'I am sorry if I've made you angry, miss.'

'No, I am not angry,' Emma said. 'But this is a foolish
tale, Lily, and I want you to forget it. If there is a highwayman haunting the road between Cambridgeshire and
London, it is not my brother.'

'No, miss…if you say so.'

'I do say so,' Emma said. 'Now, go back to the inn and
see if you can make yourself useful to his lordship. Knock
at his door and ask if he wants anything, and then go to
my room and wait for me.'

'Yes, miss.'

Lily hung her head as she retraced her head to the inn.
It was clear that she felt her mistress had been sharp with
her, which was a pity and not what Emma had intended—
but she could not allow such tales to reach Lytham's ears.

She decided that she would take up his offer to try to
trace Tom. She had already been toying with the idea of
employing an agent to try to find her brother, and now she
realised that it might be more important than she had previously thought.

She wandered as far down the road as she dared, finding
a wooden seat that overlooked a pretty view of the river,
and sat down to ponder her situation. Could Tom have
taken that shot at Lytham? Were the rumours of his having
arranged an accident to bring about a man's death by some
remote chance true? No, she could not believe it and yet…

Emma sat there for some moments, staring at the brown water as it weaved its way sluggishly through reed beds and lapped against willow-fronded banks. She had wondered how Tom was managing to live, cut off from home and family. She had thought he might have joined the army, for he had spoken of wishing he might when they were children—but to become a highwayman!

That was indeed a desperate act, and one that made Emma feel shivers down her spine. It was a hanging matter if he was caught…but…no, she would not believe it. The servants had got hold of some foolish tale and made it more than it was…

'Emma? It is you, isn't it?'

Emma jumped as she heard the voice, spinning round to stare in bewilderment at the man who had spoken so tentatively. She rose to her feet, feeling as if she were in a nightmare. Tom here? Then it must have been him Lily had seen following them.

'Tom…is that you?' Her face was as white as a sheet, her heart beating wildly. 'Oh, Tom! I was just thinking about you.'

'Lily spotted me, didn't she?' Tom came towards her a little awkwardly. 'I saw her looking out of the window and thought she might have seen me—that's why I dodged off into the woods.'

'Oh, Tom!' Emma went to greet him, her hands outstretched. 'Why didn't you come home for the funeral? Why didn't you come to see Mama and I after Father died?'

'I wasn't sure I would be welcome,' Tom said. 'Besides, I've only just recovered from…a nasty chill.'

Emma was sure he had been going to say something else.

'Tom…' It was a terrible thing to ask, but she had to be sure. 'You didn't take a shot at someone earlier today, did you?'

His eyes lost their look of uncertainty, becoming angry. 'If that's what you think of me, I may as well go now.'

'No!' She took a step towards him, catching at his arm. 'I didn't think it was you, but Lily told me…'

Tom pulled a wry face. 'I can imagine what she said.' He paused and then squared his shoulders. 'It's true, Emma. I did take to the road for a while. I was desperate and I fell in with someone…a bad lot.'

'Oh, Tom…' Her heart caught and she looked round as if fearing someone might hear his confession. 'That is so dangerous.'

'I know.' He looked rueful. 'Someone took a pot-shot at us some months ago, and I was wounded. I've been ill of a fever, and then I went into hiding because I was told they were looking for us. That's why I couldn't come home for the funeral—because I might have been arrested.'

'Are you in danger of being arrested now?'

'I've given up the life,' Tom said. 'I doubt if anyone has proof that I was involved in any of the crimes we committed. But the man I was with is threatening to murder me if I don't help him with something he has in mind.'

'What is that?' Emma sensed that he was nervous. 'You might as well tell me, Tom.'

'I think he took that shot at Lytham,' Tom said after a moment's hesitation. 'He had me watching the house for Lytham's arrival but…when I guessed what he intended, I refused to help him with the rest of it. But I saw someone skulking in the woods just after the shot, and I think it may have been him.'

'The rest of it?' Emma felt the chill run down her spine. 'What are you talking about, Tom?'

'I shouldn't have told you so much.' Her brother glanced over his shoulder. 'He would kill me if he knew—but I wanted to warn Lytham to be on his guard. If *his* attempt to murder the marquis has failed this time, he will try again. He hates him and has vowed to see him dead.'

'Who is this man?' Emma hung on to his arm as he tried to turn away. 'You have to tell me, Tom.'

'I don't know his name, not his real name—and that's the truth,' Tom said. 'All I know is that he hates Lytham. He swears he has a score to settle…and that was said when he was drunk one night. Usually he is tight lipped and keeps his plans to himself.'

'You are afraid of him, aren't you?'

Tom nodded but said nothing.

'Why did you get involved with him?'

'I was drunk and near to desperate,' Tom said. 'It seemed I had nothing left to hope for…I thought I might as well be hung as a thief since everyone already thought the worst of me.'

'Oh, my dearest brother…' Emma saw the hurt in his face and her throat tightened with emotion. 'What can I say?'

'Only that you believe me,' Tom said. 'Believe me, Emma, however desperate I might be, I would not kill, except in self-defence. I am not a murderer, and I did not arrange the death of Alexander Lytham's brother.'

She stared at him in horror. 'It was Lytham's brother— the man with whose wife you were supposed to have had an affair? It was Lord Lynston who fell from his horse and was killed?'

'Yes. I thought you must know.'

'I had no idea. Mother told me a part of it, but Father never mentioned the man's name. I don't think she knew that.'

'There was something between Maria and I,' Tom admitted, his cheeks pink. 'You are not to tell anyone else that, Emma. Give me your word!'

'Yes, of course.'

'I did not do anything that might have caused him to fall that afternoon. I give you my word.'

'Of course you didn't! I never believed it,' Emma cried.

'Thank you.' She was rewarded by a slight smile from Tom. 'But you thought I might have taken a pot-shot at Lytham today—why?'

'Because of what happened to Father and the estate.'

'He is welcome to the estate,' Tom said, a note of bitterness in his voice. 'Had I inherited there would have been nothing left. What I hoped for—what I wanted—was a career in the army, but Father would not fork out for a commission for me. He insisted I must look after the estate, but he had ruined us before I had the chance to try.'

'I am so sorry, Tom.'

He shook his head. 'It was not your fault—or Mama's. I have thought of you both often, but I believed it better not to involve you in more trouble. I'm going to find honest work if I can and then I'll do something to help you and Mama.'

'How can I reach you?' Emma asked as he began to move away from her again. 'Tom…don't go just like that, please?'

'It is better you do not try to contact me,' he said. 'If I need you, I'll be in touch.'

Emma stared after him as he ran towards the woods, where she thought he must have tethered his horse.

What was she going to do now?

Chapter Three

Emma had the rest of the day to consider her options, for the marquis did not appear before seven that evening when he came downstairs to join her in the private parlour for dinner. She saw that he had somehow managed to dress himself, struggling into his coat, which was foolish and unnecessary since they were to dine privately. He looked tired and pale, but seemed otherwise no worse for his injury, and denied feeling any great pain when she inquired.

'Thank you, but apart from a little soreness I believe I have taken no ill, Miss Sommerton.'

'Should you not have supped on a little broth in your room?' Emma asked. 'I am certain the innkeeper's wife would have been happy to have brought up a tray.'

'And that would have left you to fend for yourself,' Lytham said. 'I have already caused too much distress, and I can only apologise for it, Miss Sommerton. I thank you for remaining here and not finding yourself an alternative way to finish your journey.'

'I should not dream of abandoning you while you are unwell,' Emma said. 'And I could quite easily have had my dinner upstairs—could do so now, if you would prefer to return to your bed.'

'This is not the first time I have been wounded,' Lytham said. 'I had the privilege of serving under Wellington, and received a slight injury in the Spanish campaign. I was with him in France, too, and left him only after Boney had been beaten.'

'You were a soldier…' Emma nodded as if that confirmed something in her own mind. 'That was what my brother wanted above all things—a commission in the army.'

'It would probably have saved much unpleasantness had your father allowed him to have his way.' Lytham's gaze narrowed as he saw her blush. 'Have you considered that your brother may have joined the army already?'

'I…I am not sure that he would have joined the ranks, and anything else would have been out of the question.'

'Because he did not have the money?'

'That, and the shadow hanging over him.'

'Ah, yes, that accusation of cheating.'

Lytham's gaze narrowed as she avoided looking at him. Now what was she hiding? She had told him she knew nothing of her brother's whereabouts, but it seemed she had not told him the entire truth. He was certain she did know something, but his questions had to wait because the innkeeper's wife was bringing in their supper. She had prepared vegetable soup, which smelled delicious, and informed them that stuffed pike and a tender roast duckling would follow it.

'For I didn't want to cook anything too heavy for his lordship, miss,' she explained. 'Not but what there ain't a nice bit of roast beef if he should fancy it.'

'You are too good, madam,' Lytham said. 'We shall see how we go on, thank you.'

'So, what is it you don't want to tell me?' he asked once the woman had retired after serving the soup. 'It would be best if you deal honestly with me, Miss Sommerton. Be sure that I shall know if you lie—and I do not care for liars.'

'Lily saw someone following the carriage from the moment we left Sommerton House.'

'But she did not see fit to tell us?' He arched his brows. 'Why was that, I wonder?'

'I dare say she was frightened of you,' Emma replied. She glanced down at her dish, toying with her spoon. 'Besides, it does not follow that the man who was riding behind us took that shot at you.'

'It is not necessarily the case,' he agreed, but his eyes were hard and suspicious. 'Who was following us—your brother?'

Emma's gaze flew to his face in surprise. 'What makes you say that?'

'Although some may make the mistake of thinking it, I am not a fool, Miss Sommerton. When did you know your brother had been following us?'

'Not until after—' She bit her lip. 'Tom said it was not he who shot you and I believe him.'

'Indeed? Should I believe you? I wonder?'

'I am not in the habit of lying.'

'I do believe that,' he said. 'You should never play cards, Miss Sommerton. You have the most expressive face and it gives you away every time.' He studied her as she choked over a spoonful of soup. He had hardly touched his own, she noticed. 'Come, now, it cannot be that bad.'

'You are pleased to mock me, sir!'

'Yes, it does please me,' he admitted. 'But tell me—what has your brother been getting up to now?'

'Nothing…why should he?'

'You told me he had not been home since his father's death. There must be some reason for that, would you not agree? I would have thought it was an excellent opportunity for him to visit his mother and sister. And yet he approaches you now.'

'He has been ill...'

'Ah, so he has been ill. I wonder what kind of illness?'

'A fever, I believe.' Wild horses would not have dragged the truth from her!

'Yes, but what had he been doing before he became ill?' Lytham mused. 'Clearly you do not mean to tell me, Miss Sommerton. Has your brother given you an address where we may contact him?'

'No. He...he said he would come to me if he needed me.'

Lytham nodded. 'Then, whether you know it or not, he is involved in something.' He saw that she was staring at the table again. 'You may tell me the truth, you know. I have no intention of bringing more harm to your family— any member of your family.'

Emma glanced up, meeting his eyes. 'My brother is in some kind of trouble,' she admitted. 'I cannot tell you what exactly for I do not know—but he said that I was to warn you of danger to yourself.'

'It is a little late for that, do you not think?'

'He did not know you would be shot at,' Emma said, though she could not be sure that Tom hadn't had some idea of it. Why else would he have been following them? 'He says that someone... A man he knows has a score to settle, but he does not know the man's name, only that he is a bad lot. I believe this man may have been committing acts of highway robbery these past few weeks.'

'Ah, now we are getting to it,' Lytham said, nodding his head. 'Your brother has been involved, but draws the line at murder—is that it? No, you do not need to answer, for it would incriminate both you and your brother.'

'Tom is not a murderer. He told me that he did not arrange your brother's death.'

'I am sure that John's death was the result of his own recklessness,' Lytham said. 'Your father should have known better than to believe such rumours. There were bound to be some after what happened—but I shall make inquiries and do my best to clear your brother's name...of this at least.'

'I do not believe he cheated at cards either,' Emma said, holding her head proudly. 'He always maintained his innocence, but he was not believed.'

'It is a difficult thing to disprove,' Lytham said. 'But this also I shall look into—there, does that make you more inclined to trust me?'

'I have had no reason to distrust you, sir.'

'And yet you continue to hold me at arm's length.'

'How else should I behave, sir? We are destined to part in another day or so.'

'Perhaps.' His mouth curved in a mocking smile. 'Why is it that I do not believe that, Miss Sommerton?'

Her heart raced wildly as she saw the laughter in his eyes. He was a very provoking man and she had a good mind to tell him so, but she did not quite dare.

'Perhaps because you do not wish to believe it, sir.'

'That may be true. I have always taken my responsibilities towards others seriously. Until I believe you safely settled, I could not simply abandon you.'

'Even if I prefer to be abandoned?'

'Even so.' He inclined his head. She thought he looked a little uncomfortable, but he was intent on questioning her and she did not ask if he was too warm, though his face was flushed. 'Did your brother give you a name or any other clue to this rogue's identity?'

'None, sir. He said merely that you should be on your

guard. I do know that Tom is afraid of him, whoever he is. Apparently, he has threatened to kill him if he does not help him do whatever it is he intends to do.'

'Murder me, do you think?' Lytham's brows rose. 'And yet will there ever be a more perfect opportunity than this morning in the woods? I feel that the shot that winged me was a warning in itself.'

'But why?' Emma frowned as she posed the question. 'Have you an enemy, sir? Someone who would like to make you suffer…someone for whom a quick death would not be enough?'

'That seems a likely explanation, does it not?' His brow furrowed. 'I have not been able to think of anyone I have offended to that degree, except your brother. I believe he may feel he has cause to wish for my death. There is the matter of the quarrel with his father, which led to his being disowned, and, if that were not enough, I am responsible for your father's death. Please believe me when I tell you I wish I could have prevented that, but it happened and there is no denying it. Your brother has more than one grievance that might make him wish to kill me.'

'It was not Tom who shot you!'

Lytham looked at her gravely, then nodded. 'You know, I am inclined to think you may be right. Your brother is clearly a hot head, Miss Sommerton—and whoever planned this has taken his time.'

'Who would benefit from your death, sir?' Emma asked. 'Have you no brothers or cousins?'

'I have distant cousins in the north,' he admitted. 'But I do not know them. I cannot think they covet my fortune to such a degree—and I am the last of my immediate family.'

'Then you must have an enemy—someone who hates you,' Emma said. 'Are you sure you cannot think of anyone? Perhaps someone with a grudge against your family, if not you personally?'

'I believe my father and John may have made enemies,' Lytham said, looking thoughtful. 'Your brother was not the only one to have been ruined by them.'

'Then that is perhaps where you should look.'

He shook his head and she noticed again that he looked flushed. He was sweating now. Was he ill and too stubborn to admit it?

'But they are dead,' he said as if to convince himself. 'Would such hatred continue beyond the grave?'

'It seems unlikely, sir—but unless it was merely a poacher...' She left the sentence unfinished, hesitating for a moment, then, 'No, Tom risked much to warn me. You do have an enemy, sir. You must look deeply into your past and think of someone you have injured.'

Lytham frowned. 'There was once a man who might have hated me, but he is dead. I heard that he had been killed in a bar in Spain after he was court-martialled.'

Emma saw that he was thoughtful. 'You have remembered someone who might have cause to hate you enough to kill you?'

He drew a deep sigh and did not answer at once. She could swear that he was feverish and his eyes had an odd brightness about them. She believed that it was taking a supreme effort of will to sit there talking to her as if nothing was wrong.

'He was reported killed,' Lytham said. 'But if he lived...yes, Pennington might hate me sufficiently to make me suffer before he killed.'

'What did you do to him?'

His face was hard as he returned her accusing look. 'What makes you imagine that I did anything?'

'Forgive me, but you did say he might have cause.'

'I was unwittingly the cause of his downfall,' Lytham said. 'He committed the unforgivable sin of raping another officer's wife while under the influence of drink, and I was the first on the scene afterwards. I did what I could to help her, and then went to her husband. He challenged Pennington to a duel, and for that he received a severe reprimand— but Pennington was court-martialled and dismissed from the service in disgrace.'

'And so I should think!' Emma cried. 'In my opinion, he deserved more than that.'

'He received more,' Lytham said and something flickered in his eyes. 'Some of the other officers got together after he was dismissed. They whipped him and spat at him, humiliated him in all manner of unspeakable ways, and finally drove him out without a decent rag to his back.' He saw that she had turned pale. 'Forgive me, that was not a tale to repeat to a lady.'

'It was no more than he deserved,' Emma said, recovering from the shock. She rather liked it in him that he had told her the whole tale. Most gentlemen would think it too terrible for her to hear. 'But why should that make him hate you? Unless you were one of those officers?'

'No. I was aware of their plans, but I did nothing. I have often thought that I ought to have reported them, but I was disgusted at what he had done, and although I did not join them, I condoned what they did. That was wrong and has been a shame to me ever since, Miss Sommerton. I have told no other.'

'Then I am honoured by your confidence, sir. You may rest assured that it will go no further.' She looked at him uncertainly, taking note of the beads of sweat on his brow. The stubborn man was obviously ill, but refusing to admit it. What ought she to do?

'Thank you. You are a remarkable woman, Emma Sommerton.'

'You are certain this man was killed in a brawl?'

'I was told it was certain, but I had no evidence. I wished to put the whole incident from my mind.'

'Yes, I can understand how you felt,' she agreed. 'But I think you should try to make further inquiries—don't you?'

'Yes, perhaps.' He laid down his spoon. 'This is excellent fare, but I do not feel I can eat much more. Will you excuse me if…?' He rose to his feet, gave a sigh and then staggered, crashing into the table.

Some instinct had Emma on her feet in time to prevent him falling. He leaned on her heavily, muttering an apology as she assisted him to a wooden bench.

'You are ill, my lord. You should have stayed in your room.'

'Forgive me,' he said and gave her the sweetest smile. 'I was feeling perfectly well when I came down.'

Emma placed her hand against his brow. 'I think you have a slight fever, sir. Will you allow me to help you upstairs?'

'Call the landlord,' he said thickly. 'It is not fitting for you to help me to bed.'

'I dare say he is busy just for the moment,' Emma said. 'If you can lean on me I believe we might make it up the stairs…if we go slowly.'

'Yes, I think I could manage if you help me. I am so sorry.'

'Hush, you foolish man,' Emma replied. 'Put your arm about my waist and we shall do the best we can.'

He obeyed her, clearly feeling much worse than he would allow. Emma marvelled that he had managed to hold a sensible conversation with her for so long. He was obviously suffering both a great deal of pain, and judging by the heat coming from his body was also in fever.

She drew him from the parlour into the hall, just as a party of rather rowdy gentlemen was being ushered into the larger parlour next door. One of them laughed and nudged his friend, who leered at Emma suggestively. They seemed to imagine she was assisting a drunken man, and probably thought the worst.

Emma ignored them, concentrating on getting him up the stairs. She had managed to get halfway when one of the maids came hurrying to help them.

'Is the gentleman ill again, miss?' she asked. 'He was very hot earlier and I offered to fetch the doctor, but he wouldn't hear of it.'

'I think we must send for the physician as soon as he is in bed,' Emma said, ignoring the muffled protests of the man she was half-carrying by now.

It was difficult to get him to his room, but once they had him on the bed the maid hurried away to fetch the stable lad, who would ride at once for the doctor. Emma left the marquis for a moment as she went down the hall to her own room and summoned Lily.

'The marquis is ill,' she said. 'We must get him into bed and sponge him down to cool some of the heat before the doctor gets here.'

'You can't do that, miss,' Lily said, looking horrified. 'You can't go into a gentleman's bedchamber—not a lady like you.'

'I have already been into his bedchamber,' Emma said, ever practical. 'Besides, no one need know if we do not tell them. It will be our secret, Lily.'

'Why don't you let me look after him, miss?'

It was exactly what she ought to do, of course—but Emma could not simply abandon the marquis to his fate.

'We shall do it together,' she said. 'No one can say it was improper if you were there, can they?'

Lily opened her mouth and then shut it again. She had not forgotten that her mistress had been sharp with her earlier, and she did not want to upset Miss Sommerton again.

'No one need know, miss…if that's what you want?'

'It is what I want,' Emma said and smiled at her. 'Thank you, Lily—and I'm sorry if I was sharp with you earlier.'

'Oh, that's all forgot now, miss.'

'Follow me, then.' Emma led the way back down the hall to the marquis's bedchamber. He was lying where she had left him, but as she entered he moved restlessly and called out a name. Emma could not make out whom he was calling to, but she imagined it was a woman—perhaps the woman he loved, she thought. She laid a hand on his brow, frowning as she felt the heat. 'It is all right, my lord, the doctor will come soon.'

He muttered something she could not hear again, and Emma turned as Lily brought a bowl of cold water to the bed.

'Had we better undress him, miss?'

'Yes, I think we ought,' Emma said. 'You start with his boots and I'll bathe his face, and then we'll take off the rest of his things.'

'You'd better turn your back when we get to his breeches,' Lily said. 'I've seen a naked man before when I nursed my father, but I dare say you haven't, miss.'

'No…' Emma swallowed hard. 'Yes, perhaps that would be best, Lily. I'll help with the rest and leave that to you.'

She bathed his face, and then began to take off his neckcloth and then his coat, waistcoat and shirt. He winced as she tugged at his coat, and she wondered at the strength of mind that had got him into it with his wounded arm in the first place. He was clearly a stubborn man, but now he was suffering for his reckless behaviour.

Lily had discarded his boots, and she began to pull down his skintight breeches, warning Emma when it was time to turn her back.

'It's all right, miss. I've covered him with a sheet. He's decent now. You can turn round again.'

Emma turned back to the bed. She saw that the top half of his body was still uncovered, which was enough to make her stomach clench with the oddest sensation. She had never realised that a man's naked body could look so beautiful, and half-regretted that she had dutifully turned her back as Lily finished undressing him.

Lily had begun to sponge his shoulders and arms while Emma looked on. He muttered in his fever a few times, but she thought that he was not really aware of what was happening.

'He's proper poorly,' Lily said. 'It's a terrible shame, miss—and him such a fine figure of a man, too.'

'Yes, he is, isn't he?' Emma said, her voice sounding husky. 'I should imagine he is quite strong.'

'Oh, yes, miss—but it's often the strongest what the fever takes.'

Emma wished that her maid would be a little more cheerful, but she held her tongue. Lily might be needed in the next few days and she did not want to upset her again.

'I think you should go back to your own room now, miss,' Lily said. 'It would be better if there was just me here when the doctor comes—don't you think?'

'Yes, I suppose so. But you must tell me what he says as soon as he has gone.'

Emma was reluctant to leave, but it would not do her reputation any good if she remained, and so she went out into the hall and started to make her way towards her own room.

'Ain't he no good to you this evening, lovely lady?' a voice asked, and Emma looked into the flushed face of one of the men she had seen downstairs a few minutes earlier. 'I could show you how a proper man behaves with his woman.'

'Please allow me to pass,' Emma said haughtily, disliking the suggestive leer on his face. 'Stand aside, sir—or I shall call for the landlord.'

'No call to take offence,' the man replied, swaying slightly on his feet. 'Just being friendly—doxy!' His taunt was clearly meant to wound because she had refused him, but Emma did not care to answer, merely going into her own room and locking the door.

It would stay locked until Lily came!

Several hours passed before Lily came at last to tell her that the doctor had been.

'Doctor Fettle gave the gentleman something to ease him, miss. He says someone needs to sit with his lordship all night—and the innkeeper's wife is there now. She told me to get some rest. You should too, miss. You haven't slept at all, have you?'

'I couldn't rest until you came,' Emma said. 'But I shall try to do so now.'

It was in any case difficult to sleep since Emma was unused to sharing a bed. She dozed for a while, but when Lily began to snore got up, dressed, and went down the hall to the marquis's room.

The innkeeper's wife put a finger to her lips as Emma entered.

'You shouldn't have come, miss. It isn't fitting for a young lady.'

'I had to know how he was faring.'

'A little better, I think. Go back to bed, miss. I can manage here.'

'I would rather just sit here quietly for a while. You have been sitting with him for hours now. Why don't you go and get some sleep? I am sure you have much to do in the morning.'

The woman looked at her uncertainly. 'That's true enough…if you're sure, miss?'

'Perfectly sure,' Emma said and took her place by the bed. 'Thank you for being so kind to us.'

'It was no more than anyone would do. Such wickedness to shoot down a fine man like that. 'Tis a wicked shame that such a thing should happen, that a man cannot be safe anywhere these days. I hope they catch whoever did it and hang him!'

Emma nodded, but did not speak again. She was watching the marquis as he slept, and got up to place her hand on his brow as the other woman went out. Was it her imagination—or did he seem a little cooler than he had earlier in the evening?

She wrung out a cloth in cool water and bathed his face and neck, smoothing the cool linen over his shoulders, then sat down by the fire again. The logs were still smouldering, though no longer giving out much heat and she shivered as the chill went over her. Had Tom been telling the truth when he said he had not shot Lytham? She did hope so for she did not think she could forgive him if he had… especially if the marquis should die. But he would not die! He was strong and despite what Lily had said earlier, she believed that he would beat this fever.

'Please, God, let him live,' Emma prayed aloud. 'Do not let him die. But he will not die! He is much too strong to let something like this defeat him.'

'Water…' She heard the harsh whisper and went to him, seeing that his eyes were open. 'Please…water…'

There was a jug of water beside the bed. She poured a little into a cup, and then saw that she would have to help him to drink.

'Help me…'

'Yes, of course,' she said and put her arm about his shoulders, lifting him so that he could sip from the cup she held to his lips. 'Just a little at a time, not too much at once.'

'You are a good nurse,' he muttered and she realised that the fever had broken. His eyes were open and looking straight at her. 'But you ought not to be here.'

'Others have been sitting with you,' she said. 'Lily and the innkeeper's wife. I have merely come to give them a rest.'

He sighed as she laid him back against the pillows. 'Damned fool…all right now. Go to bed, Emma.'

'In a little while,' she agreed. 'When I see you are settled.'

'Sleep now,' he said and his eyes closed.

Emma sat with him for another hour or so, but he seemed to be peaceful and she believed the fever had gone. It was as she had thought; he was strong and had been able to fight the sickness off more easily than some others might, and she thanked God for it.

Lily came just as dawn was breaking.

'You should get some rest, miss,' she said. 'I'll sit with him now—unless you need me?'

'No, you stay here,' Emma said. 'But I think you will find he is much better. I dare say he will wake and call for his breakfast soon.'

'He's sure to be weak for a few days,' Lily said in a

voice of doom. 'And just because he's settled it doesn't mean the fever's gone. It can come back worse, so they say—the fever does for many a man what seems strong as a horse.'

'Thank you, Lily,' Emma said and smiled inwardly. Did Lily enjoy being the forecaster of ill fortune?

She was fairly sure in her own mind that the danger time had passed and was able to rest on her bed for a few hours before she rose and went down the hall once more to look in on the marquis.

As she had suspected, he was propped up against his pillows and eating what looked like a milky porridge. He set the bowl aside as she went in and gave her a disapproving look.

'I believe I told you last night—you ought not to be here, Miss Sommerton.'

'In fact, you called me Emma last night,' she said and smiled at him. 'I see that you are feeling more yourself, my lord. I shall not stay to disturb your sensibilities, but go down at once and break my fast.'

'I shall come down later.'

'You would be foolish to try. Why do you not stay in bed for today? You should rest for the morning, at least.'

'But you will wish to continue your journey. Mrs Flynn will be expecting you.'

'She will not worry too soon. Travelling is always uncertain, and she will merely think there has been some delay.'

He looked amused. 'Are you always so calm?'

Emma smiled, but would not be drawn. She had felt less than calm on several occasions recently, and most of them were due to this man.

'You know that is not so, my lord. I believe I treated

you to a most unseemly display of temper the first day you arrived at Sommerton.'

'Ah, yes, but I took you by surprise, didn't I, Emma? It was Emma I met that afternoon, and it was Emma who gave me water last night—but you are Miss Sommerton now.'

'Surely Emma and Miss Sommerton are one and the same?'

'Oh, no,' he said and his eyes gleamed with humour. 'I can assure you that they are two very different people.'

'I shall not question your judgement,' Emma replied. 'One should always humour an invalid, especially when fever is present.'

With that she went out, a little smile on her lips as she heard his laughter. How was it that he had penetrated her secret self in a way that no one else outside her family had for years? She was not sure that even her beloved mother truly knew the real Emma. She had subdued her passionate nature long ago, knowing that a life of duty caring for her mother quietly at home was likely to be her lot, but just now and then she had allowed herself to dream.

She shook her head, dismissing the foolish dreams that had started to come into her mind since...since never mind! She would not be wise to let Emma loose, and would do better to keep up the pretence of being the calm, serene Miss Sommerton who was always ready in an emergency.

Fortunately, the emergency seemed to be over. Lytham took her advice and stayed in his room until late that afternoon, coming down in time to order dinner for them both in the private parlour.

'Are you feeling better, my lord?' Emma asked, noticing that he had sensibly not tried to force himself into his elegant coat this time, but allowed it to rest over his injured arm. 'You certainly look less flushed than you did yesterday evening.'

'My wound is still a little sore and my shoulder feels stiff, but I believe I am on the mend now. I must apologise for causing you so much trouble last night, Miss Sommerton.'

'I really had very little trouble from you,' Emma assured him. 'You should thank Lily and Mrs Bennett—she is the innkeeper's wife, you know. It is Mrs Bennett who has been put to some trouble, for we are occupying rooms that were promised to someone else.'

'Yes, I dare say,' Lytham said. 'I shall have to give her a handsome present to make up for it—and Lily, too.'

'Shall you feel able to continue your journey tomorrow, my lord?'

'Yes, certainly. I am sorry to have delayed you, Miss Sommerton.'

'As I believe I told you, it is no matter.'

Lytham inclined his head, but made no further apology. He sat with her in the parlour and they discussed various books they had read, discoursing on the merits of Byron, Shelley and the quieter, whimsical work of Charles Lamb, exactly as they might have had they been in any London drawing room.

Dinner was served at six o'clock, which was early by town standards but quite late for country hours. Mrs Bennett had done them proud with soup followed by roast pork, a baked ham, trout and a side dish of baked potatoes and parsnips.

Emma was pleased to see that the marquis did this excellent fare justice, and she herself indulged in two of the custard tarts provided as a sweet course. Afterwards, they took their mulled wine to sit by the fire, the evening having turned quite chilly.

Their conversation had graduated to music and politics, and they had a lively debate on the merits or otherwise of the Corn Laws. The law had been passed that March to forbid the importation of foreign corn until the price was sufficiently high to enable the farmers to make a decent profit, but had unfortunately led to a four-pound loaf rising to the astronomical price of one shilling and tuppence.

'Well, I dare say we shall never see eye to eye on such matters,' Emma said with a smile after they had argued the subject long and hard. 'For I think of the poor villager in his cottage, and you think like a wealthy landowner.'

'Commerce must have its way,' Lytham said, amused that she had forgotten to be Miss Sommerton during her impassioned defence of the rights of the common man. 'But if the villager in his cottage were paid a fair wage might he not make his own choice about whether or not he wished to buy a loaf or bake his own?'

'Now that is another debate altogether,' Emma said and was startled by the striking of the clock in the hall. 'Do you know it is ten o'clock, sir? We have sat here all evening talking, and it is time you were in bed if you are to be fit to travel on the morrow.'

'And you must be tired since I kept you from your bed last night.'

Lytham rose with her, catching her hand, as she would have turned away. She gazed back at him, and something in her face got through to him. Before he realised what he was doing, he had drawn her close to him and, as she made no attempt to pull away but looked up at him fearlessly, her eyes dark with emotion, he bent his head to kiss her lips. His kiss was soft at first, but deepened, becoming fiercer and more passionate than he had intended.

The effect was startling for them both. Emma felt a sensation such as she had never experienced before; it seemed to burn its way through her body like slow fire, making her melt into his embrace helplessly, all resistance gone. Dimly at the back of her mind she knew that she ought not to allow this, but the overwhelming pleasure she felt prevented her from breaking away. She had never dreamed that a kiss could be so sweet! For his part, Lytham was aware of a fierce desire to scoop this woman up in his arms and carry her off to his bedchamber.

The madness lasted no more than seconds, for both remembered where and who they were and broke away almost simultaneously.

'Forgive me,' Lytham muttered, fighting the urgent need she had aroused in him. 'That was unforgivable in the circumstances.'

'It was foolish,' Emma replied. 'But understandable, my lord.'

'How so?' His brows arched. How would she seek to make such a kiss commonplace?

'You have had a brush with death…men must be forgiven much in such a case, so I have heard.'

He gave a crack of laughter. 'No! That is doing it too brown, Miss Sommerton. I am not in the grip of a fever now, I promise you—at least, not a fever induced by that slight wound to my shoulder.'

'Not so slight, my lord. You were quite ill last night. Lily was very fearful that you would succumb to your hurts.'

'Then Lily is a foolish girl,' Lytham said and frowned. 'There was never any danger of my dying from such a paltry injury. Goodnight, Miss Sommerton. I would debate this matter further with you—but the hour is late and I have taken too much advantage of your good nature already.'

'Goodnight, my lord. I wish you pleasant dreams,' Miss

Sommerton said, but Emma's heart was saying something very different.

She went from the parlour hurriedly, knowing that once again she had betrayed herself into unseemly behaviour. It was fortunate that the marquis was a gentleman, for otherwise she might have been in some trouble.

Hurrying up to her room, Emma found that Lily had turned down the bed and passed a warming pan between the sheets. She assisted Emma into her nightgown, and then retired to the truckle bed that Mrs Bennett had set up.

'I thought it best, miss,' Lily said. 'You did not sleep well last night, and my snoring will not disturb you so much if I am not beside you.'

Emma thanked the girl for her thoughtfulness, but she was so tired that she did not think anything would keep her awake, even the memory of that kiss.

She closed her eyes and soon drifted into a pleasant dream...of kisses that never ended and a man who spoke of love.

It was a fine dry morning, and Emma woke early to discover that Lily had brought a breakfast tray to her room.

'The marquis requested that you breakfast early, miss,' she explained. 'He has been out already, making sure that everything is ready—and one of the grooms from the inn is to ride with us so that his lordship's own groom may keep a sharp eye out for anyone who might follow us.'

'Has Lord Lytham asked you anything about the horseman who followed us the other day?'

'He did ask me when I first saw the man, miss,' Lily said and blushed. 'And he asked me to tell him if I noticed anything in future. I said I would, miss—was that all right?'

'Yes, of course.'

*   *   *

Emma discovered that the marquis was wearing his coat
in the normal fashion, and from his manner when she went
down seemed perfectly recovered. Indeed, had she not seen
him in the fever, she would not have thought that he had
had a moment's illness in his life.

'I am sorry to appear impatient, Miss Sommerton,' he
said. 'But I thought we should continue with all speed. Mrs
Flynn will begin to worry if you do not soon keep your
appointment with her.'

Since he seemed impatient to deliver her to her employer, Emma could only think that he had regretted his
impulse of the evening before. It was as she had suspected,
a moment's madness on his part. She imagined that he kept
a mistress, and that he was used to dealing with experienced
women. He had had no intention of encouraging any pre-
tensions in her, and she was sure that she would not have
been his choice had he been considering marriage. So it
was just as well that she was a sensible woman who could
put an unimportant incident from her mind and behave as
if nothing had happened.

'I am certain you also have business, sir,' she replied
briskly. 'The sooner we arrive in town and you can deliver
me to Mrs Flynn's door, the better.'

Lytham nodded, but made no further comment. When he
had helped first her and then Lily into his carriage, he
climbed in himself, settling down with his long legs
stretched out before him and his eyes closed.

Emma waited for him to begin a conversation as he had
on the first day, but as the miles passed and he did not
speak, she realised that he had withdrawn into himself.

Clearly he did not wish to become further involved with
a woman whose family had caused him nothing but trouble,
and she could not find it in her heart to blame him. She
could wish that he had allowed her to go her own way from

the start, but there was no sense in repining over what could not be altered.

She had suffered reverses before and coped…but something told her that it would be many nights before she ceased to dream of that kiss.

Chapter Four

Lytham roused himself from his reverie to make casual conversation for the final hour or so of their journey. He was, he told Emma, planning to go out of town for a few weeks.

'I have some business to complete, but after that I may be gone for nearly a month.'

'You are to visit your estates perhaps, sir?'

'I must visit my aunt,' he said. 'She has complained that I never do so, although I spent a month at my estate earlier in the year.'

'I dare say she is lonely. Perhaps you should bring her back to town with you?'

'I have suggested such a visit, but she has always declined,' Lytham said. 'However, the idea of a companion was a good one. I must see what can be done.' His gaze was thoughtful as it rested on Emma. 'I shall not forget your affairs whilst I am away. You may expect a visit from me on my return to town.'

'As I believe I told you, I am not certain where we shall be.'

'A letter to my London address will keep me informed.' The tone of his voice made it a command rather than a request, and Emma gave him a speaking look. However, it was reasonable to suppose that he might have some business to discuss with her, and she nodded once to show that she acquiesced.

'Good.' He gave her a look of approval. 'We made an unfortunate beginning, Miss Sommerton, but there is no reason why we should not progress.'

Emma was not certain what he meant by this, but she made no demur. Indeed, she was pleased rather than dismayed at the idea of seeing him again.

'There is, of course, no need for us to meet in the future as other than friends,' she agreed. 'Should I be able to assist you in the matter of disposing of my father's estate, I shall be happy to do so.'

'As to that…' Lytham paused. 'Well, we shall see. I have not made up my mind yet.' He glanced out of the window as their carriage slowed to a decorous halt. 'It seems we have arrived.'

Lytham jumped down as soon as they had stopped outside the tall but narrow house in an elegant square, handing both Emma and Lily from the carriage. The front door opened instantly at his knock, and a very pretty young woman dressed in an elegant lilac dress came flying past the rather staid-looking servant who had answered it. Her pale spun-gold hair was caught up in ringlets that bobbed about her face and were tied with satin ribbons.

'Emma!' cried Bridget Flynn. 'I have been worried to death thinking that some accident had befallen you. But you are here now and all in one piece so everything is all right.'

Emma saw the expression on Lytham's face and smiled inwardly. She was not sure what he had expected, but the very fashionable young woman who spoke without the trace of an Irish accent was evidently a surprise to him.

'Bridget...or perhaps I should say Mrs Flynn.' Emma accepted her friend's impulsive hug and laughed. 'May I introduce you to the Marquis of Lytham, who very kindly brought me to London in his own carriage.'

'But isn't he the one—?' Bridget bit back the embarrassing words and offered her hand to him in a friendly manner that robbed the situation of any awkwardness. 'It is a pleasure to meet you, sir. Especially if you have been kind to my dearest Emma.'

'Thank you, ma'am.' Lytham's mouth twitched slightly. This dazzling creature was far from the wretched widow he had been imagining as Emma's future employer. 'No doubt you are eager to be alone with Miss Sommerton, so I shall not trespass on your hospitality.' His eyes challenged Emma. So this was the reason for that odd, secretive look in her eyes! 'I had not perfectly understood your situation. Please excuse me, I have other business.'

'Pray do call on us another day,' Bridget invited with an appealing innocence that he did not believe for one moment. She was a minx and those flashing eyes would be the downfall of many a man, especially now that she was a wealthy widow. 'As yet we have few engagements, though I hope for more once it is known we are in town.'

'This is not the best time of year for social occasions in town,' Lytham said. 'My advice would be to visit Bath for a few months and come back in the spring, ma'am. I believe you might find that quite diverting.'

'Yes, perhaps we may once I have something decent to wear. I have only recently come out of blacks for my dearest Bertie, you know, and I am eager to buy a new wardrobe—in fact, we shall both buy new clothes. I must tell you, sir, Emma was my dearest friend at school, and I am determined to make up to her for the unhappy time she has had of late.'

'I wish you both good fortune.' Lytham bowed to her, gave Emma a very odd look and took his leave without more to-do.

'Well…' Bridget said, glancing naughtily at Emma as she drew her into the house. 'That was a shock. I had no idea that the dastardly marquis was so attractive. No wonder your journey took so much longer than it ought.'

'Pray do not imagine anything until I tell you the whole story,' Emma said, but her heart lifted as she looked at her friend. It was such a long time since they had been together at school, and although they had always exchanged letters, she had almost forgotten how much fun it was to be with Bridget. 'Let me start from the beginning. We have had such a time of it!'

Her story unfolded, leaving nothing she considered of importance out, apart from that kiss…which had been a mere moment of madness and consequently not worth repeating.

'So you did not tell him about us,' Bridget said. 'That must account for his look when he first saw me. Do you suppose he thought I was a woman of the lower orders?'

'He may very well have done so,' Emma said and gave a little giggle. 'Perhaps it was wrong of me to deceive him, Bridget—but he was so autocratic at first. He had come to make us his dependants and it quite took the wind out of his sails when he discovered that Mama had escaped to Italy with friends, and that I was determined to become a companion.'

'Oh, pooh to that!' Bridget cried. 'It sounds very well— and we must appear to be completely respectable, Emma dearest—but you know that I invited you here to be my friend.' She pulled a naughty face. 'I shall need you to protect me once Lindisfarne arrives. He is determined to seduce me, and I am determined that he shall not.'

'Oh, Bridget,' Emma said. 'If only I could believe you.'

Her friend gave a little giggle of sheer pleasure. 'You cannot imagine how good it feels to be pursued again, Emma. I was married for nine months to my dear Bertie and I have been a widow for more than a year. Does that sound fair to you?'

'Not at all,' Emma replied. 'I told you in my letter how sorry I was for your loss.'

'I wept forever when he was killed.' Bridget pulled a face, her eyes shadowed by sadness. 'It was just like him to race his horse like that…in such a mad fashion. Bertie was such a dashing man, Emma. I wish you could have met him.'

'So do I…' She looked at Bridget and saw the haunted expression in her eyes. 'But I am sure he loved you and would not want you to grieve forever.'

'Oh, no, he absolutely forbade it,' Bridget replied. 'When we were courting he told me he'd had a premonition that he would not live long, and he made me promise that if I were to become a widow soon after we were married I would return to England and set the town on fire with his money.'

'Did he really say that?' Emma felt a little shiver down her spine. 'What a very exceptional man he must have been.'

'Oh, he was, the best,' Bridget said. 'He had nothing when we first met, you know, but then his uncle died and left him lots of lovely money—and Bertie was going to buy himself out of the army. We had planned to come back to London and set up house here.'

'And so you decided to come alone. I think that is very brave of you.'

'It is a promise, you see,' Bridget said. 'Only I didn't expect to like Lindisfarne as much as I do.'

'Ah, I see…'

'I went to call on him because Bertie talked about him so often. Lindisfarne is the black sheep of the family, Emma. The wicked earl—a terrible rake, gambler and altogether not the kind of man a young woman should know. She especially shouldn't fall in love with him.'

'Except that you have?'

'I think I may have,' Bridget admitted. 'I did not believe that I would ever love anyone again, but this is different. Bertie was like a part of me. We were so close that we might have been twins. Lindisfarne is different. He excites me and yet he terrifies me.'

'Yes…' Emma nodded her understanding. 'It is strange that you should say that, but there is a difference.'

'That is how you feel about the marquis, of course.' Bridget laughed and clapped her hands. 'Oh, do not bother to deny it, Emma—I saw it in your face. You never were very good at hiding your thoughts.'

'So I have been told. I hope that Lytham could not read me as easily as you could.'

'Oh, I doubt it,' Bridget replied blithely. 'Men are not as perceptive as we are…as the general rule. But were you in love the other way once?'

'It was during my first season,' Emma said. 'He was a very shy young man and we met only a few times. He picked up a glove for me once, and smiled at me. He sometimes sought me out at gatherings. I thought he liked me because he read poetry to me and told me I was different to the other young women he had met…but then he discovered Papa's estate was heavily encumbered and married an heiress.'

'Oh, poor Emma,' Bridget said. 'At least I did not have my heart broken in that way. I may have lost Bertie, but I know what it is like to be truly loved, and to be happy.'

'Yes, you were lucky and you must never forget that,' Emma said. 'I cannot truly say my heart was broken, though my confidence received a severe setback. I did not take well in my first season, you know, and I was never given another chance.'

'You were a late developer,' Bridget said, looking at her consideringly. 'I think you could be startling in the right clothes.'

'That sounds ominous,' Emma said. 'I am not sure that I wish to be startling.'

'You know what I mean,' Bridget said. 'You have that remote, proud look, rather like a princess or a queen. I think you could be a heartbreaker, and I shall take great pleasure in dressing you as befits royalty.'

'A few clothes I can accept, but there is no need to go overboard, Bridget.'

'Oh, pooh to that,' Bridget replied. 'I have far too much money to spend it all on me, Emma, and I am determined on this. I want us both to take the town by storm. Would you not like to be all the rage…just for once in your life?'

'Well, I suppose…' Emma was tempted and the mischief in her friend's eyes made her laugh. 'Just what are you planning?'

'Oh, nothing very much,' Bridget said. 'But I shall be very interested to see what the Marquis of Lytham makes of you when he sees you next time.'

Lytham frowned as he flicked through the pile of letters awaiting him at his London house. Even after a few days there was always some pressing matter of business that must be attended—and for once in his life he was not in the mood for making more money.

He tossed the notes aside as he went over to the sideboard and poured himself a brandy—far superior to any that he had tasted in the past week. He sipped it reflectively as he went to stand by the fireplace, one immaculate boot resting on the fender.

His valet had near fainted at the sight of the Hessians he had worn into the country, but these were superbly polished and he was once again dressed in the elegant but understated dress he adopted for town.

It seemed that Toby had made some headway with his heiress, and he was invited to an intimate gathering of friends, which might possibly turn out to be an engagement party. It was in two days' time, and would mean that he would need to stay in town a day later than he had planned.

He could make his excuses, of course. Or he could request an invitation for two friends.

A smile tugged at the corners of Lytham's mouth as he recalled the wistful note in Mrs Flynn's voice. An endorsement from him would mean that she was launched into society, here or in Bath…and that might be amusing.

He had seen something in the widow's eyes that touched a chord in his own heart, and he believed she meant to cut a dash in town. She had an unusual style, and he imagined that, once started on her way, she would cause quite a sensation.

And if the widow were invited everywhere…that would necessitate her companion accompanying her and their paths were bound to cross—especially if Lytham dropped a few hints.

'Now what are you up to?' he asked himself softly, lifting a glass to his own reflection in the mirror.

He had been unable to separate Emma from Miss Sommerton, but perhaps Mrs Flynn might succeed where he had failed. And whereas he had felt only a passing interest in the fate of the calm, reserved Miss Sommerton, he was very much more concerned with Emma. For it was Emma who had given him water when he woke from his fever, and Emma who had returned his kiss in a way that had made him want her with an urgency he had not felt in an age.

As for his ultimate intentions? That was something that even he did not know as yet. He had not thought that he cared to marry, his only experience of family life having been far from happy.

His parents had neither loved nor liked each other, both taking lovers whenever the fancy suited them, and his elder brother had picked a cold beauty as his wife, which was perhaps the reason that they had had no children.

Did he want children? Lytham stared broodingly into the fireplace. He certainly would not want to subject any child to the kind of childhood he and his brothers had been given, left to the care of servants who might sometimes be kind and at others take a cruel delight in punishing the offspring of their employers. Perhaps that was why his brothers had grown up the way they did, taking their pleasures with no thought of others, hurting any who offered them love. Was he not the same in his way? For he had never allowed himself to love and there was an emptiness within him that he had never found a means of banishing as yet.

Were all families the same? His brow wrinkled as he considered. Emma had suffered at the hands of a careless father, though she had not complained of him, had seemed to care for all her family...even the troublesome brother.

Lytham frowned as he finished his brandy. Emma was a challenge, and might prove amusing to watch over—but what was he to do about the brother?

Tom had been involved in crimes that would lead to a hanging if he were caught. And that would be disastrous for them all. Before Lytham could even consider his own affairs, he must rescue Emma's brother from his folly and set him straight—if that was possible.

The first step was probably to clear Tom Sommerton's name of any lingering scandal, and that might in part be achieved by a visit to his own home in the north-east of England. He had not bothered himself with John's personal papers, but he knew that his wife Maria still lived in the Dower House. He had seen her a couple of times briefly, to ask if she needed anything, but he usually left the day-to-day running of the estate to Stephen Antrium. Maria was his responsibility now that he was the head of the family and he had told Stephen to make any repairs to the Dower House she requested. She had retired there after she was widowed, refusing to think of coming out of her mourning, but as far as he knew she had made no demands of the estate.

He could call to see her on the pretence of business and then ask casually what she knew of the affair. She might be prepared to tell him the truth of that quarrel between Tom Sommerton and his brother, which could set the rumours of murder straight—but the charge of cheating at the card table was another matter.

It needed to be investigated further, and for that he must talk to a few of his late brother's friends. They would remember the tale and if there was any truth in it.

There was much to be done, he thought. In the meantime, Toby would oblige him with that invitation.

'Oh, look,' Bridget cried as she opened the exciting envelope the following afternoon after they had returned from a rewarding visit to her dressmaker. 'We are invited to a small evening party tomorrow.'

'Mrs and Mrs Dawlish invite you to dinner and a musical entertainment,' Emma read as Bridget handed her the card. 'That is curious. I would have expected to be invited to something more formal for a start. Do you know these people, Bridget?'

'No...' Bridget had seen something scrawled on the back and leaned over to read it. 'Ah, that explains it. Turn the card over, Emma.'

Emma did so and read aloud, 'I understand you are friends of the Marquis of Lytham, and he has personally requested that you be included, and it is therefore my pleasure to request your presence at what is to be an intimate gathering.'

'Wasn't that sweet of the marquis?' Bridget said. 'I shall wear my blue silk—and you must wear the green gown we bought today. It was fortunate that Madame Fontaine had something to fit you, Emma. It needs to be taken in a fraction at the waist, but it will be ready for tomorrow.'

'Do you mean to accept?' Emma stared at the scrawled message a little doubtfully.

'Oh, certainly,' Bridget said. 'This is just what I hoped for. Lindisfarne will take us up once he arrives, but he seems to have been delayed for some reason. Besides, it will be very much more comfortable to know some people before we go down to Bath.'

'You have made up your mind to take Lytham's advice, then?'

'Oh, yes—and if Lindisfarne is not here by the time we leave so much better,' Bridget said with a naughty look. 'It will show him that I am not to be taken for granted.'

Emma nodded, but her mind was wandering. Why had Lytham gone to the trouble of securing an invitation for them? Something warned her that he would be present at the gathering, even though he had expected to be leaving town almost at once.

'You look wonderful in that gown,' Bridget said the next afternoon as Emma twirled in front of the long mirror for her. 'Now, let me see—what shall we do with your hair?'

'What is wrong with my hair?' Emma glanced at her reflection. 'I think the style very suitable for a companion.'

'Perhaps—but not for my best friend,' Bridget said and began to unwind the plaits. 'It suits you back off your face, but I think we could make it a little fuller at the sides, and then catch it back in a big swirl like so…' She glanced at Emma's reflection in the mirror. 'Yes, that is much better. I shall instruct my maid to teach Lily how to achieve this style, and I shall lend you some of my pins to make it look special for the evening.'

It was impossible not to catch Bridget's enthusiasm, and Emma was suddenly looking forward to the prospect of their first evening engagement since she had come to town. She was vain enough to know that she would be looking very much more stylish than she had for years, and to wonder what Lytham might think of the change in her.

'You're a deep one,' Toby said, giving the marquis an old-fashioned look. 'I thought you meant to banish the old-maid daughter off to deepest Yorkshire?'

'It seems she had other plans,' Lytham replied coolly. 'And since neither she nor Mrs Flynn has any acquaintance in town, I thought it behoved me to give them a helping hand.'

'You're up to something,' Toby said. 'I know you too well, Alex, and I ain't a slowtop. No cause to imagine you can pull the wool over my eyes. Besides, Mama has seen Miss Sommerton, and she says she is rather—' He had been going to say attractive, but happened to be staring across the room as two young women entered the salon. 'Good grief! Are they the widow and the companion you asked

Lucy's mother to invite? Pray tell me at once, which is the widow and which the companion?'

'The dark one is Miss Emma Sommerton,' Lytham replied with a lift of his brows. 'The blonde beauty is Mrs Bridget Flynn—why do you ask?'

'Because they are both beautiful, but *she* is stunning.'

'Mrs Flynn?' Lytham gave him a quizzing look. 'I thought your interest was fixed with Miss Dawlish?'

'Yes, of course it is. You know I am devoted to Lucy,' Toby said, a faint colour in his cheeks. 'Matter of fact, there may be something announced this evening…but that doesn't stop me appreciating beauty and *she* is rather special.'

'I admire a woman with style,' Lytham said, deliberately obtuse. 'And I grant you that Mrs Flynn has a certain dash about her.'

'You know very well I meant Miss Sommerton.' Toby gave him an indignant stare. 'Mrs Flynn is lovely, but her companion—' He broke off, lost for adequate words.

'Puts her in the shade? I dare say most women would find it difficult to compete with Emma.' He had spoken the name without thinking and cursed himself as he saw Toby's gaze sharpen with curiosity. 'I meant Miss Sommerton, of course.'

'So that's the way of it,' Toby said and grinned, delighted at having caught his friend out, which was exceedingly rare. 'Mama was sure of it. She said she had never known you to take the slightest interest in a decent young lady before and that there had to be a reason for your doing so now.'

'Your mama always was inclined to let her tongue run away with her,' Lytham said, brows lifting. 'It would be most unfortunate for Miss Sommerton's chances if such an unfounded rumour were to take hold, Toby. I have no thought of making her or any other lady an offer of marriage.'

'Can't be thinking of making an offer of *carte blanche*,' Toby said. 'Not to Miss Sommerton, anyway—the widow is another thing, of course.' Lytham fixed him with a stare that made him subside into silence. 'Sorry, mind my own business.'

'May I offer you congratulations on your own engagement?' Lytham said. 'I shall have to find a pretty gift for Lucy before I leave town.'

'Oh, are you going to Yorkshire?'

'Tomorrow—and now you must excuse me. I ought to greet Mrs Flynn and Miss Sommerton.'

He nodded, feeling slightly off balance as he walked leisurely across the room in the direction of the newcomers. He had known Emma would dress well, but that gown brought out reddish highlights in her hair. Or perhaps it was the new style that did that. She had looked beautiful when he first saw her, hair windswept and a fresh colour in her cheeks, but this evening she had been transformed into another person. There was a brilliance about her, a vitality that shone from her lovely eyes, and he felt that he was witnessing the awakening of a woman who had lain dormant for too long.

Toby had been right, she was stunning. She had poise, style…and watching her smile at her hostess, charm. With the right backing she could be the toast of the town. He was sorry that he would not be here to oversee her success, but he believed that she would need little help from him.

It was a pity she had no fortune, of course, but that need deter only the fortune hunters. A man of sense would admire her for all the qualities she possessed. She turned to him as he approached, a slightly guarded look in her eyes.

'Miss Sommerton,' he said. 'How delightful to see you

here this evening—and Mrs Flynn. I had hoped we might meet again before I left town. I have something I wished to tell you. It could have been put into a letter, of course, but I always prefer to communicate in person where possible.'

He offered her his arm and they walked through the first reception room into the next, which was less crowded. Lytham steered her towards a small sofa set near the long French windows.

'Will you not be seated for a moment, Miss Sommerton?'

'Thank you, my lord.' Emma glanced at him as he sat beside her. She was not sure what she had expected, but his serious manner had set off flutters in her stomach, and she was a little disappointed that he had not mentioned her appearance. 'Something has happened? I do hope you have suffered no more attempts on your life?'

'You may rest easy on that,' Lytham assured her. 'I dare say you were right in the first place and that it was merely a poacher misfiring.'

'Oh, but…' She was quelled by his look.

'The matter concerns your brother. I was able to make certain inquiries last night, and I discovered that the accusation of cheating came from a close friend of my own brother…' His gaze was intent on her face. 'You do realise what this may mean?'

Emma was silent for a moment, then, 'You think your brother may have put his friend up to it—because he wanted to ruin Tom?'

'I think it possible,' Lytham said. 'My brother—indeed, both my brothers and my father were capable of such behaviour. There is or was bad blood in my family, Miss Sommerton. My father and his heir did their best to ruin us, and my second brother was little better. Had he inherited instead of me…' He shrugged his broad shoulders. 'I doubt there would have been an estate by now. My mother's loose behaviour in her youth may only be excused by virtue of her having been badly treated by her husband.'

Emma was a little shocked by this revelation, which she absorbed in silence and without comment. 'But what would your brother have gained by such vindictive behaviour, my lord?'

'For all his faults, I believe John was in love with his wife. That does not mean he treated her well or that he gave up his pleasures for her sake…any of his pleasures. You understand me?' Emma nodded. She understood perfectly, for, if her mama were to be believed, even her papa had taken a mistress when he was young. 'If Maria decided to console herself in the arms of a young and handsome man, I think John might have done almost anything in his rage.'

Emma's face had turned pale. 'Then the whipping…it was all part of the same plan to destroy Tom because he had dared to flirt with your brother's wife.'

'That part of it is mere speculation as yet,' Lytham said. 'I tell you only what I think possible. If Maria is willing to tell me her story, I may soon have more to report.'

Emma nodded, her eyes dark with emotion as she gazed up into his face. 'It would clear Tom's name of cheating, but would it not make it all the more likely that—?' She halted and could not go on.

'You think that anger might have driven Tom to take his revenge?' Lytham read the answer in her expressive eyes. 'But did he not swear that he was innocent of all the crimes of which he stood accused?'

'Yes, but…'

'Have faith, Emma,' Lytham said. 'Believe that I shall

do nothing that would harm either you or your family more than they have already been harmed.'

'You are generous, sir. I do not know how to thank you.'

'You will thank me by enjoying your life, Emma. You now have an opportunity that has, I believe, been denied to you for a long time. You should take what is offered with both hands.'

She blushed as she realised he had now twice called her by her name, and his mouth twitched at the corners as he saw the look of accusation in her eyes.

'You *are* Emma tonight, you know—and it suits you very well.'

So he had noticed the change! She chided herself for having expected a more effusive compliment. Bridget had called her stunningly beautiful, but of course she was not really.

'It is an elegant gown,' she said. 'I dare say that makes the difference.'

'Ah, but the woman maketh the gown,' Lytham said and she could see the mischief in his eyes. 'I believe you will receive more exquisite compliments before too long has passed, Emma—but I am not in the habit of flattery.'

'I do not require flattery, sir!'

'Oh, Miss Sommerton!' His tone and look mocked her. 'I have never yet met a woman who did not enjoy being complimented—if she spoke truly.'

'You, sir, are a rogue!'

'Yes, I believe you are right,' Lytham agreed, a smile on his lips. 'I have been called worse by some, I dare say. But it does not hurt me so I do not regard it—though I should not like to think I had offended you. Are you cross with me, Emma?'

'Will you not be serious, sir?' Emma fixed him with a straight look. 'You are leaving town soon, I think. Please take care—and do nothing that might endanger your own safety for my sake. Or, I may add, that of my brother.'

'Why, Emma, I believe you are concerned for me,' he teased and laughed softly as he saw her blush. 'No, no, I am the veriest rogue to tease you so. I promise I shall not be caught by surprise again as I was in the woods. I shall be very careful, I promise you—there, will that content you?'

She shook her head at him, but her hostess was bringing a young man and a young lady towards them, and she was obliged to give her attention to the introductions.

'Miss Sommerton—may I make you known to Mr Tobias Edgerton and my daughter, Miss Lucy Dawlish.'

Lytham got to his feet. He bowed to the younger lady, and congratulated her on what he said he expected to be a happy night for her, threw an outrageous wink at Mr Edgerton, stayed only a moment to wish them both happiness and then turned to Emma.

'For I must be early to bed if I am to rise early.' He bowed to Emma. 'It has been a pleasure to spend a few moments in your company, Miss Sommerton. I shall hope to see you on my return—if not here, then I shall most certainly see you in Bath.'

With that he walked away, leaving her to stare after him while everyone else in the room nodded to one another and considered that his most particular behaviour had confirmed what they all suspected.

The Marquis of Lytham was obviously very interested in Miss Sommerton and that could surely mean only one thing! Since she appeared to be a respectable young woman, he must be thinking of taking a bride.

Emma, of course, had no such thought in her head. His revelations had given her much to think about, and her rather absent-minded manner that evening did nothing to dispel the rumour that had firmly taken root.

It was obvious that Miss Sommerton was interested in the marquis, and he had made his intentions perfectly clear.

Emma had no idea that Lytham's interest in her was the reason that several invitations—to dinner, card parties and even a small dance—began to arrive the next day. There were nowhere near as many as there might have been had it been during the season, of course, but there were still a number of hostesses in town who had for various reasons not yet retired either to their country houses or Bath for the winter. Sufficient anyway for both Emma and Mrs Flynn to discover that they had not one free evening for the whole of the two weeks they planned to spend in town.

'This is such fun,' Bridget said to Emma as they discussed what they would wear to the dance, which was being given to celebrate Miss Dawlish and Mr Edgerton's engagement. 'I think I shall wear the crimson silk—and you must wear that blue gown we bought from Madame Veronique. It suits you very well, Emma.'

'You should not have bought it,' Emma replied. 'It is beautiful, Bridget, but it was so very expensive.'

'And worth every penny,' Bridget replied. 'If you had not come to me, Emma, I should have had to employ some crabby old matron to lend me consequence, and I dare say we should not have been invited to a half of the houses we have been these past few days.'

If Bridget had some idea of why they were being so well received by the cream of society, she did not enlighten her friend. Although the daughter of gentry, Bridget knew that her marriage had done nothing to give her the entrée into London drawing rooms, and had Bertie brought her to London himself as they had planned, it would have taken much longer for them to be accepted.

It was a stroke of good fortune to be introduced by someone like the Marquis of Lytham, and Bridget was determined to make the most of her chances. She had let it be seen that she was not averse to dancing now that she was out of her period of mourning, and her fortune saw to it that she was never short of partners at Lucy Dawlish's dance.

She was asked to dance by several men she shrewdly assessed as being fortune hunters, but there were others who could not be said to have come from the same melting pot. She was enjoying herself very much, and if the truth be known had hardly given Lindisfarne a second thought until he walked in towards the end of that evening.

He came towards her as her partner returned her to Emma's side at the end of that particular dance, and her heart missed a beat as she saw the look in his eyes. It was the look of a predator hunting its prey!

'He is here!' She touched Emma's arm, her pulses racing. 'He has come at last.'

'Lindisfarne?' Emma turned to look at the man approaching them, and she felt an icy trickle down her spine. There was something about the earl that she instinctively distrusted. 'Oh, Bridget...'

Bridget was gazing at him in much the way a rabbit might gaze at a stoat. The earl was undoubtedly one of the most handsome men Emma had ever seen, in a dark, almost saturnine way, his eyes piercingly blue, his hair as black as jet, thick and wavy, but cropped short to his head. He had full, sensuous lips that seemed to Emma to curl back in a sneer, and he had an air of menace about him that she found slightly threatening.

Why did Bridget find him so fascinating? Emma could not understand it. There were several gentlemen here this evening that had as much and more to recommend them, and to her dismay Emma found herself immediately disliking him.

'My dear Mrs Flynn,' Lindisfarne said, his voice softly purring as he bowed over Bridget's hand. He reminded Emma of a great cat prowling around a helpless mouse, waiting its time to pounce. 'Have I come too late to secure a dance with you?'

'I fear my card is full,' Bridget said in a slightly breathy voice. 'I did not expect you. Had you sent me word, I might have saved one for you.'

'Business delayed me,' he said. 'But I am here now, and I shall claim my rights in future, believe me.'

The look he gave Bridget was so blatantly sensual that Emma gasped. What did he mean by behaving in such an intimate manner in company? Had he no thought for Bridget's reputation? And *she* seemed to have lost all her natural common sense as she stared adoringly up at him.

'Mrs Flynn, I believe this is our dance?'

'Oh…yes, of course.' Bridget gave her hand to the young man who had come to claim her. 'Excuse me, Lindisfarne. Please—you must stay and keep Miss Sommerton company.'

Emma frowned as her friend was whisked away to the dance floor. She herself had no partner for this particular dance, and she wished that she had not been left to make conversation with a man she instinctively felt was dangerous for her friend, and perhaps for both their reputations.

'Miss Emma Sommerton…' Lindisfarne's eyes turned on her, narrowing with sudden interest. He had ignored her in his assault on Bridget's senses, but now he was aware of her. Emma squirmed inwardly as she felt his gaze intensify.

'Ah, yes, Mrs Flynn's companion. I believe she did mention having invited you to bear her company for a while.'

'Yes, my lord,' Emma replied coolly. She could have wished that she was not wearing the blue gown that became her so well or that she had dressed her hair in the prim style of old. She did not like the way he looked at her! 'We have been friends for a long time. I am very fond of Bridget.'

She was not sure why she had stressed that to him, unless it was to make it clear that she knew his intentions and had decided to do all she could to thwart them. For she felt that Bridget would be making a terrible mistake if she consented to be this man's mistress—or, indeed, his wife. He was not a nice man, Emma felt it deep down inside her, and was sure that he would cause Bridget only unhappiness if she allowed him his way.

The earl's eyes narrowed, and she knew that he had sensed her hostility. 'I am sure Mrs Flynn's generosity must make her generally liked, Miss Sommerton.'

Emma blushed. Was that a hint that he knew Bridget had paid for the gown she was wearing?

'Bridget is a good friend.'

'Mrs Flynn has no notion of how to take care of her fortune,' the earl said. 'That is why she came to me—and I intend to take care of her, to make sure that she does not fall foul of hangers-on and fortune hunters.'

Was that a warning? Emma knew that this man would make a bad enemy. She believed that her expressive eyes had betrayed her. He had seen that she neither liked nor trusted him, and was on his guard now—and he would do all he could to lessen Emma's influence on Bridget.

Bridget would do as she pleased in the end, of course. Emma had no right to influence her one way or the other, unless she asked for advice. Should she do so, Emma would

advise severing any connection at once. This man was a
ravenous wolf and he would gobble up her poor friend and
her fortune in an instant.

Bridget would be a fool to trust either her person or her
fortune to his care, but she had fallen under his spell. Emma
was not sure that it was not already too late to save her
from him.

Emma knew she would have to take the greatest care or
she too might find herself being devoured by this man.

Chapter Five

'Should you care for a visit to Bath, Aunt?' Lytham asked as he handed Lady Agatha Lynston a glass of her favourite port. 'You could take the waters for your health and gossip with old friends.'

'Most of 'em are dead,' his great-aunt snorted with something between triumph and disgust. Her face was deeply ingrained with the lines of old age, but her eyes were as intelligent and bright as those of a much younger woman. 'Gave up that lark when I realised they were dropping about me like flies. Might be contagious.'

'Not you, Agatha. You'll live to be a hundred, I dare say.'

'Buttering me up, Lytham?' The sharp, knowing eyes swept over him. He was the best of his family, most of whom had been bad to the core. Of course, if Lady Agatha's suspicions were correct, he wasn't the old marquis's son. And a good thing, too! Not that one word of the forgotten scandal would ever pass her lips. There were cousins ready to pounce on the estate he had restored and extended. He deserved his good fortune, and her suspicions would die with her. 'What are you up to?'

'I was thinking of visiting Bath myself.'

'Who is she?' Lady Agatha demanded instantly. She was like a little terrier after a rabbit as she sensed a secret. 'Or ain't she decent?'

'Miss Sommerton is a very respectable young lady.'

'Good thing, too! We don't want more bad blood in the family. We've had enough of that.'

'I couldn't agree with you more, Aunt.' He smiled at her fondly. She was the only person who had ever offered him affection and he always enjoyed his visits with her.

'Thinking of getting hitched at last, eh?' She looked at him with satisfaction. 'I never expected to see the day, thought your parents had given you a distaste for it.'

'It wasn't that so much,' he told her. 'I saw no reason to marry.'

'And now you do? She must be an exceptional gel.'

'Yes, she is.' Lytham smiled as his memory jumped back in time to the moment Emma had brandished her knife at him in the woods, ready to bind up his wounds. 'I believe you will like her.'

'Want me to look her over for you?'

'Good lord, no!' He laughed. 'I merely want you to meet her—without appearing too particular.'

'Not still shilly-shallying? Pull yourself together and take the plunge, Lytham. You're not getting any younger.'

'I am not quite in my dotage yet.'

'Want a son, don't you? Better get on with it before it's too late. You'll be past your prime soon and we don't want a knock-kneed runt as the heir, do we? Old men's children are always sickly creatures.'

Lytham choked on his port. He had been used to thinking himself at the height of his sexual powers, and to be told that he would soon be past his prime in such a forthright manner was something of a shock.

The gleam of mischief in the elderly lady's eyes amused

him. Agatha Lynston had been born in a more bawdy age and had never hesitated to call a spade a spade. Or anything else by its right name, come to that. Emma was not quite as forthright, but she too had the courage of her convictions, which might be why he admired her.

'I don't know where you got your spirit, Agatha Lynston, but they should bottle it and feed it to the army.'

She cackled with laughter, her skinny, age-spotted hands clapping in appreciation of his reaction to her provocation.

'Say one thing for you, Lytham. You ain't high in the instep like your father. For all his selfish, bad ways, he was a damned snob. You must be a throwback to your great-grandfather. He was a fine man, but his son married into bad blood.'

'Perhaps…or perhaps Mama went astray,' Lytham replied with a lift of his brows. He had never been able to dismiss his father's last words to him, spoken in anger, but unforgettable.

'You are no son of mine!'

'Stuff and nonsense!' Agatha lied stoutly, though she knew it was very likely the truth. 'Your father would have disowned you from birth if he'd thought that.'

'Perhaps he couldn't be bothered. He had two elder sons, after all. He could not have expected that I would inherit the title.'

'Only Lady Helena could have told you the truth of it,' Agatha said. 'And she can't because the old devil finally broke her heart.' She snorted as she saw Lytham's sceptical look. 'You may be a rogue, Lytham, but you are unquestionably a gentleman. It's time the family became respectable again.'

Lytham looked at her affectionately. 'It always has been, Aunt—and always will be while you live.'

'I ain't going to live forever—so oblige me by producing

an heir, Lytham. And now I think about it, a trip to Bath might be just the thing to set me up for the winter.'

The chaise carrying them towards Bath was both fast and comfortable. Emma could only be grateful that Lindisfarne had chosen to travel on horseback. It was bad enough that he had insisted on escorting them, and she did not think she could have put up with his company the whole way, for her dislike of him had grown each time they met.

The earl's arrival in town had meant that Bridget had delayed their journey a week to fit in with his plans. She seemed to be completely under his dominion, willing to do anything he asked—other than become his mistress.

'I am certain he loves me,' she told Emma on her return from being driven to the park the afternoon following Lucy Dawlish's dance. 'But he insists that we have no need to marry.'

'You should continue to hold out for marriage,' Emma told her, hoping that she would come to her senses in the end and see him for what he was. 'It is all very well for him to say there is no need for you to marry, but if you wish to continue to visit the best houses you must protect your good name. An affair could only tarnish it.

'I know that Maria Fitzherbert was received everywhere when she was the Prince of Wales's mistress, but that was a different case. Many believe he went through a form of marriage with her, that she is in fact his true wife, but even had that not been so they would have accepted her. And other women do carry on affairs without censure, but they usually have some consequence or the protection of an influential man. Remember what happened to Lady Caroline Lamb. She made a scandal with Lord Byron and that led to disastrous consequences for her and the family. It would be even worse for you. I dare say some hostesses would receive you, but have you considered what might happen if you should part from Lindisfarne?'

'I know you are right,' Bridget said. 'But sometimes when he kisses me I feel... Oh, you cannot imagine how it feels to be kissed like that!'

Emma could imagine it very well. She had not forgotten the kiss Lytham had given her that night at the inn, and the temptation she had felt in his arms. In that heady moment she might have counted the world well lost for love, but she had no fortune and no prospects. Bridget was a wealthy widow with every chance of remarrying if she did not throw it all away for the sake of a man who would only ruin her.

Emma was becoming increasingly wary of the earl. She had not been invited to drive out to the park with them on three separate occasions during the week they remained in London. She was aware that the earl had every intention of excluding her whenever possible. However, he had reckoned without Bridget's genuine affection for Emma and she refused to attend parties without her. She also retained enough sense not to be alone with him in the parlour. A drive in an open carriage was another matter, of course, and even Emma could not find reasons why she might not go with him.

Emma reflected that she was fortunate not to have been consigned to the baggage coach with their maids. Lindisfarne had made it clear that he thought her presence unnecessary and she knew from little things that Bridget had let slip that he was actively discouraging her from giving Emma presents.

Since Emma had herself tried without success to curb Bridget's excessive spending she did not object to this, though she did wonder why the earl seemed to take such an interest in her friend's fortune.

She knew that it would be impossible to warn Bridget against trusting him. Even a hint of censure was enough to bring a frown to her friend's brow. Emma was wise enough to realise that she must only offer advice when it was asked for; to press her opinions when they were unwelcome could only destroy their friendship.

In her heart, Emma knew that Bridget was already too deeply involved with Lindisfarne to draw back. It was, she believed, merely a matter of time before she became either his wife or his mistress.

In either case it would mean an end to their arrangement. Emma knew that the earl would never allow her to remain in his home if he decided to marry Bridget—and if she became his mistress it would not be possible for Emma to stay with her.

Besides, he would probably carry her off to his castle in Ireland, and Emma had no intention of ever living under the same roof as the Earl of Lindisfarne!

Glancing out of the window, Emma saw that they had drawn up outside an inn. It was almost evening, and they would be staying here overnight.

Lindisfarne came to assist Bridget from the carriage and escort her inside. He did not offer assistance to Emma, and she was left to jump down herself. She followed the others into the inn, feeling rather like a gatecrasher at a private party as she watched them laughing and putting their heads together.

Lindisfarne glanced back at her once, and the cold expression in his eyes sent a shiver through her. She knew that he was her enemy, and she wondered how long it would be before he tried to dislodge her from her position as Bridget's companion.

It was clear to Emma that she must start to make plans for that eventuality. She would have to make discreet inquiries while they were in Bath, and in the meantime she must be careful.

Lindisfarne was ruthless, she felt it instinctively, and he would not hesitate to use any means at his disposal of making it impossible for her to stay in Bridget's employ.

Emma pondered that word employer… For her first few weeks with Bridget there had been no reason for her to feel other than a valued friend, but she had noticed a slight difference recently. Had Bridget withdrawn from her slightly?

'Oh, do come on, Emma,' Bridget called looking back at her. 'It is chilly out here. Let us go into the parlour and get warm while Lindisfarne sees to the matter of our rooms.'

Bridget's smile allayed Emma's fears for the moment. Lindisfarne was doing his best to dominate her friend, but he had not quite succeeded yet.

Emma stood watching from the side of the bath as Bridget moved about in the warm waters of the spa. She was not the only woman to indulge, for there were several dowagers taking advantage of its medicinal benefits. However, she was the youngest and most beautiful, and it was she who was attracting the attention of the gentlemen who had come more for the sights than the waters, for her bathing gown clung most revealingly to her figure.

On this their second visit to the baths, Emma had taken a few sips of the drinking water in the pump room, finding it unpleasant to the taste, and the idea of stepping into the bath with only the flimsiest of garments to cover her naked body was something she had steadfastly refused.

'Why do you not follow Mrs Flynn's example?'

Emma had been allowing her attention to wander, and the earl's soft voice startled her. She turned to look at him, seeing the menace in those cat-like eyes as they watched her.

'Mrs Flynn is much braver about these things than I, sir.'

'I suppose you think it beneath you?'

'Indeed, I think no such thing, sir. It must be perfectly proper if Lady Thrapston feels it respectable to indulge. It was she who recommended it to Bridget.'

The earl's full lips curled back in a sneer. 'But you know differently, do you not? You despise those who are prepared to show off their charms in such a vulgar way, is that not so?'

'Please do not put words into my mouth, sir. I have no opinion one way or the other. I dare say it is a very pleasant experience, but I do not care to try it.'

'You are a little prude, Miss Sommerton,' the earl said, his eyes sweeping over her. Emma had taken to styling her hair into the staid coronet of plaits about her head rather than the softer style Bridget favoured. 'I doubt a man has ever laid a finger on you.'

'That, sir, is my business and not for discussion.'

The earl's hand snaked out, catching her wrist. She could feel the burn of his fingers bruising her flesh, but resisted the temptation to snatch her arm away.

'I've a mind to see if I can get beneath that prim mask you wear. I would swear there is a whore wriggling beneath that delicate skin of yours.'

'Take your hand from my arm, sir. Or you will force me to make a scene. I think that would be most embarrassing for us both, and Bridget would not care for it.'

Lindisfarne's eyes narrowed with anger. 'There are other places and other times,' he hissed. 'Do anything to turn Bridget against me and you will wish you had never been born.'

Emma turned as he released her, walking from the bathing chamber into an adjoining room and then into the pump room. She was outwardly calm, but seething inside. It was the first time the earl had put his hostility into words, and she had a feeling that she had not handled it as well as she might. She must try harder to keep her distance from him, but she would not allow his spite to overset her.

'This is foul stuff, Lytham. Give me a glass of good Madeira any day.' The words accompanied by a cackle of laughter drew Emma's eyes across the room to a rather odd-looking lady. She was clearly of advanced years, but her hair, which she wore in a mass of curls beneath a rakish hat more suited to a woman half her age, was bright red. 'Pah—that stuff will kill anyone fool enough to take it regularly, and as for the baths…'

Emma's gaze travelled on to the gentleman standing beside her. He was tall, broad of shoulder and well dressed, though in a more casual style than many of the gentlemen present, and the sight of him made her heart turn over.

She saw that he had noticed her, and he smiled as he touched the arm of his companion, nodding in Emma's direction. The elderly lady looked towards Emma, then raised her hand and beckoned imperiously. Emma had been wondering whether she ought to approach them or not, but now felt able to do so without fear of intrusion.

She realised that she was being intently scrutinised by the lady, who had very bright, inquisitive eyes, and felt her cheeks getting a little warm as she instinctively made a slight curtsey.

'Well met, Miss Sommerton,' Lytham said a faint smile on his lips. 'I had hoped we might see you somewhere. Please tell Mrs Flynn that it is my intention to call soon.'

'Good morning, my lord.' She smiled at his companion. 'Did you wish to speak with me, ma'am?'

'Know my nephew here, don't you? He tells me your

name is Miss Emma Sommerton, and that you are a respectable young woman—is that right, miss?'

Emma was a little startled to be addressed in such a
forthright way, but found it amusing. 'Yes, ma'am, I believe I am. I try to behave properly whenever I can.'

'Not too mealy-mouthed, I hope? Can't stand all these
modern young woman who are too frightened to say boo
to a goose. We were not like that in my day, miss.'

'No, indeed, ma'am, I can see that you were not.'

Lady Agatha Lynston stared at her for a moment, and
then gave a shout of laughter, which caused a few heads
to turn in their direction.

'I like the gel, Lytham. She has spirit…yes, I think we
shall deal well together.' She turned her eagle eyes on
Emma. 'Give me your arm, gel. Walk me about a bit. I've
a mind to see what they are getting up to in the baths. Now
that ain't decent, though I indulged when I was younger—
when I had a figure to show off. You don't care for it,
miss?'

'No, though my employer Mrs Flynn is bathing at the
moment. I came to bear her company.'

'Got bored, did you? Thought you would see what the
gentlemen looked like in the pump room. Young woman
like you, bound to be thinking of marrying. Take my advice, gel—get yourself a good man with a sense of humour
and plenty of money. I never married. I had the money
through my grandfather and didn't see why I should be at
some man's beck and call all my life. Besides, the right
one never asked me.'

'I do not imagine I shall marry,' Emma replied. 'I am
not in the happy position of having my own fortune,
ma'am, and I dare say I shall need to work for most of my
life.'

'Oh, I dare say you may marry,' Lady Agatha said, giv-

ing her a knowing look. 'Men ain't all fools, m'dear, and
some of 'em ain't even bothered by the lack of a fortune.
Mind you, there ain't many I could recommend to you as
a husband, but if you're sensible you may do well enough.'

'Perhaps,' Emma said, not wishing to argue. Lady Agatha's hand was gripping her arm tightly as if afraid she
might make a bolt for it.

'That fellow over there—the one staring at us in that
peculiar manner.' Emma looked and saw that she meant the
Earl of Lindisfarne. 'Now I wouldn't recommend you to
take someone like that. He's a scoundrel by all accounts. I
knew his father. Bad blood there.' She glanced at Emma.
'Why is he staring at you?'

'He is a friend of Mrs Flynn's,' Emma replied. 'He is
staring at me because he does not like me…and I do not
like him.'

'Be careful of him, Miss Sommerton,' the old lady said.
'Lytham is a rogue, but he is also a gentleman—that one
is not.'

'I shall be careful,' Emma told her. 'But I thank you for
your warning, ma'am.'

'You are a sensible gel,' Lady Agatha said, her eyes
sweeping over the ladies and gentlemen in the water. 'Look
at those old fools! What do they think they look like? Only
one of them shows to advantage, and that's the blonde
beauty. I'll bet she's no better than she should be.' She felt
Emma stiffen and glanced at her. 'Your employer, is she?
Well, my advice to you would be to find a new position.
You may take me back to my nephew now. All this splash-
ing about in water has given me an appetite. Lytham shall
take me somewhere for something decent to drink and a
slice of cake.'

Emma made no reply as she escorted Lady Agatha back
to the pump room, where she discovered that Lytham was

deep in conversation with another man. He glanced in her direction, smiled, but made no attempt to delay her as she turned away.

Emma was slightly disappointed that he had been content to let his elderly aunt monopolise her, for she would have liked some conversation with him. However, it was not for her to push herself, and he would no doubt seek her out when and if he had news for her.

When she returned to the baths it was to discover that Bridget had left the water, and she hurried to the dressing rooms, arriving only just in time to help Bridget gather her things.

'Where have you been?' she asked in what was an unusually irritable tone for her. 'I thought I should have to leave without you. Lindisfarne wants me to drive out with him to a beauty spot this afternoon, and I must go home and change.'

'I happened to see the Marquis of Lytham and made the acquaintance of his great-aunt, Lady Agatha Lynston,' Emma said. 'She is a remarkable lady, but she kept me talking and I was perhaps longer than I ought to have been. I am sorry if I kept you waiting.'

'So the marquis has come to Bath, has he?' Bridget's mood of irritation seemed to slip away. 'I wonder why?'

'To accompany his aunt, I imagine.'

'Oh, surely he would not come just for that—would he?' Bridget wrinkled her forehead. 'Well, it does not matter. We must hurry. I do not want to keep Lindisfarne waiting.'

Bridget shivered as they went out into the keen air of a dull winter day, and Emma looked at her in concern.

'Do you think it wise to drive out in an open carriage this afternoon, Bridget?'

'Why ever not?' Bridget said with a slight frown. 'It is just chilly after the heat of the baths. You did not bathe, so you cannot realise what it feels like to come straight out into the cold air.'

'Did you enjoy bathing, Bridget?'

'It was well enough as an experience,' Bridget replied with a shrug of her shoulders. 'I only did it because Lindisfarne thought I should—and Lady Thrapston recommended it.'

'Was it Lindisfarne's idea?'

'Yes. Why do you ask?' Bridget looked at her oddly, but Emma merely shook her head. 'Oh, don't look like that! I know you didn't approve. He told me that you thought I was making a show of myself, that it was indecent.'

'No! That is not true, Bridget. I said nothing of the sort. It is perfectly respectable, but I do not care for the idea for myself, that is all.'

Bridget was silent for a moment as they walked along the street together, clutching their scarves and shawls about them. The wind was much cooler and Emma saw her friend shiver several times.

'You dislike him very much, don't you?'

'Who?' Emma glanced at her, seeing the stubborn set of her mouth. 'I am not perfectly sure what you mean, Bridget.'

'Lindisfarne. You disapprove of him, and he feels it dreadfully. He is afraid that you will turn me against him.' Bridget looked at her accusingly. 'Is that what you want to do, Emma?'

'I would not dream of turning your mind against anyone,' Emma replied carefully. 'I do not particularly like the earl, but it is not my place to influence you in such a matter.'

'He said that you despise him!'

'Surely it is not what I feel that matters?' Emma said. 'I am here only as your companion, Bridget—because you asked me to come and help you resist the temptation he offered. If you wish to dispense with my services, you must say so. I do not wish to interfere with your pleasures.'

They had reached the house Bridget had rented, and she swept in ahead of Emma, two spots of bright colour in her cheeks. It was obvious that she was angry, but undecided what to do. Emma waited as Bridget unburdened herself of her scarves and shawls, then ran upstairs. She followed more slowly, knocking at the door of Bridget's room.

'Oh, come in,' Bridget answered impatiently. She was at the wardrobe, pulling at some of her gowns. 'What shall I wear? The white muslin or the yellow silk?'

'The silk would be a little warmer,' Emma said. 'Would you like me to leave, Bridget?'

Bridget whirled on her. 'For goodness' sake, don't look at me in that prim and proper way. I did not think you had changed so much from the girl I used to know.'

'I am sorry if I have changed.' Emma thought it was Bridget who had changed under the influence of Lindisfarne. 'I have tried not to be critical, even though I cannot like him, Bridget. I cannot think you would be happy as his wife.'

Bridget looked at her haughtily. 'I did not ask for your opinion, Emma. Please go away now. I need to send for my maid. I haven't time to argue with you. We shall talk about this another time...when I have made up my mind.'

Emma felt herself dismissed, exactly as if she were a paid companion, which of course she was. It would not have hurt so much if Bridget had not insisted at the start that they were friends and Emma was to think of herself as guest in her house.

She turned away and went into her own room, sitting on the edge of the bed and staring at her pale reflection in the dressing mirror. The rebellious spirit inside her wanted to start packing immediately, to leave before the situation deteriorated too far, destroying happy memories. But she knew she could not afford to be so impetuous. Bridget had showered her with costly gifts, but she had not actually given her money. Emma had only a few shillings in her purse, which would not even pay her fare home.

Besides, she was going to have to learn to accept this sort of behaviour. Employers were often fickle and could be pleasant one moment, and demanding or irritable the next. She had been led to expect something different from Bridget, but it seemed that their old relationship was over.

It was at about four that afternoon when the maid came to call Emma and tell her that they had a visitor.

'The gentleman asked for Mrs Flynn, but when I told him she was out, he said he would talk to you, Miss Sommerton.'

'What name did he give, Maisie?'

'The Marquis of Lytham, miss.'

Emma's heart skipped a beat, her mood lifting a little. 'Very well, I shall come down at once.'

She glanced hastily in the mirror, smoothing her gown and her hair, which were both immaculate. Her complexion was a little pale, but that could not be helped and she refrained from pinching her cheeks to make them pinker.

'Ah, Miss Sommerton,' Lytham said as she walked into the small parlour. 'Forgive me. I thought Mrs Flynn might have been at home, but I came to deliver an invitation from my aunt and could not leave without delivering it.'

'That was kind, sir,' Emma replied. 'I am sorry Mrs Flynn was not at home. She will be sorry to have missed you, I am sure—but she went out driving this afternoon.'

'Not in an open carriage, I hope?' Lytham glanced at the window. 'It has been raining this past hour or more.'

'Has it?' Emma had been engaged in reading a book to take her mind off her problems, and had not noticed. She crossed to the window to look out. The rain was heavy, slating down on the pavements, and it looked as if had been raining for some time. 'Oh, it is a heavy downpour. Bridget will be soaked to the skin if she is caught in this.'

'We must hope that her friends have had the sense to take shelter somewhere.'

'Yes, we must certainly hope that is the case.' Emma did not tell him that Bridget had gone with only the earl, for she sensed that he would not have approved, and his next words confirmed it.

'My great-aunt tells me that Mrs Flynn has formed a friendship with Lindisfarne, Miss Sommerton.'

'Yes. I think they met in Ireland when she went to him for advice after her husband died. I understand he is a distant relative of the late Captain Bertram Flynn.'

'It is none of my business, of course—but I think you should warn your friend that Lindisfarne is not the kind of man she wants to know. He is dangerous and bad...I mean really bad, Miss Sommerton. I am not talking of a charming rogue who gambles and drinks a little.'

'What do you mean?' Emma felt a little shiver run down her spine.

'There are unsavoury rumours connected with Lindisfarne's name,' he replied frowning. 'Rumours of women treated in an unfortunate way and other things that I would not care to repeat to a lady, even one as broad-minded as yourself.'

'I fear that it is useless to speak to Bridget,' Emma said and looked anxious. 'I believe that she is besotted with him and will listen to no criticism of him at all.'

'Indeed, then, that is a pity for he may ruin her—financially as well as her reputation.'

'She will not listen to me. I have no influence with her in this matter or perhaps in any other.' She was still smarting from Bridget's behaviour towards her earlier and something showed in her manner.

'Emma! You must listen,' Lytham said suddenly urgent. 'My aunt is not the only one who disapproves of Lindisfarne. I have been here but one day and already I have heard whispers. If Mrs Flynn continues to be seen everywhere with him, she will soon begin to be thought of as fast—and if you stay with her some of that may rub off on you.'

'I am aware that she must not be seen to be alone with him.'

'That is not enough,' Lytham said. 'Surely you must realise that people love to gossip? His pursuit of her is so blatant, and some think that she may already have succumbed, that she may be his mistress.'

'No, that is not true. I know it to be a lie.'

'I did not say that it was true, only that people may begin to believe it, and then you know it would not be long before some ladies refused to meet her at social gatherings. They would cut her if she attended the assembly, and she would not be invited to the best houses. What is permissible in a lady of high rank is not tolerated in someone of Mrs Flynn's position. Unfair, I grant you, but unfortunately the case.'

'I am sure she knows that…' Emma raised her head a little. Why must he lecture her when she had already warned Bridget of the pitfalls associated with the relationship? 'But I do not believe that will change her if she has made up her mind to have him.'

'She would not think of marrying him?' Lytham was shocked.

'It is all she dreams of—and who am I to lecture her?'

'You must warn her against such an idea,' Lytham said. 'For her own sake, Emma. He would run through her fortune in no time, and then he would mistreat her. He has been married once before, you know.'

'Married? I had no idea. I do not think Bridget is aware of that—indeed, I am sure she is not. What happened to his wife?'

'She died a few months after their wedding...' Lytham frowned. 'He was much younger then, of course. She was an heiress, a sweet child by all accounts, though I cannot claim to have known her. I have heard stories, however, and they are not pleasant.'

'How did she die?'

'In an accident, I am told. She fell down the stairs and broke her neck, apparently when she was feeling unwell. There was some talk of her having been mentally disturbed, but the rumours were hushed up and have been forgotten by all but a few.'

'Your aunt remembered it?' Emma nodded as he was silent. 'Yes, she told me to be careful of him because he was a bad man. Was the earl thought to have been involved in his wife's death?'

'Nothing could be proved, but it was rumoured at the time, I believe.'

'This is terrible. Bridget may be in some danger.'

'You should warn her, Emma.'

'I do not think she will listen. She is already angry because I have shown my dislike of him.'

'Then you will think about leaving Mrs Flynn's employ?'

For some reason Emma could not give him the answer he sought. She had already given the matter some thought, but she knew he meant to offer her help and her pride would not let her accept.

'I shall think about it,' she agreed. 'But I cannot simply walk out on Bridget just like that. If tongues have already started to wag, think how much worse it would be for her if I were to leave too suddenly. Besides, if Lindisfarne is so dangerous…' Emma shivered as she thought of her friend at the mercy of such a man.

'If she insists in her foolish behaviour it is no more than she deserves.'

'But I cannot—shall not do it,' Emma said. 'I shall talk to Bridget when she returns, but if she decides that she can dispense with my services I shall stay with her until she can replace me.'

'Do not be a fool, Emma!'

'I cannot desert her,' Emma said. 'She has been generous towards me, and though I do not approve of her behaviour I cannot desert her.'

'You refuse to listen—because the advice comes from me, I suppose?' Lytham glared at her. 'You can be too stubborn for your own good, Emma.'

'That is a ridiculous statement!'

'Ridiculous, is it?' His brow furrowed. 'Or have I mistaken your intentions? Can it be that you approve of Mrs Flynn's behaviour, that you see nothing wrong in her becoming that man's mistress? Perhaps you hope that one of his dubious friends will show an interest in you?'

'How dare you?' Emma lost her temper. 'I believe you have said enough, sir. Will you please leave now?'

'Is that it?' Lytham advanced on her, a glitter in his eyes. 'Did you come to her knowing her intention from the start?' He saw something in her eyes and thought he understood. 'That's it, isn't it? You always knew that it might happen.'

'Please leave,' Emma said. 'I do not think we have anything further to say to one another.'

'Do you not?' Lytham towered above her, anger sparking

out of him, driven beyond reason by her apparent calm. 'Then let me tell you this, Emma—I have much to say on the matter. Should you decide to sell your favours to the highest bidder, think of me. I am perfectly willing to offer you *carte blanche,* and I am far richer than Lindisfarne or any of his cronies—but I never take another man's leavings. Think carefully before you make your choice.'

Emma's hand shot out, catching him a glancing blow across the cheek. He grabbed her wrist, pulling her in hard against him so that she could feel the heat of his breath on her face, and the anger pulsing through him.

'Let me go!' she demanded. 'Let me go this instant, sir.'

But he would not let her go. He held her fast, imprisoned against him so that she could feel the throbbing of his manhood, feel the heat of him as his mouth took possession of hers, her lips parting to the insistent probing of his tongue. Emma struggled, angry at this abuse of her feelings, but her body would not deny him much as she wished it; she felt herself melting into him, her mouth responding to the delicate touch of his tongue.

She tangled her fingers in his hair, unable to resist as his kiss explored and thrilled her, his leg curved around her so that she was pressed into him, moulded to him like a second skin. She felt that she would faint from the sheer pleasure of being in his arms like this and almost stumbled as he abruptly let her go.

He was breathing hard, a strange look in his eyes as he stared at her. She felt that he was angry and yet triumphant, as if he did not understand his own feelings.

'Do not look at me that way,' she said, a hot flush creeping up into her cheeks. 'You took advantage. I—I forgot myself. I did not mean to allow you to do that again.'

'You lie, Emma—you lie with every breath you take.' He grabbed hold of her arm and thrust her in front of the mirror. 'Look at yourself in that mirror! Where is the woman I saw that first afternoon—where the elegant creature I met at Lucy Dawlish's house? You hide her but she is there. Beneath that prim exterior is a passionate woman. Why do you hide her, Emma? Or is it that you only wish to hide her from me?'

She turned away from the mirror. Did he not understand that she was trying to protect herself from Lindisfarne and others like him? He had lectured her and now he accused her of doing the very thing he had been advising! He was an impossible man, and she did not understand him.

'Please go away, my lord,' she said in a choking voice. 'We have nothing more to say for the moment.'

'I am going, Emma, for I must. If I stayed, I could not trust myself to behave as I ought. Remember what I have told you.'

Emma did not turn to look at him. She was ashamed that she had once again betrayed her feelings for him. If he misunderstood them, then so much the worse.

'I have no wish to be your mistress, sir.'

'Oh, Emma—you know I did not mean to insult you.'

'Please go away!'

'Emma…' He hesitated but she shrugged away when he laid a hand on her shoulder. 'Well, I suppose you are angry with me, and perhaps I deserve it. I shall leave you to think about things, and we shall speak again another day. You know that I would help you if you needed my help. If you are in any trouble, you must come to me. Promise me you will!' His eyes bored into her, making her tremble inwardly but she turned her face aside, refusing to be won by his passionate appeal.

She would not answer him, and at the last he turned and went out without speaking again. Emma waited until she heard the front door slam and then she ran upstairs to her own room, locking the door behind her.

Chapter Six

Bridget did not return to the house until quite late in the evening. Emma had sat for hours alone in the parlour, having taken a light supper on a tray when it became apparent that Bridget would not return in time.

'I believe Mrs Flynn must have decided to dine with friends,' she told the servants when they asked her what they should do. 'But you must be prepared to provide a cold supper should she require it when she returns.'

By half past nine Emma was beginning to think that there must have been an accident and was wondering whether she ought to raise the alarm. However, just as she was thinking of setting a search in motion, Bridget came in, looking slightly flushed and guilty.

'Forgive me,' she said, glancing awkwardly at Emma. 'We were caught in a terrible storm and had no alternative but to take shelter at an inn. Lindisfarne bespoke dinner and there was no way I could let you know what had happened.'

'I was beginning to be a little anxious,' Emma replied in a dignified manner. She had no wish to quarrel with Bridget over this unfortunate business. 'But I thought perhaps you might have met friends and gone on to dine with them?'

'Oh, yes, that was the way of it,' Bridget said airily. 'It was all quite respectable and we were not alone.'

Emma saw the flush in her cheeks and sensed that she was lying. Bridget could not meet her eyes and there was something different about her this evening. She looked excited and yet nervous. Surely she had not done anything foolish? Emma's heart sank. She was truly fond of Bridget and felt real concern for her.

'Lytham called this afternoon with an invitation to dinner for tomorrow evening. I was not sure of your engagements, but he said a reply in the morning would do well enough.'

'Oh…yes,' Bridget said carelessly. 'We may as well go. I have nothing else planned. Lindisfarne has to go up to town for a day or so.'

'Then perhaps you will send a note in the morning.'

'Yes, of course.' Bridget looked at her awkwardly. 'Are you still cross with me, Emma? I did not mean to quarrel with you this morning, and of course I do not wish you to leave.'

Emma hesitated. For her own sake she ought to look elsewhere for employment, for Lindisfarne's reputation could only do her own harm, but Bridget was giving her a tentative smile by way of an apology and she did not want to leave her in the lurch.

'I shall stay for the moment if you want me to,' Emma said. 'But I must tell you that people have begun to talk—about you and Lindisfarne. It is not serious as yet, but I think you should be careful.'

'Lindisfarne says the same,' Bridget replied, surprising her. 'We shall be more discreet when he returns. I may decide to take a house in the country for a few months.'

Emma felt a sense of foreboding. What had happened that afternoon to bring about this change in Bridget? Had she given into the earl's persuasion to be his mistress? Had she allowed him to make love to her? Just where had they spent the evening?

It was Emma's sincere hope that she had not been foolish. She would not have censured her friend had Lindisfarne been other than he was. There were discreet affairs going on around them all the time, but Bridget had been careless and Lindisfarne blatant in his pursuit. Society would forgive the rich and titled much, but Bridget was in no position to flout the rules so openly. Even Caroline Lamb had been censured for her behaviour with Lord Byron, and Mrs Flynn was a mere nobody in comparison. If she went too far she would be cut in the street, and then her hopes of cutting a dash would be at an end.

Emma worried about her friend as she undressed that night. It was not that she did not understand Bridget's feelings. She did—oh, she did! But it was so dangerous. Bridget might lose her heart, reputation and her fortune. Even her life…

The thought came unbidden and was terrifying. No, surely there was no danger of that! Lindisfarne was not so evil—was he?

She was letting her imagination run away with her! There could be no benefit in Bridget's death for Lindisfarne. Or could there? He was a distant relative of Bridget's husband and the money had been inherited from another cousin. Wills were sometimes strange. Might it be that Lindisfarne would inherit if Bridget died?

Emma struggled to put her fears from her mind. She was being ridiculous. Lytham's tale of the earl's tragic first wife had filled her mind with foolishness.

'Lytham…' Emma had tried not to think of that last stormy interview. All evening she had struggled to put him out of her mind but now it came back to her. How could he offer her *carte blanche?* It was cruel and insulting, and it made her want to weep.

His kindness to her, his apparent concern for her brother, and his teasing had given her cause to hope for something more. She had been foolish to do so, of course, but his manner had misled her. He did find her attractive, that had been evident from his physical arousal that afternoon—but he thought of her as someone he would appreciate as his mistress.

She knew that many young women in her situation, with no prospects of improvement, would have accepted such an offer, had it been made in a different way. Lytham had flung it at her in a temper, making her feel it was an insult, but of course it was not.

Lytham was a generous man. A woman in Emma's position need not fear that she would be cast off without a penny at the end of their affair. He would no doubt settle enough on her to enable her to live quietly somewhere. It might be preferable to a life at the beck and call of a selfish employer.

What was she thinking? Such an arrangement was an outrageous suggestion! She was the respectable daughter of a gentleman. She would never consider becoming any man's mistress for a moment. When she thought about it, she decided that Lytham had probably only said it to punish her for her stubbornness in refusing to leave Bridget's employ.

Yes, that must be it. She would allow herself to believe in the excuse that she had invented for him, otherwise she might find it difficult to meet him in company. And she must do so. She could not ignore the man who had introduced her to society in the first place.

Emma and Bridget spent the next day visiting the shops and the lending library. They met several ladies they knew and were greeted politely, though Emma thought with less warmth than on previous occasions. But perhaps that was merely her imagination?

Whenever she was given the chance she made a point of telling their acquaintance that they were dining with Lady Agatha Lynston and the marquis that evening. She was asked straight out by one lady where Lindisfarne was, and replied that she believed he might have gone out of town, hoping that her tone implied that she neither knew nor cared—which was the truth.

Bridget looked at her sulkily when they returned to the house to discover that only two visiting cards had been left that morning, when they had been used to receiving a dozen or more—and both belonged to gentlemen whose own reputations were dubious.

'I suppose the old tabbies have me down as a hussy?' she said to Emma with a scowl.

'I think there has been some gossip, but if you are careful in future perhaps no real harm has been done.'

'Oh, I do not care for them,' Bridget said and shrugged carelessly. 'Besides, when I marry Lindisfarne they will have to acknowledge me.'

'Are you going to marry him?' Emma asked. 'Has he proposed to you?'

'No—but he will. He will…' There was a note of near desperation in her voice. 'He must!'

Emma did not press her further. She sensed that Bridget was unhappy, but was reluctant to risk another quarrel. At this moment they were relieved of Lindisfarne's presence and for Emma that represented a breathing space—time for her to decide what she ought to do.

The evening went off better than she had imagined. Lytham was a perfect host, taking care of his aunt's guests and behaving in exactly the same way with the elderly ladies who were old friends of his aunt's as he did with Emma and Bridget. There was no hint of censure in either his manner or his speech, and she could almost have believed that their quarrel had never happened had it not been for the look in his eyes.

However, it was for her one of the most pleasant evenings they had spent since coming to Bath and Emma was feeling more relaxed as they prepared to take their leave.

'I hope we shall see you at the Assembly next week, ladies,' Lytham said as he kissed their hands before they departed. If he held Emma's for a fraction too long she tried to ignore it, and the beating of her heart. 'I shall expect two dances from each of you.'

'I am sure we shall be pleased to save them for you— shan't we, Emma?' Bridget fluttered her eyelashes at him flirtatiously.

'Yes, of course,' Emma replied, but did not look at Lytham.

She was very conscious of his attentions as he escorted them to their carriage, handing them in and remaining on the path to watch as they were driven away.

'Well,' Bridget said when they were finally alone. 'It is obvious that Lytham is interested in you. If you were to give him the least encouragement, he might marry you.'

'I am very sure he would not,' Emma replied. 'I am seven and twenty and I have no fortune. If Lytham were looking for a bride it would be to a young woman of some consequence.'

'Then why do his eyes seem to devour you wherever you go?'

'If Lytham were to make me an offer, it would not be of marriage.'

'Oh…' Bridget sighed. 'And of course you would refuse any other. Men are beasts sometimes, aren't they? I wonder why we love them?'

'I suppose it is a woman's nature to love,' Emma said thoughtfully. 'Mama still cared for Papa despite his gambling.'

Perhaps that was why she had this persistent ache in her heart, Emma thought. Of course she didn't love Lytham! Oh, why was she lying to herself? She had loved him almost from the beginning.

Perhaps not immediately; she had been prepared to hate him for what he had done to her family, but somehow she had not been able to sustain that first anger he had aroused. When had she begun to love him? Certainly she had known from the moment he had become ill. She had realised then that she could not bear it if he should die, and yet she had subdued her feelings, hiding them as she had so often in the past.

Lytham had once accused her of being two people, and perhaps she had been, but it was becoming harder and harder to subdue the Emma who wanted to live and love.

Two gentlemen called to take tea the next afternoon, and Mr Howard brought his sister Jane, who was a lively intelligent girl. Emma liked her and gathered from hints Jane let fall that Edward Howard was more than a little interested in Bridget.

Since he was a personable young man of moderate but adequate fortune, Emma thought how wonderful it would be if her friend were to marry him or someone like him. She mentioned the idea to Bridget as they went up to change for the evening.

'Oh, Edward is very pleasant,' Bridget said with a little pout. 'But not exciting. He does not make my heart race the way…someone else does. Edward might be a good husband, but do you not think he is a little dull?'

Emma made no reply. If Bridget enjoyed playing with fire there was nothing she could do to stop her, and perhaps she ought not to try.

Bridget seemed a little pensive when they left for the theatre that evening, but she remarked on Emma's appearance.

'That blue dress always looks lovely, and I'm glad you've done your hair in the softer style. It makes you look altogether different, Emma.'

A faint blush stained Emma's cheeks. She felt a little self-conscious, as though there was something wrong in having tried to make the best of herself for once. Of course there wasn't! Why shouldn't she look attractive? It didn't mean that she was setting her cap at Lytham.

Yet in her heart Emma knew that she did want him to think her attractive. She wanted him to smile at her, and she did not wish to quarrel with him.

She looked for him at the theatre that evening, wondering if he might be there with his aunt, but he was not and she was conscious of a sharp disappointment. Nor did she see him about the town on several occasions that she visited the library or the shops in the next day or so.

Could he be avoiding her? She tried to tell herself that she was imagining things, but her hopes of seeing him by chance before the Assembly were dashed.

For the next few days they lived an unexceptional life, walking in the town, driving out with the Howards to a beauty spot, and dining al fresco on a clear bright day that seemed to deny the season.

But the evening of the Assembly arrived at last, and Emma wore her blue gown once more. It was by far the most elegant of the gowns she owned, and made her feel special. She dressed her hair in the softer style, which she was adopting most of the time now and was moderately pleased with her appearance.

Her heart was fluttering as they set out, which was nothing to do with the fact that Lytham had said he and his aunt would be attending, of course.

Their arrival at the Assembly that evening seemed to cause a little stir. At first Emma was not particularly aware of anything amiss. They were greeted by several gentlemen, who took spaces on their dance cards as usual, and one or two of the younger ladies smiled and nodded in passing. It was only after some twenty minutes or so that Emma realised that the stricter ladies, who were the important hostesses, had not appeared to notice them. It was not that they were being deliberately ostracised—not yet—but some of the ladies had clearly decided they would not go out of their way to be friendly.

However, Bridget seemed quite content in the company of several young women, who were actually thought to be a little fast, and she was certainly not short of dance partners. Her laughter rang out often, and Emma wondered if she had noticed the difference and was putting on a show of bravado or whether she really wasn't aware of the slight coolness towards them that evening.

It was not until they had been at the Assembly for an hour that Lytham and his aunt arrived. They did not immediately come to greet Emma, for they were made much of by several dowagers who had not seen Lady Agatha at such a gathering for an age. However, after perhaps fifteen minutes, Lytham approached Emma. His eyes seemed to go over her and approve of what he saw.

'You look well this evening, Miss Sommerton,' he said. 'May I ask if by some chance there is a dance left for me?'

'You instructed me to save two for you,' Emma said, a flicker of amusement in her eyes. 'I believe there are actually four spaces remaining, so you may choose what you will.'

Lytham took the card she offered and scribbled his name in three places, including the supper dance. Emma made no comment, although to dance with him three times might cause some comment.

'Thank you, my lord,' she murmured as he returned the card to her. Since he had left the immediate dance free a partner did not claim her, and they had time to stand and talk to one another for a while.

'Lady Agatha looks as if she is enjoying herself,' Emma remarked. 'I believe you told me once that she did not go out much in company these days?'

'Foolishly, she had allowed herself to become almost a recluse,' he said with an affectionate glance towards his aunt. 'I believe I have convinced her that she ought to take a companion and make her home in Bath for a few months of the year.'

'I am sure it would be more congenial for her than being alone in the country.'

'I spend most of my time in London, which Agatha finds too rackety these days,' Lytham said. 'But I may perhaps be spending a little more time in the country in future.'

'Oh…' He did not elaborate and Emma was not inclined to ask for more than he wished to tell her. 'I am sure that will please your aunt.'

'Should my plans proceed as I hope, my aunt will soon have little cause for complaint.'

The enigmatic look that accompanied these words caused

Emma's heart to miss a beat. Just what was he saying? She could not guess for his expression gave nothing away.

At the start of the next dance a young and rather shy young man claimed Emma. He was not a good dancer, and several times almost stepped on her toes, but she smiled at him encouragingly, not wanting to make him feel embarrassed.

'Thank you so much, Miss Sommerton,' he stammered awkwardly as their dance ended. 'I am afraid I am very clumsy.'

'Not at all, Mr Exening,' she replied. 'It was very pleasant. I enjoyed myself.'

'You are so kind,' he said and blushed a fiery red. 'And so pretty. I do not care what Mama says, I hope we shall be friends, Miss Sommerton.'

'I hope so, too, sir,' Emma replied and wondered what his mama had said to cause him to look so embarrassed. However, she did not ask and in another few moments she was claimed for the next dance by a man who held her a little too tightly and gave her what she could only construe as suggestive leers.

Emma survived the dance and thanked him politely, reminding herself to do her best to avoid that particular gentlemen in future until her card was safely filled. His hot hands had made her feel rather too warm and she made her way to the ladies' cloakroom to splash her face with cool water.

It was as she was refreshing herself behind one of the screens provided that she heard two ladies enter and begin at once to talk in rather loud, excitable voices.

'I tell you she is Lindisfarne's mistress,' one of them said. 'They were seen, my dear—coming from the direction of the bedrooms at that inn. Jonathan said it was quite obvious what they had been doing...'

'What a fool she is,' the second woman replied. 'Has she no idea of his reputation…or of what this will do to her own?'

'She is obviously beyond caring. Men of that ilk cause women to lose their heads, Ellen. It is so foolish of her. They say she has a considerable fortune and could do much better for herself.'

'It is the companion I feel sorry for. She cannot know what is going on, surely?'

'Well, as to that—how can one be sure?'

Emma did not wait to hear her own character torn to shreds. She emerged from behind the screen and was given the satisfaction of seeing the ladies turn bright scarlet. She nodded to them but did not smile, leaving the cloakroom with her head held high.

Inside she was churning with fury. Of course she had known that people were talking, but surely Bridget had not been so foolish as to share a bedroom with Lindisfarne at an inn? She must have known that there was a chance she would be seen!

Returning to the ballroom, Emma looked for her friend and saw that she was dancing. She seemed to be perfectly happy, though whether that was a front to cover her embarrassment Emma could not tell. She herself was smarting with humiliation and wished that she had not happened to overhear the women gossiping.

She recovered her composure in time for her first dance with Lytham, though she immediately noticed something a little different in his manner.

'We must talk privately,' he said to her when the music ended. 'Not this evening—tomorrow. Please be at home tomorrow at noon, Emma.'

Her heart jerked uncomfortably. 'Does it concern something you have heard this evening, my lord?'

'Yes...' He gave her a sharp look. 'Have you heard it, too?' He raised his brows as she nodded. 'For the first time?'

'Yes,' she whispered her cheeks warm. 'I had wondered, but I was not perfectly sure of the facts. And I did not wish to think it might be so.'

'I imagine it to be widely believed,' Lytham replied. 'Remember, I shall call tomorrow—and now you must forgive me. I must cancel my other dances with you, I am afraid. My aunt wishes to be taken home. I think she is feeling a little fatigued.'

'Yes, of course. I do hope it is nothing serious?'

'I am sure it is just over-excitement,' he said. 'Forgive me.'

Emma nodded, but could not smile. Her eyes were stinging with the tears she must not shed. Clearly, he had decided that he did not wish to be seen dancing with her too often after hearing what was being said about Bridget.

She watched him leaving with Lady Agatha, who did look a little tired, but she was convinced that it was merely an excuse on Lytham's part. His leaving meant she had no partner for the supper dance, and therefore no one to take her in. She was about to go in alone, when she heard a voice behind her.

'Well, if it ain't the doxy from the inn...'

Emma shivered as something stirred in her memory, and she turned to see the young man who had accosted her the night she was leaving Lytham's bedroom. He looked surprised as he saw her, and for a moment she thought that he was confused by the change in her appearance. He had believed that he had recognised her, but now he was not quite certain.

Emma looked through him, turning away to make her

solitary walk into the supper room. She was aware that the young man had followed her and was still staring at her intently. She refused to look at him or give any sign that she had recognised him, and after a few minutes he walked away to greet some friends.

Emma's heart was racing. How unfortunate that he should be in Bath—and that he should remember her! If he were sure of his facts he might talk, and with all the scandal Bridget had caused, Emma would be ruined. She knew that some of the ladies were already inclined to tar her with the same brush as Bridget simply because she was her companion—but if there were to be gossip about her having been in a man's room at an inn her reputation would be finished. She would never be able to show her face in society again and any hope of securing a post with a respectable lady would be at an end.

'Why the long face?' Bridget came up to her, accompanied by two gentlemen and Miss Jane Howard. 'Why are you all alone, Emma? I thought you were having supper with Lytham?'

'He had to take his aunt home because she was unwell,' Emma replied and forced herself to smile. 'I am quite content to have had one dance with him. Are you enjoying yourself this evening, Bridget?'

'Oh, yes, of course,' Bridget replied. 'As much as I can when…'

She left the sentence unfinished, but Emma understood. She meant as much as she could without the presence of the man she loved. Despite wishing that Bridget had not been so foolish as to give her heart to Lindisfarne, Emma could feel sympathy for her. She knew only too well what it felt like to love unwisely.

* * *

The rest of the evening passed without incident and it was not until they were being driven home that Bridget let slip her true feelings about the evening.

'If it were not for Jane Howard I think I should leave Bath at once,' she confided to Emma. 'Jane says that the old tabbies have set their faces against me, but she does not believe a word of the scandal and has assured me that she and her brother will remain my friends no matter what happens.'

'Oh, Bridget,' Emma said. 'I am sorry if you were made to feel uncomfortable this evening. I know some of the ladies were talking. It appears that you were seen at the inn with Lindisfarne.'

'I do not care what they may say.'

'But you will if you are ostracised,' Emma said. 'It did not happen completely this evening, but if the Howards were to turn against you…'

'Why should they?' Bridget hunched her shoulder. 'It is only until Lindisfarne returns anyway, which he may do by tomorrow evening.'

'What will you do then?'

'I shall go with him if he asks me,' Bridget said. She pulled a face as Emma looked at her unhappily. 'You do not understand how it feels to love as I do.'

'I understand more than you imagine,' Emma said. 'But I ask you to think carefully before you decide, Bridget. If you become his mistress openly you can never go back. I know that there will be some houses that are open to you as his mistress—but what if…?' she faltered uncertainly.

'You mean when he is finished with me, I suppose?' Bridget stared ahead of her in the darkness of the carriage. 'My life will mean nothing to me then, so what does it matter?'

Emma was silent. Bridget had clearly decided that she could bear anything but to be parted from Lindisfarne—

which was possibly why he had taken this trip to London, to teach her a lesson and bring her to heel.

They finished the short journey in silence, parting at the top of the stairs with no more than a subdued farewell. Emma was thoughtful as she undressed. Why had Lytham made such a point of wanting to see her privately? Was it to lecture her once more? Or was it perhaps to renew his offer of *carte blanche?*

It was obvious that she could not expect an offer of marriage now. Her reputation had already become tarnished by the scandal concerning Bridget, and might suffer more if that young buck from the inn spoke of his belief that she had been a man's doxy. It did not matter that Lytham would know the truth, the damage would already have been done.

Emma went to bed with her mind in turmoil. Lytham had not requested her to be at home, he had ordered it— and she did not feel inclined to obey. Indeed, she would make sure that she was not at home when he called.

Bridget awoke with renewed energy and declared that she was going shopping. She said that she felt like spending money, and was determined to spend some of it on Emma.

'I must pay you some wages, too,' she said, looking thoughtful. 'I promised I would and I haven't.'

'You've given me lots of presents already.'

'That was my choice,' Bridget said and went over to the little writing desk with its secret drawers. She took six gold sovereigns from it and gave them to Emma. 'I do not have much spare money on me at the moment. I can pay for anything I need by a draft on my bank—but I want you to have this.'

'I shall not refuse, because I may need it,' Emma said and looked at her sadly. 'You know that I shall have to leave you when Lindisfarne returns, don't you?'

'Yes…' Bridget sighed. 'You do not like him and he does not like you. It is impossible for me to have you both.'

'And you choose him.'

'I have no choice,' Bridget replied. 'He makes me come alive, Emma. Without him I might as well be dead—as I was inside after I lost my dear Bertie.'

'Would Bertie have wanted you to do this, Bridget?'

'Oh, don't ask me that, Emma! It isn't fair.'

'I think it entirely fair,' Emma replied. 'I know you will be angry—but Lindisfarne is not a good man. He will make you unhappy.'

'I am miserable without him,' Bridget replied. 'If I can have a few months of happiness with him, it is all I want. After that…' She shrugged her shoulders.

Emma decided to say no more. There was nothing she could say that would change Bridget's mind. She realised that all she could do was to enjoy this last morning of shopping with Bridget; if Lindisfarne were expected to return at any time, she would have to leave as soon as he did.

They spent the morning shopping and managed to enjoy themselves despite being cut in the street by a woman who had once been delighted to welcome them both to her home. Bridget stuck her head in the air, determined not to mind, but Emma felt it keenly both for herself and her friend.

She tried not to think of what her life would be like when she left Bridget. It would be almost impossible to find work as a companion to a lady of quality, for any prospective employer would turn her away if there was the merest hint of scandal attached to her name.

It might be that she would have to return to the country and throw herself on Mary Thorn's mercy. She could perhaps stay there for a few weeks until she made inquiries about finding a position.

Perhaps she ought to change her name? She could use her mother's maiden name. It was a risky thing to do, for should she be unmasked she would immediately be asked to leave. However, she could choose her new employer carefully and if it were an elderly lady who seldom left her country home she might possibly get away with it for a time.

Emma's thoughts on that subject were not the happiest, but she managed to conceal them from Bridget, pretending to enjoy their outing—and she tried not to think about how angry Lytham would be when he discovered that she had disobeyed him.

However, on their return to the house, Emma discovered a note waiting for her. It was from Lytham and begged her to forgive him for not keeping his appointment with her. He was pleased to tell her that his aunt was much recovered and hoped that Emma would visit her soon. He himself had been called away on business and would return within a few days, when he would call without fail.

Emma folded the letter away. She felt that it was merely an excuse, and believed that Lytham had decided against continuing their friendship.

He had warned her what would happen if she stayed with Bridget, and now he was ready to wash his hands of her. Well, she had only herself to blame. Had she listened to him in the first place, she might have been his aunt's companion and settled comfortably in the country—something that was now out of the question.

Emma found no comfort in her own thoughts, or in the cry of surprise and delight that came from Bridget as she opened her own letter.

'Lindisfarne is back!' she cried. 'He says that he will call and take me to the theatre this evening.'

'I am pleased for you,' Emma said. 'If it is what you truly want?'

'Yes…yes, it is.'

'Then all I can say is be happy.' Emma went to kiss her cheek and then walked upstairs.

She sat on the edge of her bed and looked about her. It was too late to make any arrangements for travelling today, but she would certainly start her packing first thing in the morning.

She was not sure what the future held, but she would go home and seek the advice of friends before she decided.

Lytham cursed the ill fortune that had caused him to leave Bath just at this time. He was aware that several rumours were being circulated about Mrs Flynn, and he did not like them—for Emma's sake.

Had his business not been so urgent he would have kept his appointment with her and tried to persuade her to leave her friend before it was too late. However, one of his agents had important news for him, and he knew that it was something that could not be ignored.

It seemed that the man who had accused Tom of cheating might be in some kind of trouble with his creditors, and that it was not the first time he had come close to finding himself in a debtor's prison. At that time he had somehow managed to find the funds needed to clear his debts—the very time when he had caused Tom Sommerton's name to be blackened.

His investigations so far into the scandal of Tom Sommerton being accused of cheating and then thrashed had convinced Lytham that his brother's wife had indeed taken a young lover, and that that lover was Tom. The theory followed then that John had not only arranged for his rival to be accused of cheating, but also that he had probably hoped that the young man would die of the beating he had given him.

This being the case, it could lead to the finger of accusation being pointed at Tom Sommerton over Alexander's elder brother's death. It would do Emma's brother no good to clear him of cheating and then have him arrested for murder, and so he had set agents to search for evidence that Tom could not possibly have been involved in what he was still convinced had been an accident.

There was also the matter of his enemy. Had Tom Sommerton taken that pot-shot at him in the woods—or had that been the work of a man he had believed long dead? He must set further investigations in hand if he was to get to the bottom of this mystery.

But it seemed at last that he was about to get some answers. Only then would he be able to tell Emma of what was in his mind and heart.

Chapter Seven

Bridget begged Emma not to leave until her own arrangements were fixed, and she could do no less than agree. On the morning after Bridget's trip to the theatre with Lindisfarne, Emma asked if she would mind if she went to visit Lady Agatha.

'Providing you do not wish me to come with you, I do not mind what you do,' Bridget said and sighed. 'I have such a terrible headache. I think I shall stay in my room and rest all day.'

Emma sympathised. Bridget did look unwell, her face pale and shadows under her eyes as if she had not slept all night. She promised to have a soothing tisane sent up to her, and then collected some books she wished to return to the lending library and set out.

Her trip to the library was uneventful for it was early and she saw no one she knew either in the street or while she was choosing some new books for Bridget, but on the return journey she met two ladies with whom she was slightly acquainted and was surprised when they crossed the road rather than acknowledge her.

Emma had not expected to meet with such rudeness so soon, and felt distressed. She hesitated outside the little tea-room where she had sometimes stopped for tea and cakes, and then turned away, feeling that it might be too embarrassing if she were to be snubbed again.

'Emma—do wait!'

She glanced round and then halted as Jane Howard came hurrying up to her. Jane was looking extremely stylish in a gown of green-striped sarcenet and a heavy wool pelisse to keep off the chill air. Her bonnet was dark green velvet and trimmed with curling black feathers.

'I am so glad I caught you,' Jane said. 'Were you thinking of taking tea? I should be glad of the chance to speak with you.'

'I am on my way to visit someone,' Emma replied, 'but I should be glad of your company if you would consent to walk with me.'

'Willingly...' Jane gave her an uncertain smile. 'This is a little awkward, Emma. I am not perfectly sure where to start.'

'You may have heard certain rumours, perhaps?' Emma said, deciding to help her out. 'Please do not be afraid to speak of them, Jane.'

'Yes, yes, I have. I must tell you that they made me extremely angry and I do not believe them for a moment. And nor does my brother.'

'I think Mr Howard would believe nothing ill of Mrs Flynn,' Emma said with a smile. 'And I am very glad, for she may need friends in the future.'

'My brother refuses to listen to gossip about Mrs Flynn, and he will always continue her friend—but this concerns you, Emma.'

'Me...' Emma stared at her, a cold chill creeping over her. 'You have heard gossip concerning me?'

'Yes, and most unpleasant it was, too,' Jane said, her

cheeks warm. 'You were supposed to have been seen supporting a drunken man up to the bedchambers of an inn.'

'Ah, yes,' Emma said fighting for calm. She curled her fingers into her palms and took a deep breath. 'I thought that young man had recognised me. However, he was the one who was drunk at the time, and the man I was helping upstairs was ill. He had a fever and had almost fainted. I know that the situation appears to have been compromising, but there was really nothing improper about it.'

'I knew there could not be,' Jane said and looked relieved. 'Was the gentleman a friend or a stranger you had helped out of kindness?'

'His identity and the circumstances must remain confidential,' Emma replied. 'For your own information, I will say that the gentleman was Lytham and his illness was the result of an injury. But I do beg you not to reveal that to anyone. I have confided in you alone because of your staunch friendship towards Bridget and myself.'

'Then I shall not repeat what you have told me to anyone,' Jane said. 'Shall we see you at the Assembly this week?'

'I believe not.' Emma hesitated. 'I am thinking of going home for a short visit. Mrs Flynn may also be leaving Bath soon, but I am not yet certain of her intentions.'

'My brother will be sorry to hear that.' Jane frowned as though the news that Bridget might be leaving Bath had upset her. 'I think I must part from you now. I am sure we shall meet again soon.'

Emma nodded, but had nothing further to say. She was grateful that Jane had gone out of her way to tell her about the latest gossip, but she knew that not many ladies would be so easily convinced of her innocence. Gossip, once it began, was difficult to stop. Coming on top of the gossip concerning Bridget, it made Emma's position even more difficult, and she realised that her departure from Bath could not long be delayed.

Arriving at the house where Lady Agatha was staying, she hesitated and then decided she would continue with her visit. Lytham's great-aunt would surely allow her to give her side of things. She could always confirm it with Lytham herself. Besides, Emma felt it would be impolite of her to leave Bath without saying goodbye to a lady who had treated her kindly.

A stern-face butler admitted her to the house and asked her to wait in the small parlour while he went to inquire if his mistress was in. Emma stood looking out of the window that fronted on to the street, noticing that it had just begun to drizzle with rain. She turned expectantly as the butler returned.

'Lady Agatha begs you to forgive her, Miss Sommerton, but she is not receiving visitors this morning.'

'Oh…' Emma's cheeks burned. 'I hope she is not ill?'

'As to that, I really couldn't say, miss. I was just told that she was not at home this morning.'

'I—I see,' Emma said, her cheeks flaming. She was so embarrassed! The message could not have been clearer. Lady Agatha was not at home to her. 'Forgive me for troubling you.'

'I am sorry your journey was wasted, miss.'

Emma avoided looking at him as she allowed him to show her to the door. Oh, this was so terrible! She had not minded being cut earlier by two ladies she only knew slightly, but to be refused by a lady she liked and admired hurt more than she cared to admit.

Emma's insides were churning as she walked briskly back to Bridget's house. She had called with the best of intentions and now felt humiliated. It was all so unfair. She had suffered a loss of reputation when she had really done nothing wrong.

Inside the house, she took off her bonnet and pelisse and went into the parlour to deposit the little parcel of books she had brought for Bridget. She was startled to see a gentleman standing by the window and was about to make a hasty retreat when he turned and looked at her, his cold eyes sending a chill down her spine.

'I suppose I have you to thank for this?' The tone of Lindisfarne's voice left her in no doubt that he was furious and blaming her for whatever was causing his anger.

Emma was startled by the accusation. 'I fear I do not understand you, sir.'

'Bridget has refused to see me…' His gaze narrowed in dislike. 'Do you tell me this is none of your doing?'

'I believe she has the headache.'

'A convenient excuse, no doubt.' He moved towards her, his expression so menacing that Emma's pulses jumped in fright. 'I'll swear you put her up to it. No doubt you have lectured her about the perils associated with a rogue like me?'

Emma's head went up. She had had enough for one morning, and she was not going to put up with this!

'I have told her from the beginning that I think her unwise to continue her friendship with you, sir. It can do her reputation only harm, but—'

'Damn you!' His lips had gone white with temper. '*You* to speak of reputation—when it is all over town that you are little better than a whore yourself.'

'That is a vicious lie!'

'You pretend to be such a meek little thing,' he muttered, beyond listening to her so caught up was he in his own fury. 'But I have suspected there was fire beneath the ice.

Very well, since I am to be denied Mrs Flynn I'll have you!'

Emma gasped as she read his meaning and turned to flee from the room, but he came after her, catching her arm in a viselike grip and swinging her round against him. She gave a little scream and kicked out at him, but he twisted her arm behind her back, making her cry out in pain, and then, imprisoning her with his other arm, he lowered his head to kiss her.

His kiss was horrible, meant to punish and humiliate as his teeth ground against hers and he hurt her. She tasted blood in her mouth and struggled, turning her head aside and gagging for air. He took a handful of her hair and pulled her head back, tugging it at it so that tears came to Emma's eyes. Holding her with his leg curled about her and one hand, he pulled at the neckline of her gown, and it tore in his hand as she jerked wildly, spurred on to a desperate effort as she guessed what he meant to do.

'Let me go, you beast,' she cried but he jerked on her arm and made her scream out. 'Let me go! I want nothing to do with you.'

'I am going to teach you a lesson, whore!' Lindisfarne hissed. 'You shall learn what it means to defy me. I had *her* eating out of the palm of my hand. She was ready to do anything I asked and now…'

'You want her fortune more than you want her! You are a wicked evil man and I—'

He struck Emma across the face, making her head jerk back. 'Be quiet, jade. The money is necessary, but I want Bridget—she's mad for me and I intend to have both her fortune and her.'

He grabbed Emma tighter and began to force her backwards towards the sofa, and she gasped as she realised what he had meant by teaching her a lesson. He was going to violate her!

'What is going on here?'

Bridget's voice startled them both. Lindisfarne let Emma go immediately, his face stamped with surprise and guilt. He had been sure that Bridget was safely in her room and would not venture down, but here she was wearing a loose wrapping gown and looking pale as if she really were suffering a headache.

'Bridget dearest…your companion pretended to faint,' he said and then with more confidence, 'She then flung her arms about me and made a scene because I would not embrace her. She is jealous of you, because she knows she is unlikely to stir any man to passion.'

'Liar!' Emma said. She had retreated to stand as near to the door as she could, prepared for flight. 'Don't listen to him, Bridget. You know he is lying. You know I dislike him and that I would never throw myself at him or any man.'

Bridget pressed a hand to her head. She was suffering dreadful pain and she stared from one to the other of them in indecision.

'Oh, I do not know who to believe,' she said and tears of self-pity sprang to her eyes. 'I wouldn't have believed you capable of this, Emma—and yet why should Lindisfarne want you when—' She broke off on a sob.

'She accused me of wanting only your fortune,' Lindisfarne said, pressing home what he sensed was his advantage. 'I was about to tell her that I adore you when you came in.'

'Bridget…' Emma appealed to her but saw that she was wavering, obviously wanting to believe her lover. 'Very well, if that is what you wish to believe, please excuse me.'

She walked from the room with her head lifted high,

holding on to her torn bodice and the shreds of her dignity. Bridget must know in her heart that she would never throw herself at Lindisfarne in the way he had described, but she was prepared to believe him because she could not bring herself to accept the alternative.

It was time she was leaving. Emma went up to her room and took off her torn gown, throwing it on the floor of her bedchamber in disgust. Even if it had not been ruined she could never have brought herself to wear it again. The memory of Lindisfarne's hateful lips on hers made her shudder. She scrubbed the back of her hand across her mouth and then went over to the washstand and poured cold water from the jug into an earthenware basin. She was not sure that she would ever feel clean again, but she was going to try and scrub the taste of him from her mouth.

And then she was going to leave this house.

'It is unfortunate that Mrs Flynn should take up with such a man,' Mary Thorn said as Emma unfolded her tale some hours after her arrival at the vicarage. It had taken two days on the Mail coach, but she could not afford the luxury of travelling by post chaise and had been worn out by the time she had finally walked the last few miles to her friend's home. Most of her luggage had been left behind at the depot, and she had had to arrange for it to be sent on by carrier. Mary had taken her in instantly, insisting that explanations could wait, and now it was after supper and they were comfortably settled in Mary's small but pretty parlour in front of a warming fire. 'If I may say so, I think you have been treated shamefully, Emma dearest. And I am very glad you came to us.'

'It is only for a short while,' Emma assured her. 'I shall write to various agencies and see if they can advise me of any vacancies for a lady's companion, and I shall read the advertisements. I dare say it will not take too long to find something.'

Emma sounded more confident than she felt, for she knew that many prospective employers would expect a reference from her last employer and she was not sure that Bridget would give her one should she apply to her.

Emma had not spoken to her former friend after that unpleasant scene in the parlour, feeling that she did not wish to be accused of throwing herself at a man she had always disliked. If Bridget could think that of her then their friendship was clearly at an end, and the only sensible thing left for Emma was to put the whole sorry episode from her mind.

She had left a note for Bridget before she left, telling her the truth of what had happened, and assuring her that she wished her only happiness in the future, and then she had sent for the porter to fetch her trunk to the coach station. She had taken only one or two of the gowns Bridget had bought for her, leaving the most expensive behind. She would, after all, have no use for elegant ballgowns in future, and Bridget might be able to have them altered for herself—or more likely give them to one of the maids as a gift. Emma had no wish to keep them after the way her former friend had behaved. She was not bitter, but she knew that if they were ever to meet in the future, she would not be able to feel towards Bridget exactly as she had previously. Bridget ought to have taken her word, the fact that she had not had been both hurtful and humiliating.

During the uncomfortable journey on the Mail coach, which had involved a stay overnight at an inn and contrasted vividly with the one in Lytham's carriage a few weeks earlier, Emma had had a great deal of time to think. She made up her mind that the only way to deal with all that had happened to her was to bury it deep in her sub-conscious.

Emma had managed to subdue her feelings many times before when it was necessary, but she had already begun to discover that it was not going to be so easy this time. Lytham would not be banished from her thoughts no matter how she tried, and the memory of those kisses he had given her had disturbed her sleep too often already.

However, she had accepted that she could expect nothing more exciting of life in future than a position as companion to an elderly lady, and knew she must expend all her energies on seeking that post. Mary Thorn had welcomed her warmly, but she could not stay with her kind friends for more than a few weeks.

Emma had wished several times since her departure from Bath that she had taken Lytham's offer to become a companion to Lady Agatha, and yet perhaps that would not have served. For her foolish heart would still have misbehaved, and she knew that if he were to be wounded again she would not hesitate to do exactly as she had the first time.

Emma reflected that it was a sad thing to be a woman and at the mercy of spiteful tongues. Had she been a man and noticed on the stairs of an inn with a whore, she would have been thought a bit of a devil and no one would have censured her. It was unfair that she should have suffered a loss of reputation through a kind act, but it would just have to be forgotten along with all the rest.

Emma tried not to think of what might become of her if she could not find the kind of situation she was looking for—but she would not allow herself to have such thoughts. It was surely only a matter of time before the right opportunity presented itself, and in the meantime she would keep busy helping Mary with all her parish work.

* * *

'I believe it may be my fault that she left Bath so abruptly,' Lady Agatha said to Lytham as he towered over her that morning some six days after Emma's departure. 'Please do sit down, Lytham. This is a small parlour and you make it seem smaller when you stand there so aggressively. I did not mean to offend her, of course. I had not heard those unkind rumours then, and I was feeling unwell the morning she called. I told my maid to give Miss Sommerton the message herself, but she delegated it to Smithers and goodness knows what he said. He must have upset her for she went off that same day.'

'If she had heard the rumour herself, she may have thought that you did not wish to receive her,' Lytham said and frowned. 'It is my fault. I should have kept my appointment with her that morning before I left for town and made all clear.'

'Do sit down, Lytham, and stop pacing like a caged animal,' his aunt said a trifle impatiently. 'Your restlessness is disturbing.'

'Forgive me.' Lytham sat in the large wing chair opposite her but still looked as if he were a coiled wire spring ready to snap.

Lady Agatha smiled inwardly, wickedly deciding to tease him a little more. 'This story going around—you think there is no truth in it?'

'My dear aunt,' he replied between his teeth, 'I can only imagine that the young fool spreading this gossip is referring to the night I was taken ill of a fever on our journey to town. Since I was the gentleman in question, I can assure you that I was in no case to ravish her that particular evening.'

'I trust you would not have done so had you been perfectly well,' his aunt reproved him with a frown. 'Emma

Sommerton is a lady—and although you are a rogue, Lytham, I believe you to be a gentleman. Gentlemen do not take advantage of innocent young ladies, however much they might wish to sometimes.'

Lytham's mouth twisted in a wry smile. 'You are telling me that I am to blame for Emma's predicament, I think.'

'Well, if it was you she was helping upstairs, you are certainly the indirect cause of her loss of reputation, and I think you must instantly repair it.'

'You are very right, Aunt,' Lytham agreed. 'I shall see the young idiot in question—Rotherham's boy, I believe? By the time I've finished with him he will be ready to grovel to Emma on his knees.'

'All that is necessary is that a correct version of the story be circulated,' his aunt reproved. 'It would be best to make a jest of the tale if you can find the way to do it. People will always wonder a little—no smoke without fire, as the saying goes—but if you handle this properly no permanent damage may result.'

'You know my intentions, Aunt.'

'Yes, but Emma may feel differently,' Agatha said. 'You must do what you can to re-establish her reputation before you press your own desires on her, Lytham.'

'You mean she might feel that she is being forced to accept me because she has no other choice?'

'Yes, that is exactly what I mean,' Agatha said. 'Your first duty is to put the story straight here in Bath, and you must also call on Mrs Flynn and ask her if she knows why Emma left so suddenly—and where she went.'

'Yes, I believe you are right,' he replied thoughtfully. 'I think I shall have a few words with Jane Howard. She and Emma had been quite friendly I think, and she may be able to shed some light on Emma's decision to leave.'

* * *

Lytham was thoughtful as he set out for the Howards' lodgings, and was fortunate enough to meet with Jane, as she was about to set out on a visit to the pump room.

'I was hoping we might have a word, Miss Howard?'

'Why, certainly, my lord,' she replied and smiled at him. 'If you mean to ask me about these ridiculous rumours circulating about Miss Sommerton, I can tell you my mind is quite at rest over them. Emma told me in confidence that you were unwell that evening, and that she merely assisted you up the stairs. I have told anyone who will listen that that is the case, though I did not use your name as Emma particularly requested I should not.'

'Did Miss Sommerton seem upset to you when she spoke of the affair?'

'No, indeed, she was remarkably calm,' Jane Howard replied. 'I should have been most distressed had she been upset as it was I who told her about the stupid tale going around. I believe she was on her way to visit someone.'

'Yes, my aunt,' Lytham said, 'who was unfortunately not well enough to receive her.'

Jane looked at him thoughtfully. 'I had wondered why she left Bath that day, for she had mentioned a visit to her home but she had not said it was imminent. When I spoke to Mrs Flynn concerning Emma, she seemed a little odd. It was in my mind that they might have quarrelled, but I cannot be sure of that.'

'Thank you for your confidence,' Lytham said and smiled at her. 'I think I must call on Mrs Flynn immediately.'

'You will not find her at home,' Jane told him and smiled a little oddly. 'My brother has taken her driving this afternoon, but I believe she means to visit the Assembly this evening.'

'Then I shall see her there and make an appointment to call—' Lytham's gaze narrowed as he caught something in

Jane's look. 'Forgive me if I presume too much—but am I right in thinking your brother and Mrs Flynn have an understanding? When I left Bath I thought someone else was her constant companion?'

'That is all changed now, I am happy to say. There is nothing official as yet,' Jane assured him with a little blush. 'But now that Mrs Flynn has ended her friendship with Lindisfarne, I expect to hear happier news of her very soon.'

'That nonsense is definitely ended then?' His brows rose.

'Oh, yes, my brother says it is quite over. She had found *him* out, you see, and turned to Edward for advice in the matter of some investments a certain person had been trying to force her into—and of course he told her that they would be a mistake. He assured her that she would be much better not to break the trust her husband's lawyers had set up for her, which was what any honourable person would do, of course. It is rumoured that the very next day Lindisfarne left Bath in a terrible rage. I believe there was also a personal reason for the split, but whatever the cause...' she gave a little satisfied nod '...I am perfectly certain that it is over.'

'All Mrs Flynn's friends must be glad of it, I am sure.'

'Oh, yes,' Jane said and gave a little shudder. 'One should not speak ill of another if one can help it, but that man is despicable!' She made an expressive face of disgust.

'Exactly,' Lytham said. 'You are a sensible young woman, Miss Howard, and I am glad I came to you first.'

'I do hope you will go after Emma,' Jane said. 'Her friends will always support her, for none of us could believe that kind of Banbury tale.'

'I am sure she will be glad to hear that, and as I hope she will either return to Bath or spend some time in London next spring, I hope you will call on her.'

'You may depend that I shall.'

They took their leave of one another in perfect harmony, Jane convinced that her suspicions about a certain gentleman's intentions towards her friend had been correct all along, and Lytham to make his rounds of the fashionable meeting places in order to begin the reparation of Emma's reputation.

'Oh…' Bridget gave Lytham a guilty glance as he came up to her at the Assembly that evening. 'If you are looking for Emma…'

'I believe I am seeking an explanation,' he said before she could continue. 'Did you perchance quarrel with Emma, Mrs Flynn?'

'Yes, and it was most unfair of me,' Bridget replied with a shamefaced look. 'She had warned me that Lindisfarne would ruin me and indeed he would have had…he not made that mistake. I heard some of their quarrel, you see.' Her voice tailed away to a whisper.

'I imagine your tale would be better told in private,' Lytham said as he saw her embarrassment. 'May I call on you in the morning—say at eleven-thirty?'

'Oh, yes, I am sure that is best,' Bridget said and turned as Edward Howard came up to her. 'Pray excuse me, sir. I have promised this dance to Mr Howard.'

And most of the others on her card from what he had been able to observe, Lytham thought. Clearly Mrs Flynn had recovered from her passion for Lindisfarne much more quickly than would have seemed possible, and was probably seeking a safer attachment for the future.

He wondered what Lindisfarne had done to cause her to come to her senses so suddenly, and wondered if it concerned Emma. If that swine had harmed her…! But he must wait for the morning in patience. It would not do to march

Mrs Flynn from the ballroom and force her to repeat what was sure to be a harrowing tale.

It was in any case too late to set out for the country that evening, and Emma was probably quite happy staying with her friends for the moment.

He stayed only to dance once with Jane Howard, and then took his leave. As soon as he learned the truth of Emma's hasty departure, he would set out to find her.

It was only when he arrived back at Lady Agatha's lodgings that he realised his journey would have to be delayed for a few days.

Almost two weeks had passed since Emma left Bath, and her hopes that Lytham might follow her had faded. It had been foolish of her to allow herself to hope even for a moment, but she could not control her heart. Despite everything, it continued to race wildly at the mention of his name—something she tried hard to hide from Mary.

'Why do you not apply to the marquis for help?' Mary asked when her first two inquiries for the post of companion ended in disappointment. Both positions had been advertised in a local paper and she had thought it might be easier to get work locally, where she might be known as Sir Thomas's daughter. Indeed, she had received a very kind letter from one lady who said that she knew Emma's mother and would have gladly given her the position had it not already been filled. 'I am sure he would recommend you to someone he knows.'

'Oh…I prefer not to ask for favours if I can avoid it,' Emma replied. She had been encouraged by the kind letter and was only waiting for the next edition of the paper to see if any more likely situations were offered within its pages. 'I believe I shall—' She had been about to say that she was thinking of placing an advertisement herself when

Mary's little maid came in with a silver salver. 'Is that for me, Annie? Thank you.'

She slit the letter open with a pearl-handled knife, and saw that it was from one of the agencies she had approached soon after her father's death. She had written to them again to ask if they knew of anything, and it seemed there was a suitable position with an elderly lady living in Northumberland.

'This sounds as if it may suit me,' Emma said, holding it out to Mary when she had finished reading it. 'What do you think?'

Mary read the letter and frowned. 'It says that their client is a difficult lady and that her recent companion left suddenly. I think she may be the sort of person who makes life uncomfortable for her employees, Emma.'

'Yes, I dare say,' Emma replied, for she had guessed something of the sort herself. 'But I do not have a great deal of choice, Mary. I must find a position soon.'

'You know we are delighted to have you here.'

'You have been very kind,' Emma said. 'But I must not stay too long, Mary dearest. If I do not wear out my welcome, then I may come back to you whenever I am in need of a temporary home.'

Mary made no further protest. She would have liked to offer Emma a permanent home, but she knew that would not be comfortable for any of them. At the moment her two sons were sharing a room, but when Mary's daughter was old enough to leave the nursery she would need a room of her own. For a week or two at a time they could manage, but the Vicarage was not large enough to accommodate them all indefinitely.

'I thought I would take a walk up to the house this afternoon,' Emma said. 'Lily told me that they go on as usual and I wanted to see how everyone is. Lytham will surely not let things continue as they are forever, and when I return next time there may be new people living there.'

'Well, it is cold, but I do not think it will snow,' Mary said, glancing out of the window. 'A little walk may do you good, Emma. You may use the time to think about this position you have been offered and decide what you wish to do for the best.'

'Yes, that is what I thought,' Emma agreed. 'I shall write this evening and let them know one way or the other.'

It was easy to speak of making a decision, Emma thought as she began the walk to what had once been her father's estate. She had chosen to take the longer route through the village for the fields were muddy and, though it was cold, she did not think it cold enough to freeze. Better to take the road and avoid getting stuck in the mud. The trees were beginning to lose their leaves and it would not be long before winter set in. The prospect of spending the coming months at a place she did not know with an employer of uncertain temper was not a happy one but, try as she might, Emma could find no alternative.

Everyone was delighted to see her up at the house. It was clear that Lily had told her fellow servants that they had left Bath hurriedly after a quarrel with Emma's employer, though she had been unable to give them more details since Emma had not communicated them to her.

Lily was back to her old work as a parlour maid, apparently quite content to be home from her travels. She welcomed Emma to the servants' hall, but did not stay to listen because she was summoned by the ringing of the doorbell.

'Well, miss, you're looking very healthy,' Cook told her as she sat down at the table with them as she had often done in the past. 'You could have knocked me down with a feather when Lily said you was back so soon. Shall you be staying long, miss?'

'Only for a few weeks,' Emma replied. 'I am looking for—' She turned as Lily came back in, looking pink-cheeked and flustered. 'Did you want me, Lily?'

'It's his lordship, miss…the marquis himself,' Lily said in a voice breathy with excitement. 'He recognised me and asked me how I was.'

'I hope you didn't tell him I was here?' Emma's heart sank as she saw the look on Lily's face. 'You did and he asked to see me, of course?'

'Yes, miss. He said he would take it as a favour if you would consent to take tea with him in the parlour.'

Emma cursed the ill fortune that had caused Lytham to arrive on the very afternoon that she had chosen to visit her old servants at the house. He would think she was taking liberties, but there was no help for it. She could do no other than comply with his request.

'I shall go up at once,' she said. 'Please wait a few minutes before you bring the tea, Lily.'

'Yes, miss—his lordship said twenty minutes and no sooner.'

Clearly Lytham was in charge here, but she must expect that. The estate belonged to him now, and she was merely a guest under his roof—an uninvited one at that. She put her hands to her cheeks in an effort to cool them, taking a moment to recover her composure before knocking at the parlour door.

'Come!' Lytham barked, then glared at her as she entered. 'I imagined it was Lily. Why did you knock? This is your home, you may enter without seeking my permission.'

'It was once my home,' Emma corrected with dignity. 'I must ask you to forgive me for this presumptuous visit. I came only to see old friends before—'

'Running away again, Emma?' His brows arched. 'You

have less courage than I believed. I did not think you so easily cowed.'

'Forgive me. I do not think I understand you.'

'Why did you run away from Bath—was it because of that stupid tale making the rounds? Or because you quarrelled with Mrs Flynn?'

Emma clasped her hands in front of her, trying for calm. He had obviously been listening to the gossip, and though he knew the truth of the scurrilous tale put about by one young gentleman, he must think ill of her or he would not be giving her such looks!

'If you know that I quarrelled with Bridget, you must know why I left,' she said, refusing to be drawn.

'I know that that rogue Lindisfarne told Mrs Flynn you had thrown yourself at him, and that for a few moments she chose to believe him.' He glared at Emma. 'But that was no reason for you to run away. You might have known that she would realise the truth of the matter when she'd had time to reflect.'

'I knew no such thing,' Emma retorted. 'Bridget was in love with him, and I believed she had chosen to believe him over me. I did not care to be disbelieved in that manner. Besides, there were other reasons for me to leave.'

'Such as that stupid tale circulating?' His brows rose. 'I have put that to flight, Emma, and I think you will hear no more of it—and my aunt was unwell that morning. You were supposed to have received that message, but perhaps it was not put to you in quite those terms?'

'No, it was not,' Emma replied, a flush in her cheeks. 'I believed Lady Agatha had heard the gossip and did not want to receive me.'

'She was afraid that was what had happened,' Lytham said, 'and she asked me to beg your forgiveness if indeed you were made to feel unwelcome in her house.'

'It was not exactly that,' Emma said, not meeting his eyes. 'Jane Howard had told me about the gossip, and I fear I may have jumped to a hasty conclusion. When Lindisfarne also accused me of being a whore—'

'Damn him! The man deserves to be horsewhipped for the way he behaved towards you—and Mrs Flynn. Had he not taken himself off to Ireland I might have been tempted to teach him a lesson myself.'

'Has he indeed gone?' Emma was relieved as he inclined his head. 'Poor Bridget must be desperately unhappy.'

'That was not the case when I last saw her,' Lytham said. 'She seems to be making a remarkable recovery under the tender care of Mr Howard and his sister.'

'Oh, I know they will take care of her, but Bridget was desperate. I cannot believe her nature to be so shallow that she is not hurting inside.'

'Then it is your own nature you follow, not hers,' Lytham replied with a frown. 'I have found most women to be inconstant, and to find comfort very quickly in another lover.'

'That is unfair of you, sir!' Emma's eyes flashed fire at him. 'I do not know what you may have experienced in the past, but not all of us are so easily content to pass from one man to another. Some of us having once given their heart may never give it to another if disappointed.'

'Is that what happened to you, Emma? Is that why you have hidden your feelings for years?'

'I do not know what you mean.' Emma turned away from him and went to stand by the window, looking out at the park. Her pulses were racing and she did not trust herself to speak for the moment. She must do and say nothing that gave her feelings away, though her heart raced wildly when he looked at her.

'So—what are your immediate plans?' Lytham asked, his change of subject surprising her.

'I have been seeking for work as a companion,' Emma replied, without looking at him. 'There is a post that I might consider with an elderly lady.'

'Is that really what you want?'

'I may have no choice. Once there has been talk there are always some who will believe it, and I may not be able to find more congenial employment.'

He was silent for a moment, then, 'There is always my offer...'

Emma's heart stood still. She felt a tingling sensation sweep over her. He was asking her to be his mistress! For a moment she was angry that he could press his scandalous offer at a time when she was so very low. Yet in an instant the anger was gone as she realised how wonderful it would be to be held intimately in his arms...to sleep in his bed after having experienced his loving.

Her cheeks were burning as she felt the confusion and shame mingle in her mind, and knew that she was sorely tempted to accept his offer. She ought to refuse it, of course. She ought to storm from the room and never speak to him again ...but it was her last chance of ever knowing the happiness of a man's love. Even if that love were a transitory thing that would burn itself out.

She couldn't do such a wicked thing! She would be throwing everything away, her reputation, the respect of her friends, all hope of a return to society. But as she gripped her hands together tightly, she knew that she was going to be reckless for perhaps the only time in her life.

'You are asking me to be your mistress,' she said, still not looking at him. 'I refused you the first time, but have given your offer much consideration since we parted, sir, and—and I have decided to accept.'

Lytham was stunned. Surely she could not mean it? He was not sure what devil had prompted him to remind her. In Bath, he had thrown the offer that she might care to be his mistress at her in a moment of temper and never for a second had he believed she would accept—nor had he truly wished for it. Even now, he had expected her to fly at him in a rage, and then of course he would have taken her in his arms and told her that she was quite wrong. He had always had something quite different in mind for Emma, but now that little devil was on his shoulder, tempting him to see how far she would really go. Supposing he let her believe that he truly wanted her as his mistress?

'If you mean that, Emma, I should be both honoured and delighted with the arrangement. I assure you that you will be well taken care of financially.'

'Oh, I know that, my lord.' Emma turned to face him. She was in command of herself now, though her heart was pumping madly and she thought her cheeks might still betray her inner agitation for they felt heated. 'I have realised for some time that you were both generous and fair. I am therefore quite prepared to be your mistress for—for as long as you are satisfied with the arrangement—and to retire to a discreet distance when you are...tired of the situation.'

'That may be a very long time, Emma,' Lytham replied. If she was struggling for composure, then he—the rogue!— was struggling to stop himself laughing out loud. 'You are a lovely woman, and I admire beauty for its own sake, but I think you also know that I enjoy your company, and that I have certain feelings for you.'

'Yes...' Emma's cheeks were definitely burning now and she could not have met his eyes to save her life. 'I was aware of that when...when you kissed me, my lord. I—I found it a pleasant experience. Had I not, nothing would have induced me to accept your offer, but I think we may deal well together and—' She found it too difficult to continue.

Lytham decided to rescue her. He moved swiftly towards her, taking her into his arms and pulling her close to him so that she felt the heat of him. As he pressed his mouth to hers in a kiss of possession that left her close to swooning, Emma felt an overwhelming surge of relief and happiness.

It did not matter that this would not last, that one day she would taste bitterness and despair when he no longer wanted her—for now, she was happier than she had ever been in her life.

'Does that answer your question, Emma?' He gazed down at her, a look of devilish amusement in his eyes. 'If you were in any doubt about my feelings for you, that must surely tell you that I want you very badly.'

'Yes, my lord,' Emma said, a smile tugging at her mouth. 'Had this been a conventional arrangement, I should have had to pretend that I was ignorant of your meaning or that I was too shy to respond—but I believe you would have known that to be a falsehood?'

Lytham chuckled, realising that she was an even more remarkable woman than he had believed, and that he was extremely fortunate that he had found her.

He ought, of course, to tell her at once of his true intentions towards her, but the pleasure to be got from teasing her a little longer was irresistible.

'Your response was very satisfactory for a beginner, Emma,' he replied. 'But I shall teach you the way a passionate woman behaves with her lover—there are many things for you to learn, my darling. Shall you be willing to learn them, Emma?'

'I think you will find me an apt pupil,' she replied. It

was so good of him to make a jest of this, she felt, easing her through what might otherwise have been an awkward situation. She was well aware that her behaviour was shocking in the extreme, but just for the moment she did not care.

'Oh, I am convinced of it,' Lytham said, eyes alight with mischief. 'But I think we shall not begin your lessons just yet, Emma. I do not want to shock your friends and household. No, I shall take you somewhere that we may be private…a little love-nest that will enable you to become the woman I know you can be.'

'You are always so thoughtful, my lord.'

'I really must insist that you call me Lytham, Emma.'

'Yes, certainly, Lytham,' she replied and her lovely eyes were brilliant with the love she had no idea that she was betraying. 'You see, I shall be very good from now on.'

'Oh, yes, I see it,' he replied and smiled inwardly. It was a good beginning, but he could not wait for her to wake up and realise just what she had agreed to.

Chapter Eight

Lytham insisted on accompanying Emma back to the Vicarage, declaring that he would have the carriage brought round since dark clouds had blown up and there was a likelihood of rain. She could not but be grateful; it did indeed begin to bucket down long before she could have walked to the Thorns' house.

'There you are, my love,' Mary said welcoming them into her parlour where a fire was merrily burning. 'I was beginning to think you would get a terrible soaking, but his lordship has seen you safely home as I might have expected he would.' She smiled at the marquis, clearly approving of him. 'My husband had heard you were come, sir. It is nice to see you back again.'

'Thank you, Mrs Thorn,' he responded warmly to her welcome. 'Emma could have remained at Sommerton for as long as she wished, of course. However, she wanted to return here until we leave tomorrow. I am taking her to my family estate, ma'am, where she will be quite safe.'

'There—did I not say his lordship would make all right if you applied to him, Emma?' She beamed at him. 'My mind is completely at rest now, sir. I know *you* will take care of her.'

'Thank you, Mrs Thorn. You may indeed rely on me to do just that.'

Emma wondered how he could respond so easily. For herself she was determined to say as little as possible about her intentions for the future. If Mary knew the true situation she would be terribly shocked. Emma hoped that she would never need to tell her.

Her courage ebbed during the night when she lay for some hours, staring into the darkness and trying not to think about what she had done. By agreeing to become Lytham's mistress, she had effectively cut herself off from her family and friends, none of whom would approve of what she was doing. She knew that she was being reckless, but the alternative was so bleak…and she did love him. It would be heaven to be with him, to be loved by him, even if for only a short time.

No, she did not regret her decision, not for a moment! She would think only of the time to be spent with him, the man she loved, and forget that a lonely future might await her one day.

Emma slept at last, dreaming sweetly of a cottage with roses growing up the walls and a man who looked remarkably like Lytham carrying a young lad on his shoulders, who she instinctively knew was their son. All quite ridiculous, of course, she reflected on waking. Lytham lived in a large house and their relationship was hardly likely to last long enough for her ever to see him playing with children of their union.

She had slept longer than she intended and there was a last-minute rush to be ready for the carriage, with Emma searching for trinkets she had somehow mislaid, and Mary trying to organise the final packing of her bags. The last

hour went so swiftly that she did not have time to be nervous, and the carriage was at the door before she realised
it.

'You must write to me when you have the leisure,' Mary
Thorn said as she kissed Emma goodbye. 'But I know you
will do well now, dearest Emma. The marquis is a fine man
and he will take care of you.'

Emma blushed then as she wondered for a moment if
Mary had guessed the truth. She seemed to be suggesting
a relationship of an intimate kind between Emma and
Lytham, but of course she could not know anything. She
probably imagined that Emma was to live with Lytham's
aunt as a kind of unpaid companion, Lytham's dependent.
Of course that must be it.

Kissing Mary goodbye, Emma smiled at Lytham as he
came to hand her into the carriage. He nodded but said
nothing, though his eyes seemed to study her face thoughtfully before he went to take his leave of Mary Thorn.

'I wish to thank you for taking care of Emma for me,
ma'am.'

'It was nothing, sir. The Vicar and I are both fond of
her.'

'But I am grateful none the less. Should your husband
ever wish for preferment to another living you will apply
to me, ma'am. I shall be happy to promote your family's
interests now and in the future.'

'Oh, sir,' Mary said, overcome. 'I am sure I don't know
what to say.'

'You need say nothing, ma'am. Simply pass on my message to the Reverend Thorn and he will know what to do.'
He took the hand she offered, saluting it with a chaste kiss
before leaving her to climb into the carriage with Emma.

'What have you been saying to Mary?' she asked, having

witnessed their leave-taking but not overheard the conversation between them.

'Merely politeness,' Lytham replied with a careless shrug of his broad shoulders immaculately clothed in a coat of blue superfine. She could not help noticing how very good looking he was and experiencing a little shiver of anticipation. 'I am glad to see you looking so well, Emma. I trust you slept well?'

'Tolerably well,' she replied, eyes downcast, lashes long and dark against her cheeks. 'There are always slight anxieties when one embarks on a new venture, but I am content now. I know that you are experienced in these matters and I need only follow your lead.'

Lytham's mouth twitched at the corners, but he managed to hide his amusement. Did she imagine that it was his habit to carry off innocent maidens and make love to them? What a delicious idiot she was! This was proving even more enchanting than he had thought. He was a wicked rogue to carry on this deception, but he had not been so diverted in an age. She would make an entrancing mistress!

He gave her no answer, stretching out his long legs as he leaned his head back against the squabs, and admiring her lovely face and apparent composure from beneath lowered lids. She was a picture of serenity. She could not possibly be that calm inside—could she? A young woman of good family about to become an outcast from society by becoming his mistress—what must be going through her mind? Had she thought ahead, to a time when he might no longer want her? No, he was sure she had not. She was behaving recklessly in a way that was foreign to her nature and soon now she would wake up and realise that she could not go through with this masquerade—and then he would tell her that he had something else in mind for her.

He reviewed in his mind the women who had been his

mistresses in the past. Not one of them could hold a candle to Emma for poise or looks, although all of them had been exceptional in some way. Some had been young and beautiful, others had possessed different qualities, but none had been everything that he could desire in one woman.

The first woman he had ever made love to had been a lady some twenty years his senior. He had been fifteen and she had been married, a friend of his mother's. Lady Lytham had died a few days previously and Alexander had been feeling bewildered by his grief; although his mother had never shown her love for him, he had cared for her.

Anne Hemsby was a gentle, pretty woman who had initiated him into the pleasures of the bedroom, teaching him how to please her as well as himself. He had always been grateful to Mistress Hemsby for her patience and forbearance with a clumsy youth, and they were still good friends.

He was on good terms with most of his former lovers, though there was the notable exception of the fiery opera dancer who had driven him from her dressing room with a vase directed at his head at the stormy end of their relationship.

'Why are you smiling like that?' Emma asked, bringing him out of his reverie. 'You have a positively wicked expression on your face, Lytham. Tell me what you are thinking?'

'I was contemplating all the pleasures in store for us, my darling,' he replied in a tone that caressed her, sending a flush of heat through her body and making her tinglingly aware of him. 'I think we should have a period of retreat so that we may get to know one another well—and then perhaps a trip to Paris to buy a wardrobe fit for—my love.'

Her cheeks were on fire now, her heart racing wildly. He had deliberately avoided using the word *mistress* so as not to embarrass her. His consideration for her feelings was remarkable.

'I should enjoy that very much,' she said once she could trust herself to speak. 'I—I am not perfectly sure what you expect of me, Lytham. Oh, I know that there are…certain duties…but do you intend me to live in a separate establishment and…' Her voice tailed off in confusion as she saw the expression in his eyes. 'No, do not laugh at me, Lytham. I really do not know how these things are conducted.'

'Be assured that I know exactly what I require of you,' he said. 'You need only give yourself up to the pleasures in store for you, my love. You should, however, be aware that my passion for you is no slight thing. I intend to spoil and indulge you, Emma. You need not worry about anything.'

'Then I shall not,' she replied. 'I shall rely on you entirely to show me what is expected of your…' Once again she hesitated and he came to her rescue gallantly.

'My lover,' Lytham supplied and knew himself a wicked rogue. A gentleman would do the decent thing and set her mind at rest, but the rogue in him was enjoying this far too much!

Emma was not sure what she had expected once they left the Thorns' house, but Lytham's behaviour was exactly what it had always been—polite, courteous, and casual. Oh, there were those burning looks, of course, and the occasional touch of his hand, which turned her insides to liquid fire, but he had made no attempt to make love to her during the three days of their journey.

She had been treated in every respect as a lady, sleeping alone in her own room after dining with Lytham in the parlour at the inn in which they stayed overnight. She had wondered on that first night whether he might wish to begin their relationship, but her look of inquiry had met with an enigmatic smile.

'We have plenty of time, Emma.'

'Yes, of course,' she had replied, her heart racing.

And now they were approaching the house Lytham had described as a perfect retreat. She was a little surprised to hear the cry of seagulls and to smell the salty tang of sea air, and then their carriage rounded a long, gentle curve in the road and she saw the sea glistening in the distance.

'Oh—are we to stay near the sea?' she cried, looking at him in delight. 'I have only been to the sea once, Lytham. Papa took us to Newquay for a few days when I was a small child.'

'I trust you do not have a dislike of sea air? Our northeast coast can be a little bracing, but there are some excellent walks and on a mild day it can be beautiful.'

'Certainly not,' she replied, eyes sparkling. 'I loved my visit and wished we might have stayed there forever. I believe I cried when it was time to go home.'

Lytham looked amused. 'This is not a developed resort, Emma, merely a small, rather private cove. My mother was advised she needed some sea air for her health's sake soon after I was born and she bought a house here with a legacy from her aunt. She came alone often, but a few times I was allowed to accompany her and I have retained some good memories of the place. The house was left to me when she died and I have maintained it in good order. I visit from time to time.'

'I am glad you brought me to your mother's house,' Emma said, craning her head to look from the carriage window. She gave a gasp of pleasure as the house came into view. It was set in a bend in the road, sheltered by the hill from the full blast of the sea wind and from public gaze as it faced the sea. The walls were painted white and looked dazzling even in the weak wintry sunshine, the long sash windows at the back were sparkling as they caught the rays. 'It looks beautiful.'

It had no front garden as such, just a sweep of grass that gradually sloped to the cliff edge. Two of the windows at the front were bowed and dressed with lace curtains, but the main entrance was at the side and approached by a gravel drive flanked by evergreen bushes of some kind. The black painted door stood between two pillars of white stone, and opened at their approach.

A woman who was clearly the housekeeper came out to greet them as they got down from the carriage. Tall, thin, dressed in a suitable grey gown with a white lace collar and a bunch of keys worn on a chain at her waist, she had obviously been expecting them and bobbed a respectful curtsey.

'Your lordship…Miss Sommerton. I am Mrs Warren. Everything is ready for you, sir.'

'Thank you, Mrs Warren. If you would be so good as to take my ward to her apartments. We have been travelling for some hours and I know Emma would like to rest before we dine.'

Emma's cheeks felt warm. He had spoken of her as his ward to the housekeeper to save her blushes presumably, but their true relationship would become apparent once… they were sleeping together. There, she had faced it in her own mind. She had become accustomed to the idea now. At first she had been shocked at her own brazen behaviour, but Lytham's casual manner had robbed the situation of any embarrassment. Indeed, his behaviour had been so circumspect during their journey that she might well have been his ward.

'Would you come this way, miss?'

Emma followed the housekeeper through a small entrance hall to a reception room set out with various chairs and sofas into a larger hall with an open and rather impressive staircase, which gave the house a light airy feel. She looked up to the floor above, thinking that it had an Italian feel about it—or as she had imagined an Italian villa might look from pictures she had seen. The marble statues of naked boys added to the feeling that the person who had furnished this house had liked the Italian style.

'It is a long time since his lordship visited,' Mrs Warren informed Emma as she led the way upstairs. She stopped in front of a pair of double doors at the end of the upper hall and opened them with a flourish. 'These rooms were always used exclusively by Lady Lytham herself. I hope you will be comfortable here, miss.'

'Oh, how very pretty!' Emma exclaimed as she stepped inside the first room.

She had never seen such elegant furnishings. The colours were gentle shades of pink and cream with the occasional touch of deep crimson, as though it had been flung there to startle the senses, the furniture of some pale wood with panels of intricate inlay. There were display cabinets containing delicate porcelain cups and tiny teapots, and some exquisite figurines that looked as if they came from the Derby factory, also a lady's desk with a leather top and a gilt rail above the little drawers. Sofas, gilt-framed chairs and an embroidery frame all combined to make it the most charming room Emma had ever been in.

Further exploration showed her an equally charming bedroom, beyond which was a dressing room and a door leading where—into another bedroom, perhaps? Emma tried the door and found it locked. She turned to see Mrs Warren looking at her.

'His lordship will be occupying the next suite, miss. He

has the key, of course, but you have a key to the dressing room.'

'Oh…thank you. I suppose these are meant for the master and mistress?'

'Yes, miss.' The housekeeper was clearly thoughtful. 'Was there anything more?'

'No, thank you. I shall come down in half an hour or so… Perhaps some tea in the parlour?'

'Yes, miss. Her ladyship always used the back parlour in the winter, miss. She said it was warmer.'

'Then I expect we shall do the same,' Emma said and turned away to look about her once more. The housekeeper's gaze had made her feel slightly uncomfortable, but she was determined not to be affected by any other consideration other than her own feelings. It did not matter what Lytham's servants thought of her. She would not allow such considerations to weigh with her.

After the housekeeper had gone she took off her heavy travelling cape and went to investigate the contents of two large armoires in the dressing room. Her trunks had been sent on ahead in the baggage coach, but although her own gowns were hanging there she saw that the clothes she had left behind in Bath had also been placed in the armoire. Had Lytham been so sure of her then?

Dismissing the unworthy thought, Emma was about to select one of the gowns when a knock at the door made her turn. A young maid was standing there, holding an elegant silk gown that Emma had never seen before.

'I'm Betsy, Miss Sommerton. I've been pressing some of the new gowns his lordship had sent from town. I brought this one back—and Mrs Warren said to ask if you needed any help, miss?'

'I was about to change into this green afternoon dress,' Emma said. 'But the one you have pressed looks rather nice. Perhaps I shall wear that instead.' Betsy held up a bronze silk gown that was more stylish than anything else Emma possessed and had clearly been chosen by someone with an eye for colour. 'Yes, I shall wear that one, please.'

Lytham must have been planning this for some time, Emma thought as she allowed Betsy to help her to change into the beautiful dress. He could not have known she would be forced to leave Bath so suddenly—and yet perhaps he had been expecting it. He had warned her of the consequences if she continued as Bridget's employee, though he could not have known what Lindisfarne would do.

Emma had found it difficult to accept Bridget's apparent change of heart. How could she be desperately in love with one man, and only a few days later be seemingly content to be courted by another?

She was glad that Bridget had come to see how unworthy Lindisfarne was, but still hurt that she could carelessly cast off her friend for a man she was now prepared to forget. Lytham had told her that Bridget was very apologetic for the way she had behaved and hoped that they might be friends in the future, but Emma did not think it would ever be quite the same between them.

If their circumstances had been reversed Emma would never have been so careless of another's feelings, especially someone who was in an awkward position, but then, she would not have become so involved with a man like Lindisfarne in the first place.

She had in her own way been as reckless as Bridget, though. The only difference was that Lytham was being discreet. They were unlikely to meet anyone who knew them here, which meant that their affair could be kept secret. At least until they went to Paris.

Surely she would not need so many new clothes? Lytham

had chosen several gowns for her himself, and she had those Bridget had given her. The trip to Paris was not necessary. Unless Lytham wished for it, of course.

He would not choose to stay here for long. Emma realised that he must mean this to be a temporary situation…just until she had got used to being his mistress. And she meant to show him that she was perfectly capable of carrying the role he had given her, which was why she had chosen to wear the bronze gown.

She was not some green girl to shy at the first hurdle. Lytham had offered his protection and she had accepted, that meant she must expect to have gowns bought for her and presented as a *fait accompli*. A wife would be given an allowance and expected to choose her own things, a mistress must accept what she was given. And, judging by this dress, Lytham had given her beautiful things.

By wearing this gown she was showing him that she was perfectly happy to accept his terms.

Lytham looked out at the pretty back garden, which was protected from the full blast of the sea air by the house itself. There were rose walks, herbaceous borders and the summerhouse at the end of the long walk. It was all rather bare at the moment, the only things blossoming a few winter heathers and shrubs. He had remembered it as a garden full of roses, but he had never visited in winter before. Perhaps he should have gone straight to Lytham Hall—and yet that perverse devil inside him wanted to see just how far Emma would push this masquerade of hers.

She would surely not go through with it to the end? She would realise what she was doing, beg his pardon for having misled him and ask to be allowed to leave—and then he would tell her of his true intentions.

He wondered what she would make of the gowns he had

ordered for her from town. They had been intended for her
use at Lytham, just a temporary measure until he could
arrange for her to join him in London in the spring, when
she would be able to buy whatever she desired. She was
certain to be outraged when they were presented for her
use with no explanation. She would never wear them…at
least until he told her the truth, which was that she would
need some warmer clothes because the winters in these
northern climes could be very cold.

'I hope I have not kept you waiting too long?'

He turned to look at her, experiencing a shock as he saw
her standing there in the bronze silk. He had always known
that the gown would suit her. It brought out the richness
of her hair and gave her skin warmth—but he had not expected to find her quite so beautiful. Nor had he imagined
she would choose to wear one of the gowns he had bought
for her. He was uncertain for the first time since he had
begun this charade.

'You look…beautiful, Emma,' he breathed, feeling a
sharp, urgent desire to make love to her now, this moment.

'It is the gown,' she said and laughed softly. She looked
so confident standing there, almost a different person. Was
it the gown—or had something else happened to her? He
could not decide, but there was one thing certain in his
mind. She was no longer the prim Miss Sommerton she
had pretended to be, but a lovely desirable woman. 'Whoever chose this had good taste.'

'I chose it for you from a range shown to me by a French
seamstress. When I mentioned your name she said that you
had visited her showrooms and she had your measurements,
though you had not bought anything from her.'

'Madame Alicia,' Emma said. 'I recognised her style.
She did indeed measure me for a gown, but I decided she

was too expensive for my gowns, though Bridget bought from her.'

'She may be expensive, but I think the cost worthwhile.'

'I am glad you approve,' Emma said. She thought he was about to say something more when a knock at the door heralded the arrival of the tea tray. It was a few minutes before they settled again, and by then the moment had passed.

'You were looking at the garden when I came in,' Emma said as she poured tea the way she knew he liked it, with just a spot of cream and no sugar. 'I imagine it is very pretty in the spring and summer. Did I see roses climbing up the wall just beneath my window?'

'Yes, I believe so,' Lytham replied. 'I had not realised it would look so bare at this time of year.'

'I should imagine the views from the edge of the cliff are quite spectacular. Perhaps after tea we could take a walk there? Is there an easy route down to the cove—or must one go all the way back along the road that brought us here?'

'There is a path,' Lytham said. 'But the incline is quite steep and I believe there has been a rock fall quite recently. If you use the path you must take the greatest care, Emma. I should not want you to slip and hurt yourself. A tumble could only result in serious injury.'

'I promise to be careful.' She sipped her tea, then picked up the silver pot. 'May I refill your cup, Lytham?'

'Thank you, no.'

His eyes watched her thoughtfully as she refilled her own cup, adding one lump of sugar with the silver tongs. She was perfectly at ease, her manner that of a lady at home in such a drawing room, which of course she was. Except that he had thought she would be nervous of being alone with him. He had anticipated the moment when she would throw herself on his mercy and then he would laugh, take her in his arms and tell her the truth.

But this woman was too assured, too confident to act in the way he had imagined. By heaven, she was not going to shy off! She was actually going to go through with it. Why? She was not that desperate—not as desperate as she had been when she left Bath, for he had told her that the rumour was scotched and she must know that many doors would be open to her if she were to return to society.

As she turned her lovely head and looked at him he saw the expectancy in her eyes…the hint of excitement. He had seen that look in other women's eyes, across a crowded room, at the theatre, and he knew what it meant.

She wasn't afraid of becoming his mistress. Indeed, she was ready for him to make love to her now if he chose. That thought made his blood race and he felt himself hardening as his desire for her burned ever brighter. It was women such as this who had turned the course of history! Cleopatra might have come to Caesar in just this way, he thought and smiled as he realised where his thoughts were leading him.

He had underestimated her courage and her determination. He had been misled because she had run away from the scandal in Bath, but now he began to see that she was much stronger than he had imagined. It was obviously time for his confession. He could not allow the masquerade to continue.

He rose to his feet and took a few steps towards her, stopping just short of the sofa she had chosen to sit on. She glanced up at him inquiringly and he held out his hand to her.

'Come here, Emma.'

She rose gracefully and came obediently, but there was nothing subdued or submissive in her manner. Her head was up, her clear eyes meeting his fearlessly. She stood without moving as he reached for her, then her lips parted invitingly as he drew her against him. As their lips met in a hungry, yearning kiss, she melted into his body, and he could feel the completeness of her surrender. Her mouth told him that her hunger was as great as his own, and he felt the throbbing need in his loins.

'I want you, Emma,' he said hoarsely. 'Oh, God, I want to make love to you so much.'

'Yes,' she said, gazing up at him. 'I think it is time.'

'Go up to your room and wait for me.'

She smiled and for just one second there was uncertainty in her eyes, but then it had gone.

'I shall lock the sitting-room door to the hall. You will come through the dressing room?'

'Yes…'

He watched as she left the parlour, his hungry eyes devouring her. This was not at all what he had planned! It was wrong, a mistake. He could not destroy her innocence this way even though she was brave enough to give herself to him, and yet he sensed that it was what she was waiting for, wanted.

Lytham paced the room like an angry beast. Why had he not spoken out? What had he done? This foolish masquerade had been carried too far. It had amused him to tease her, but to use her so basely would be a betrayal of all he felt for Emma.

He would go up and tell her that he had never intended her to be his mistress. She was the woman he loved…the only woman he had ever loved like this. He wanted her as his wife!

Yet she was waiting for him, expecting him to make love to her. His mind saw her as she would look with her hair loose on her shoulders, clad only in a flimsy nightgown and he knew that if he once touched her he would be lost. If she offered herself to him as she had a moment ago, he would not be able to control himself. No, he could not, would not use her so scurvily!

Cursing himself for creating a situation that need never have arisen, he went to the door and walked out into the hall. Instead of following Emma up the stairs, he let himself out of the main door and began to walk across the sweep of grass to the edge of the cliffs.

He needed to cool his fever before he spoke to Emma again, to control the raging desire that had sprung up inside him at the sight of her in that bronze gown. Until that moment he had not really understood the depth of his own feelings for her, and though he had known that he intended to ask her to be his wife he had not realised just how much he wanted and loved her.

It was the fault of his damnable humour, that quirk in his nature that drove him always to test others, and more often than not to find them sadly wanting. This time it had rebounded on him, for Emma was so much more than he had ever guessed, so much more than he deserved. Her reserved manner had hid so much that was valuable and fine in her, and only now did he know her for the woman she was—the woman she could become given her rightful place in society.

He was not sure that she would appreciate the jest he had played on her. Indeed, he thought she might be very angry, and rightly so. He had been a very knave to play such a trick upon her.

She might think that he had deliberately tried to humiliate her and that he had belittled the sacrifice she had been prepared to make for his sake. He knew that she was capable of anger and he feared that she might believe herself insulted.

It was that imp of mischief inside him, the perverse devil that drove him close to the edge only too often. Had it not been for that stubborn streak in his nature this situation would never have come about. Emma's father might still be living, she still residing quietly in her own home—and yet that would have been such a waste. She would have faded into a lonely spinsterhood, and the world would have been so much the poorer. With his help she could shine in the drawing rooms of society as she had always been meant to do. He comforted himself with the thought that he had at least done this for her.

In another moment he felt a surge of disgust with himself for trying to excuse the inexcusable. Emma had been forced to go against all she had been taught. What had seemed amusing to him must have been torment for her, but she had been brave enough to go through with it.

Why? Why had she been willing to go so far? He knew her too well to think it was for what she might gain financially. The only explanation that came to mind was that she cared for him sufficiently to consider her world well lost for love.

Lytham had never been offered that kind of love, had not imagined it truly existed beyond the covers of a book. Indeed, he could not believe himself worthy of it.

Most women he had known took as much and more than they gave—and yet he *had* seen love in Emma's eyes, he had known that she cared for him. He *had* known in his heart that she had not accepted his careless offer—an offer he had never truly intended to make—for the sake of his wealth.

Fool! Damned fool! He was a damnable rogue as his father had once called him during one of their frequent quarrels. He was going to hurt Emma when he told her that he had been deliberately leading her on just for his own selfish amusement. She might turn from him in disgust, refusing to believe that he truly loved her—and who could blame her? Who could blame her!

He had planned mischief and he was the one caught in his own toils. Staring down at the angry sea, as it boiled and thrashed around the jutting rocks below, driven by a bitter wind from the north, he knew a moment of utter despair. He had discovered something wonderful and there was a good chance that he was going to lose it almost immediately through his own carelessness. What a stupid fool he had been!

'Lytham!'

He turned at the sound of a man's voice and faced his enemy—a man he had believed gone to his grave in a foreign land until recently, when his investigations had warned him that Luther Pennington might still be alive and returned to England.

'They told me you were dead in a brawl...'

'I ought to have died,' Pennington replied, a bitter tone in his voice. His face was aged beyond his years, his long unkempt hair streaked with grey. He had the look of a man who had suffered abuse both at the hands of others and by his own hand through wild living, a man desperation had brought to his lowest ebb. 'You and your friends did your best to destroy me.'

'I took no part in that,' Lytham said, staring into his hate-filled eyes. 'Your court-martial—yes, that I admit. You deserved that, Pennington, for what you did to another man's wife.'

'It was a moment of foolishness under the influence of too much wine. She had been leading me on for weeks.'

'Yet that did not give you the right to act as you did. You raped a woman, a lady of gentle birth. Even a whore deserves better than that.'

'Are you so pure that you can afford to sneer at me?' Pennington snarled, his mouth curled back in a sneer of contempt. 'Why did you bring Sommerton's daughter here unless it was to make her your mistress?'

'Damn you!' Lytham said furiously, his anger directed as much at himself as the other, for he had laid her open to such rumours by his careless behaviour. 'I will not have you abuse her name. Miss Sommerton is none of your business—and for your information I intend to marry her.'

'A pity you did not marry her sooner. She might have been a rich widow,' Pennington muttered. 'I've been following you for weeks, waiting for the right moment. I don't want to make another mistake…'

Lytham saw that he was holding a pistol. Pennington's intention was clear. He had planned his revenge for a long time, feeding on his hatred for what had been done to him and his opportunity could not have been more inviting. Lytham was alone and unarmed, the last thing on his mind that afternoon the possibility that an unknown enemy might take the chance to kill him.

'You won't get away with this…'

His only chance was to keep Pennington talking. Lytham took a few steps towards him, hoping for a chance to wrestle with him, but the pistol was cocked and ready.

'Don't be a fool, man. We can talk about this…'

'You ruined my life,' Pennington said. 'Money won't buy yours.'

He raised his arm to fire, but even as his finger pressed down on the trigger another shot rang out from some distance behind him. Lytham heard the first shot seconds before the force of Pennington's ball struck him in the shoulder and sent him staggering back, teetering for a moment on the edge of the cliff. And then, losing his balance and falling over, he went slipping and sliding down the face of

the craggy cliff where the rock had fallen in recent storms.
He clawed at the loose boulders desperately, until his head
knocked against one larger than the rest, robbing him of all
conscious thought.

He did not see the man who had fired the first shot come
racing across the lawn, stop to glance briefly at the man he
had killed, and then look over the edge of the cliff. Nor
did he see the moment of indecision before Tom Sommerton began to make his way down the treacherous path.

Emma was wearing only a thin night chemise when she
heard the frantic knocking at her door. She hesitated, but
Mrs Warren was calling to her urgently and Lytham would
surely not come now. She had waited nearly an hour.
Something must have happened to delay him. Reaching for
her wrap, she pulled it on and went to unlock the door.

'Yes, Mrs Warren? I was just having a little rest.'

'You must come at once, miss. There's been a terrible
tragedy. His lordsh ɔ ..' The housekeeper choked on a sob
of near hysteria. 'Benson says he heard two shots out the
front a while ago. He went out to investigate and—'

'Has the marquis been shot?' Emma asked, her heart
catching with fright. 'Someone attempted to kill him a few
weeks ago—has he been badly hurt?'

'We—we don't know yet, miss. Benson found a dead
man near the top of the cliffs, but there's no sign of his
lordship. We think he may have gone over the edge, though
whether he fell or was pushed—'

'But how could he fall?' Emma felt sick with anxiety.
This was like a nightmare. How could such a thing have
happened? 'What are you doing to find him?'

'Benson has everyone out searching, miss. There's only
me left here to tell you what happened.'

'I shall dress and come down,' Emma said. 'Give me a

few minutes, Mrs Warren. We must get more help. Is there a village near by? Yes, I recall that we passed it. We must send there.'

'I believe Benson has already sent one of the grooms, miss.'

'Then we must pray that Lord Lytham is soon found.'

Emma's eyes were smarting with tears as she returned to the bedroom and pulled on one of her older gowns. She would join the search herself. They must find Lytham. They must!

She felt as if her heart were breaking. How could she bear it if he were lost to her now?

It was growing dark by the time the villagers began to search the beach with their dogs and lanterns. Standing at the top of the cliff, her cloak caught by the fierce wind that had blown up, Emma stared down at the angry sea and felt the despair wash over her. It was somewhere here that they thought Lytham must have fallen, for there were signs of loose rock having been disturbed. Just below her she could see what seemed to be a shelf of rock, which had been caused by the erosion of this part of the cliffs. Below that was a sheer drop to the jagged rocks that protruded from the sea like dragons' teeth.

How could he survive such a fall—how could anyone? He would either be dashed to pieces on the cliff itself or drowned in the swirling current about those spurs of jutting rocks. No one could have lived through that—and he might also have been wounded before he fell. She felt such a surge of despair that she swayed towards the edge as though she would cast herself down to join him in his watery grave.

'Come back to the house now, miss.'

Emma felt someone tugging at her arm. She shrugged away from the housekeeper's grasp.

'He must be there somewhere. They have to find him—they have to!'

'They will find him if they can,' Mrs Warren said. 'But these tides can sweep a man away. The sea does not always give up its dead.'

'He isn't dead…he can't be dead…' Emma's words were torn away by the wind and lost. 'I love him so…I love him so…'

'Yes, miss. He was a good man. He will be sorely missed.'

Her words were so final, so dismissive of any chance that they might find Lytham alive that Emma felt the rebellion surge within her. She would not give him up so easily!

'He must not be dead!'

'No, miss. Perhaps he isn't. Come away back to the house now. You can't do any good here tonight. The men will keep searching. The locals know this cove better than anyone else could. If he's there, they will find him.'

Emma wanted to defy her. She wanted to keep a vigil here at the top of the cliff until he was brought in, but she could barely see anything now other than the lights of the lanterns on the beach. Nothing could be gained from staying here and she would be needed in the sickroom when they eventually brought him home. Because they would in the end. They must! Otherwise she might as well die with him.

She took a step towards the edge, then something inside her made her draw back. No, she was not such a weak fool. She would not give him up for dead, though others might.

Chapter Nine

The wind was bitterly cold, whipping about her fiercely as she walked along the beach, constantly searching. Her eyes moved over the face of the cliff, looking for a crack or crevice where Lytham might have crawled to hide after his fall, but there were none that she could see. She turned towards the sea itself, straining as if she would penetrate its stormy waters and find him.

How could he simply have disappeared? It was more than a week now since that terrible night, a week of such anguish that Emma did not know how she had lived through it. She had hardly slept in all that time, spending every daylight hour out searching for him, and every dark hour was torment because she was forced to remain within the house.

People had been to the house, people from the village. The Vicar had tried to tell her that God had a purpose for all he did; neighbours came wishing to offer advice or con-dolence. Emma had turned her face to the wall, closing her ears to the Vicar's advice to pray.

Did he think that she had not already prayed a hundred times, her prayers sometimes an entreaty, at others a curse that this could happen? Why had Lytham been taken from her? Was it because of the sin they planned? No, no, she would not believe that. Love such as she felt for him could never be a sin. She knew that her life would be empty from now on for she would never love another man.

As yet, Emma could not even think about the future or what might become of her now that Lytham was dead. She did not want to think of a world that did not include him, her mind able to cope only with an hour at a time, counting them one by one as the darkness lifted and she could once again go out to begin her lonely vigil.

The villagers had given up the search after the second day. Everyone had told her that all hope was gone: Lytham was dead. He must have fallen unconscious into the sea and been swept under by the current. It was not possible that he had survived in such weather.

Emma refused to give up. She could not believe that it was hopeless. If they had brought her a body she might have accepted it, but without proof her stubborn nature would not give in.

He had to be alive because if he was dead then she wanted to die, too. He must be alive. He must!

'Oh, my darling,' her heart cried out to him. 'I love you. Come back to me. Please come back to me, for I shall die if you do not!'

There was only pain in the world, nothing but pain. Around him was merely darkness, no light or heat or warmth...no love or...what was it he was trying to reach? He did not know what he called for in the rare moments when he was aware of someone roughly tending him, but he knew that there was an even greater pain inside him than that in his head and shoulder.

Day was night and night was day, nothing was as it should be in this place of terrible pain. He was lost, wandering in an ocean of misery, needing something that was lost to him…lost to him forever.

'Forgive me…' he whispered as just for a moment the darkness lightened and he sensed someone bending over him. 'I did not mean to hurt you…forgive me.'

'Poor devil,' a soft, female voice said close to his ear. He felt a hand stroking his forehead. 'I doubt he can last much longer like this. It would probably have been better if you'd let him go into the sea.'

'I couldn't just let him drown. I have to keep him alive somehow.'

'I heard tell they were searching for him. Why don't you tell them where he is—fetch a doctor to him?'

'Because they will hang me,' the second voice said. 'I killed a man, Belle, and unless he vouches for me I'll be taken as Pennington's accomplice and hanged. They'll say it was thieves falling out.'

'You killed to save an innocent man's life.'

'I was seconds too late to stop that devil firing,' Tom Sommerton said ruefully as he looked at the pretty young woman bathing Lytham's forehead. 'You've got to help me, Belle. I can't watch him the whole time, and I need to collect wood for the fire. He ought to be given something…gruel or…' He shook his head despairingly. 'Damn it! I don't know. What do they give people who are this sick?'

'That wound in his shoulder looks nasty,' Belle said. 'I'll fetch Granny Robins to him, she'll know what to do.'

He grabbed her arm as she turned away. 'Can she be trusted? She won't go blabbing?'

'You don't know her,' Belle said. 'She ain't like the rest of us. Some say as she's a mite touched in the head—she sees things we don't—but she knows a bit about healing.

If the wound needs the hot iron she'll do it, and she'll give him something to ease the pain.'

'Fetch her, then—but remember, if anyone follows you here I'm done for. Unless he can prove that I saved his life I'm for the drop.'

'And wouldn't that be a pity, handsome lad like you!' Belle laughed at the man she hardly knew but had taken to her bed and her heart within minutes of seeing him hunched up in the corner of the inn parlour, looking like he had all the worries of the world on his shoulder. She had wondered where he went to when he left her father's inn, but it had taken her a week to discover his secret, and it was a fearful one. Belle knew that she could earn a fine reward for information leading to the injured man, but she wasn't going to turn her young lover in for a few pieces of silver. Besides, if his lordship recovered because of her and Granny Robins he would likely give her more. 'Don't you worry, my luvver. I'll be back and there won't be no hangman running behind neither.'

Tom watched as the saucy barmaid ran off, then went over to look at Lytham once more. He ran his fingers through his hair, wondering why he was risking his neck by staying here. If he had any sense he would cut and run, and let Belle turn the marquis in if she chose.

'Oh, Lady Agatha,' cried Mrs Warren. 'I was never so glad to see anyone in my life. I've been at my wit's end to know what to do with the poor lass. She won't eat a thing I give her—she hardly touches a cup of tea and I'm sure she never sleeps. She was a pretty girl when she came here, but she's hardly more than skin and bone now.'

'Why on earth did you not send for me sooner?' Agatha Lynston demanded. 'All I knew was that Lytham was missing, and I saw no reason to come charging up here when he might very well turn up in Bath at any moment.'

'We didn't want to worry you, ma'am. Besides, no one expected the poor girl to take on like this. I think it must have turned her mind. She seemed bright enough when she came.' She bit her lip and looked rather awkward. 'I wasn't sure you knew about her, ma'am. I thought she might be—'

'Well, spit it out, woman!' Lady Agatha said crossly. 'What bee have you in your bonnet? I am beginning to think that it is you who have lost your wits!'

'Begging your pardon, ma'am, but it did cross my mind that she might be his lordship's lady love.'

'Stuff and nonsense! Where on earth did you get that idea? Miss Sommerton is a respectable young woman. Lytham was intending to marry her, but he wanted to get to know her a little better first. I had hoped for an announcement at any time.'

'His lordship's fiancée…' Mrs Warren looked shocked. 'Oh, forgive my foolishness, Lady Agatha. His lordship said she was his ward, but he asked for her to have the suite next to… Well, that's none of my business.'

'It most certainly is not,' said Lady Agatha sharply. 'Well, I must be thankful that you decided to make me aware of the situation—what is it, three weeks after it happened?'

'We did tell you his lordship was missing, ma'am.'

'But you did not make the situation clear. Had you done so, I should have been here long before this. Now don't look so indignant, woman. I am not entirely blaming you. There are others who might have informed me. And I am here now, so we shall say no more about it. Where is Miss Sommerton now?'

'She is walking on the beach, ma'am. She begins at first light and does not return until the evening is drawing in.'

'Walking on the beach in this weather? Good grief! It's a wonder she doesn't take her death of cold. Send someone to fetch her this instant!'

'Yes, ma'am—but I doubt if she will come. She just stares through anyone who tells her to come home. I told you, I think she has lost her mind.'

'She will come if she is told that I am here and want to see her about something most urgent.'

'She will think there is news of his lordship...'

'Exactly. If that doesn't fetch her, then I shall begin to believe that you are right and she has lost her wits.'

Mrs Warren went away to detail the errand to one of the maids, a girl who had sometimes managed to get through to Miss Sommerton. It seemed a bit cruel to raise unfounded hopes, but perhaps it was the only way to shock her out of the apathy she had fallen into since that terrible night...

Emma heard the voice calling to her as she continued her walk along the beach, but she did not choose to turn round. There was only one person she wanted to see and she could not find him. She had searched and searched until her mind was so weary that she no longer really knew what she was doing, but there was no sign of him, no clue as to what had happened to him.

She was like someone sleepwalking, repeating a pattern for its own sake without knowing why. She was so tired...so terribly tired...but she had to keep on searching or she would die.

'Miss Sommerton!' Betsy caught at her arm, forcing her to turn and look at her. 'There's someone up at the house to see you. Lady Agatha Lynston has something urgent to tell you.'

'Lytham's aunt?' Emma's head went up, a glimmer of

hope in her red-rimmed eyes. There could surely only be one reason for Lady Agatha to make the long journey here! She must have news of Lytham. Gathering up her skirt in one hand, Emma began to run along the beach towards the steep path that led up to the greensward. She had climbed it many times now and it held no fears for her. Besides, it was the quickest way. And if Lytham had been found she must hurry. Pray God he was still alive! But she would not think beyond the fact that there was news at last.

Betsy had not followed her, preferring the longer, safer route to the top, but Emma did not look back. She was running as hard as she could, her chest tight with pain as she fled across the grass towards the house and burst in.

Seeing Mrs Warren in the hall, she clutched wildly at her arm, her breathing so ragged that she was gasping as she asked, 'Where is she—what news?'

'Mercy on me!' Mrs Warren cried as she saw her wild look. 'Whatever shall we do with you? She's in the parlour, miss…'

She shook her head as Emma went flying through the hall. The poor girl was out of her mind, and the disappointment of discovering that there was no news was likely to send her right over the edge. In the end they might have to lock her away for her own safety. Well, well, she had warned against it, but Lady Agatha had always gone her own way. She frowned and muttered to herself as she went back to the kitchen. Would this tragedy never be done?

'Lady Agatha!' Emma cried as she rushed into the parlour. 'Has he been found? Is he alive? Oh, please let him be alive!'

Agatha stared at her in horror. She had thought Mrs Warren must have been exaggerating until she saw Emma for herself. Her face was drawn; there were dark shadows beneath her eyes and her cheeks were hollowed. She did indeed look as if her grief might have deranged her mind.

'Come to the fire and get warm, my dear,' Agatha said, her pity aroused. 'I had no idea you were suffering all this time. That foolish woman, to leave me in ignorance.'

'Lytham,' Emma gasped. Her chest was heaving as she tried to recover her breath, but for some reason she could not. She felt pain in her chest and her head, and her vision was blurring. 'Please, tell me…'

'There is no news,' Agatha said and then wished she had not as Emma gave a scream of despair and then collapsed into a heap at her feet. 'Oh, you poor foolish child. What has that rogue done to you? Let him only come back and he shall have a piece of my mind! What can he be thinking of to upset you like this?'

She tugged at the bell rope impatiently. It was quite clear that Emma had exhausted her strength. A doctor must be summoned at once, and Emma would need constant nursing if they were not to lose her, too.

Lytham was aware that the pain had lessened since the strange old creature had begun to nurse him. She was so ugly, and so bent up that she looked like one of the witches from *Macbeth!* At first he had thought her something he had dragged up from hell—the hell of his nightmares—but now he knew that the girl had brought her here.

He tried to remember the girl, but he was certain that he had never met her in his life—but how could he be certain when he did not even know his own name?

There was a man here too sometimes. He kept in the shadows as if he were frightened of being recognised, and yet something about him seemed familiar. Why could he not remember this man—and, even more importantly, who he was?

The girl had told him that he had had a terrible accident. He had fallen from some cliffs and it was only the bravery of the man in the shadows that had saved his life.

'If Tom hadn't gone down the cliff after you, you would have fallen into the sea, been dragged under by the current and drowned. You owe your life to Tom, sir, and that's the truth of it.'

'Thank Tom for saving my life,' he muttered weakly. 'Can I have some more water?'

'Remember, just sips,' the old woman hissed at her from her chair by the fire. 'And don't be bothering him with your talk, Belle. I don't want all my good work wasted on account of your tongue.'

Belle turned away to fetch the cup, holding it while he swallowed a few sips. He grasped her wrist, as she would have moved away.

'Who am I?' he asked hoarsely. 'Tell me if you know, girl. Who am I and why am I here? Have I no home to go to?'

Since the darkness had receded a little, driven out by the light of the fire and the lanterns, he had realised that he was in some kind of a hut. It looked a bit like those used by woodcutters on the estate… What estate? Did he have an estate and, if so, why wasn't he there?

Why did he remember that there was a play about witches called *Macbeth* and yet he couldn't recall his name? There were all kinds of things jumbled up in his brain, fragments that seemed to lie just behind a curtain of mist in his mind. He thought it must be his whole life, but until he could somehow reach out and tear down that curtain he could not reclaim it.

'Ask Tom if he knows who I am,' he whispered. 'Please, I must know.'

Tom came forward out of the shadows and stood looking

at him from the end of his bed, which was little more than a pile of straw covered by sacking.

'Can you not remember anything?' Tom asked. 'Do you not remember what happened just before you were shot?'

'I was shot?' Yes, he could feel the soreness in his shoulder and he seemed to remember the old woman applying the hot iron. The pain had been so unbearable that he had fainted, returning to that place of darkness from where it was such a struggle to return. He might never have returned if he had not seemed to hear a voice calling to him, begging him to come back. Yet he did not know who called to him in his dreams. 'Who shot me—was it you? Were we fighting a duel?'

'Someone tried to murder you,' Belle said before Tom could answer. 'Tom shot him and saved your life when you fell over the cliff. If he hadn't come after you you would have tumbled into the sea and drowned for sure. And now he's in trouble with the law.'

'Belle!' Tom warned. 'Lytham doesn't want to hear this, at least not yet.'

'Is my name Lytham?'

'Yes. You are Alexander Lynston, Marquis of Lytham,' Tom replied, 'and I'm Emma's brother, Tom Sommerton.'

'Emma?' Something seemed to stir in his mind and Lytham was aware of pain, pain from within rather than physical, though he did not know what had caused it. 'Is Emma my wife?'

'I don't know what she is to you,' Tom said and glared at him. 'The last thing I knew, she was companion to Bridget Flynn, then I spotted you leaving Father's estate with her and followed you. And it's a damned good thing I did. I was coming to the house to have things out with you when I saw that devil shoot you.'

'Who shot me?'

'Pennington…' Tom frowned. 'I didn't know his name at first, but he got drunk one night and confessed the whole sorry story. He blames you for his court-martial, because you reported that he had raped a fellow officer's wife. He had been waiting his chance to kill you for ages.'

'Away with you!' Granny Robins muttered, elbowing Tom to one side. 'Enough talking for now or you will kill the poor man. Now then, sir, drink some of this good broth and rest. Time enough to talk later when you're feeling more yourself.'

'Yes, I must rest,' Lytham said and fell back against the pillows, his head spinning from weakness. 'You won't go, Tom? I need you. Help me and I'll help you, whatever you've done. Please don't leave me here alone. I need your help to find myself.'

'I wasn't going anywhere,' Tom said, but Lytham's eyes had closed.

'You've worn him out with your chatter,' the old woman scolded. 'Let him rest now. He'll be stronger next time he wakes.'

'So, you are feeling a little better,' Lady Agatha said as she visited Emma that morning, two days after her arrival. 'You foolish chit! You had me quite worried about you for a while, but Mrs Warren said you took a little chicken soup this morning.'

'Indeed, I am sorry to have caused you so much bother,' Emma said, her cheeks pink. She was feeling rested because the medicine the doctor had given her had made her sleep peacefully for the first time in an age. 'You should not have come all this way for my sake.'

'Should I neglect the lady my foolish nephew had decided to marry?' Agatha Lynston fixed her with a stern gaze. 'He would not thank me when he returns to find you wasted away to a shadow of your former self.'

Emma clutched at the straw of hope her words conveyed, ignoring the misconception of an engagement between her and Lytham for the moment.

'Do you believe he will return?'

'Lytham is not so easily disposed of,' Agatha said. 'I doubt not that there has been some mischief here. The authorities have at least established the identity of the dead man—a disgraced officer who apparently once served with Lytham. My nephew played some part in his court-martial and it was believed Pennington had died abroad. It seems Lytham had been making inquiries about the fellow recently and that he may have cause to think that Pennington was intending to murder him.'

'Murder...' Emma shuddered as another shooting incident crossed her mind. 'Oh, no! He should have been on his guard. It happened once before—the shot that scraped his arm in the woods! It occurred when he was escorting me to London. I begged him to take care.'

'That was when he was taken ill of a fever and you helped him up the stairs of an inn to his room, I presume?'

'He—he told you of that?' Emma's cheeks were heated as she met the knowing gaze of the elderly lady standing at the foot of the bed.

'Certainly. I must apologise for any distress caused you on the day you called on me in Bath, Emma. I do hope I may call you that, my dear?' She smiled as the girl nodded. 'I was unwell and I had not heard that scurrilous rumour making the rounds in Bath. I hope Lytham told you that he had scotched it?'

'Yes. He did say something about it.' Emma felt terrible. Lady Agatha was being so kind to her. What would she say if she knew the true situation?

'Well, Emma, what are we to do?' Agatha looked thoughtful as the girl was silent. 'This is a pretty coil, is it not? Lytham disappeared and you here alone, at the verge of collapse when I arrived. It won't do. It won't do at all.'

'I could not leave here while there was hope.'

'This house has never suited me, being so close to the sea, especially in winter. Those winds do my bones no good at all. I think I shall take you home with me, my dear. Lytham made Lynston Cottage over to me as a present soon after his father died. It is smaller and more comfortable than that rackety mansion of his. Yes, we shall go home and wait for him to contact us.'

'But supposing…' Emma's protest died on her lips. She had no right to remain in this house indefinitely. If Lytham was lost—her mind could not accept the word dead—she had no place here. She would have to leave eventually and she did not know where to go, for she could not impose on Mary Thorn again so soon. 'You are very kind, ma'am. I will come if I shall not be a trouble to you.'

'Stuff and nonsense!' Agatha said. 'I am not an easy person to live with, Emma, but I dare say you could fare worse. And I am all Lytham has apart from some distant cousins. We shall support each other through this trying time.'

Emma might have continued her protest, but she caught a glimpse of the vulnerability beneath Lady Agatha's show of strength. She must be more than seventy years of age and, though of stout heart and constitution, would find the loss of her only close relative hard to bear.

'I should like to stay with you for a while, ma'am.'

'If Lytham had not wasted so much time you might have been his wife.' Agatha's hand trembled, but she clutched the bed rail to steady herself. 'I dare say the wretch is caught in some card game and will return when he thinks fit.'

Emma did not reply. She could not believe any such thing, though she did wonder why Lytham had gone out when he had told her to wait for him in her room. Why had he changed his mind? Why had he gone out instead of coming to her? It was so puzzling.

In her first wild grief she had not taken the time to wonder why he had not come to her, but now the question was beginning to nag at her. Had she done something to displease him—been too eager for his kisses? Or had something lured him out to those windswept cliffs where he might have met his death? *Oh, please let him not be dead!*

Perhaps her unrestrained passion had been too revealing? Perhaps he had not wanted her to fall in love with him, fearing that she might cling, become an unwanted burden. Yet his passionate words had seemed to indicate something very different.

Why had he gone for that fatal walk on the cliffs? And why did Lady Agatha imagine that he had intended to take Emma as his wife?

It was a mystery and one that she had no way of solving. She was aware that her first tearing grief had settled to a dull ache in her breast. It would come back to haunt her sometimes, bringing tears and a return of the unbearable pain his loss had woken in her, but she was feeling calmer, more able to cope with life than she had been before Lady Agatha's arrival. And perhaps there was still a flicker of hope.

'Tell me again, Tom,' Lynston asked as he leaned heavily on the younger man's arm. They had come out for some fresh air because he was in need of it, though not yet strong enough to walk out alone. 'I have grasped who and what I am, and a few pictures have begun to remind me in flashes of my past—but though you have told me so much, I am not yet clear about your own involvement. There was some scandal linking us through my brother, you say?'

'I swear I had nothing to do with your brother's death,' Tom said. 'At least, not directly. I was with his wife that day. Maria and I had spent the afternoon together at the Dower House. It was always her favourite place, for she did not like the Hall. She lives there now, of course. She said her husband would not come to the Dower House and we met there often—but I think he may have discovered that we went there.'

'Why do you say that?'

'Because…' Tom looked awkward. 'That afternoon I saw him. I had gone to the bedroom window to look out and I saw him staring up at the house. Until that moment I had not thought he cared what Maria did. He was a careless husband, neglecting her and going his own way, but he seemed distressed, staring up at the house more in grief than anger. He may even have seen me.'

'So he rode off in some kind of a mood and was thrown from his horse.' Lytham nodded. He could not remember his brother, but something told him that he had felt no love or friendship towards the man he could not picture. Besides, he had come to trust Tom in the past few days and believed his story. 'It fits in with what you have told me. But you were accused of murder—and your father threw you out.'

'Because I told him the truth. He was in such a rage. He said that I was guilty of murder even if I had not planned it. My behaviour had driven Maria's husband mad with jealousy and so he rode carelessly—and perhaps Father was right. I had not thought John Lynston a loving husband, but perhaps I wronged him.'

'My brother was always a careless brute with horses! It

is not surprising that he was thrown, nor the first time, I dare say.'

Tom stared at him. 'Have you recovered your memory, then?'

'No. I have no idea where that came from,' Lytham admitted. 'It was instinctive. But I believe it to be true. It seems that fragments come back to me when I least expect it.'

'Perhaps everything will return in time.'

'I must hope so.' Lytham frowned. 'Now, tell me if you will, what was my relationship with Emma?'

Once again he felt that peculiar little pain about his heart. Why should he feel that way when he spoke her name, as if something very precious was lost? He tried to pull aside the curtain and remember what he knew instinctively was very important, but could not.

'I do not know,' Tom admitted. 'I had wondered that myself. You may have felt yourself in place of a guardian towards her. I know there were rumours…'

'What kind of rumours? And who told you of them?'

'Maria.' Tom went slightly pink. 'I visited her a few weeks ago and she told me you had been to see her. You asked her questions concerning her husband's death, but she had told you nothing of the afternoon we spent together.'

'Yet she might have saved you from disgrace.'

'And brought ruin on herself. I forbade her ever to speak of it.'

'That was noble if a trifle foolish, my friend.'

'Would you have done otherwise to save a lady you cared for from scandal and disgrace?'

Lytham hesitated and then smiled wryly. 'Would I? That is the question and an important one, I think. Unfortunately,

I cannot answer it for the moment. I fear that I may have done many things that might not bear the light of day.'

'I have heard you spoken of as a damnable rogue, but I do not think it, my lord.'

'Do you not?' Lytham murmured, smiling oddly. 'We must see what can be done to restore your fortunes, Tom. What is the wish closest to your heart?'

'I once wanted to be an officer in the army, but my father would not hear of it. He demanded that I do my duty by the family, but he had already ruined us. When you won the estate from my father he was deeply in debt and had sold too much land. It was not worth what you had hazarded against it.'

'Do you believe you could restore the estate—given a free hand and the necessary funds?'

'Be your agent?' Tom thought for a moment and then nodded. 'Yes, I think I should enjoy that—but are you sure you trust me? As I have told you before, you won it fairly.'

'I cannot think that I meant to take your father's estate even though he had foolishly thrown it away at the tables, though I have no memory of that night. Yet I believe I would find such business distasteful. The estate is yours by right. Show me that you can manage it properly and I shall restore it to you. As for the matter of your good name—I shall see what can be done once I have recovered my health and know a little more about my own fortunes.'

'Granny Robins has healed you,' Tom said, feeling rather emotional and wishing not to show it. 'But it is surely time you sought a softer bed to sleep in, my lord? You own a house close by and it is a matter of a short journey only.'

'Yes, you are right, Tom. I shall do so, in another day or so. At the moment I am as weak as a kitten. The day after tomorrow you will oblige me by taking me to my house for, unless you show me, I have no idea of where I live.'

'Of course,' Tom said and grinned at him. 'And I must make Belle a handsome present before we leave for she helped me care for you when you were in a fever.'

'I shall make both her and Granny handsome presents when I am in funds again,' Lytham said with a wry smile. 'I believe you did tell me that I am a wealthy man?'

'I am given to understand that is the case, my lord. There was a reward for information as to your whereabouts of five hundred guineas,' Tom told him. 'Belle could have taken it, but she did not out of loyalty to me.'

'You are fortunate in your friends, Tom.'

'Belle is an honest woman, and she has been a good friend to me in this business. It was I who begged her to keep silent.'

'You were afraid of being accused of involvement in the attempt to murder me,' Lytham said. 'We must make up some tale to cover your neglect, Tom.' He smiled a little mockingly. 'I think that will not be beyond the resources of our imaginations, my friend. Fear not, you shall not end at the hangman's noose on my account.'

Chapter Ten

'What a pretty house,' Emma exclaimed as the carriage pulled up outside the thatched cottage. The walls were of faded rose brick, the windows of grey glass and thick, but hung with pretty lace curtains. 'I have seldom seen anything I like more.'

'I am glad you approve of my home,' Lady Agatha said. 'I am very fond of it. My father restored it for the estate manager some years ago, but Lytham provided his manager with a more modern establishment. This was built in Queen Anne's time, but it has been recently refurbished to my taste and I am content here.'

'It must certainly be easier to manage than the Hall,' Emma replied with a smile. They had passed an impressive Elizabethan house on their way through the park. 'That needs a large family to fill it, I think.'

'Exactly what I've been telling Lytham since he came home from the army,' Agatha Lynston said with a harsh cackle. 'And why he spends most of his time in town, I dare say. Especially in the winter.'

'Yes. I imagine it must be very cold at this time of year.'

Emma had learned to control her feelings these past few days. Her tears were shed in private now, during the restless nights when her thoughts returned again and again to those last moments when Lytham held her in his arms and she had counted the world well lost for love.

'If my nephew had any sense he would pull most of it down and build a modern house in its place,' the elderly lady said as her groom came to assist her from the carriage. 'Thank you, Bennett. It is far too cold to stand out here talking, Emma. Come inside, my dear. I am in sore need of refreshment.'

A smiling, buxom housekeeper welcomed them into the hall, assuring Lady Agatha that tea would be served in the parlour as soon as she was ready.

'There's a good fire ready for you, my lady, for I knew you would be cold when you arrived. 'Tis a raw, bitter day so it is.'

Emma admired the warm and comfortable room to which her hostess led her. It was furnished in restful tones of blue, grey and a delicate pink, with deep cushioned couches and dainty little tables and cabinets, very much a lady's room full of knick-knacks and personal items. A sewing box stood opened on a stool by the fire, books lay everywhere as if they were always at hand when their owner needed them, and a writing box stood on the desk under the window, its lid up as though it was often used.

'Such a clutter,' Lady Agatha clucked as she watched Emma's eyes wandering about the room with interest. 'But it is comfortable so and I am a creature of habit, as you will soon discover.'

'I think it delightful,' Emma replied with a smile. 'Very like my own dear mama's parlour at home before she went to Italy with our friends.'

'Have you heard from your mother, my dear?'

'There was one letter waiting for me at home when I returned from Bath,' Emma said. 'Mama and her friends had hardly reached their destination when it was sent. I have heard nothing since, but letters are often delayed coming from abroad and I have been moving around myself a great deal.'

Lady Agatha nodded, holding her hands to the fire to warm them. 'There, that is much better. I declare I shall not stir again until the spring. Indeed, why should there be the least need? Now that I have you, my dear Emma, I shall not be in the least lonely.'

'You are very kind to say so, ma'am.'

'Not at all,' she replied. 'I have been thinking, Emma. Should Lytham not return, I should like you to make your home with me. Not as a paid companion, you understand, but as my friend. I should settle an allowance on you so that you need not be beholden to me for your personal expenses, of course. It is less than would have been yours had Lytham lived, but may recompense a little for your loss—financially. I know that nothing can repair your true loss, my dear.'

Emma dropped her head, her cheeks flaming. Now was the time to make the situation plain to Lady Agatha, but she could not find the words to tell her that Lytham had asked her to be his mistress and not his wife.

'I do not say that he will not return, for I believe he will,' Lady Agatha said firmly, though there was a slight tremor in her voice. 'But if the worst should happen, I would like you to make your home with me.'

'Thank you, ma'am. I should be happy to do so.'

Emma had not the heart to refuse for she had grown fond of Lady Agatha. As for the deception…well, perhaps it did not matter. No one but she and Lytham knew what had been said between them, and nothing had actually happened. Indeed, he had called her his ward when introducing her to Mrs Warren, and as far as Society was concerned there was no need for anyone to know the truth.

Perhaps it was wrong of her to deceive her kind hostess, but Lytham had offered her the post of companion to his aunt at the beginning and that is what she would be in all but name from now on.

And what if he returned? Emma had not solved the mystery of his apparent change of heart. Until he came to unmask her, it was surely a harmless masquerade?

'My lord!' Mrs Warren turned pale as she saw him walk into the house. 'God be praised! We thought you dead this last month.'

'I have been ill,' Lytham replied with a slight smile. 'And I must ask you for your patience, ma'am. My memory was affected by my illness and unfortunately has gaps in it. Your name seems to escape me for the moment.'

'Mrs Warren, sir. Warren and me have kept house here for the past thirty years or more, since when your mother was alive and first bought the house, God bless her soul.'

'Ah, yes, Mrs Warren.' He nodded and turned to his companion. 'This is Mr Tom Sommerton. He is my guest. It was Mr Sommerton who saved my life when I was shot and stumbled over the edge of the cliff. He found me on a rocky ledge and carried me to safety or I might have fallen unconscious into the sea.'

'Miss Emma's brother? Yes, I can see the likeness, sir. Well, fancy that. I suppose you was on your way here to see her.' Mrs Warren frowned. 'The poor lady near died of grief when we thought you lost, sir. Begging your pardon— but it seems strange your lordship did not let us know you were safe.'

'I had lost my memory and Mr Sommerton thought there might be other rogues waiting their chance to attack me.

He considered it best to tell no one of my whereabouts and kept me hidden until I was better.' His face had gone white from the effort of talking to her. 'The parlour, Mrs Warren—may I ask you to direct me?'

'Of course, my lord. You're still not well and here I am keeping you gossiping in the hall!'

She hurried before him, throwing open the door.

'Some brandy for his lordship,' Tom said. 'I think he is faint.'

'Yes, sir. At once.'

She hastened away, troubled and confused by the change in her master. He was thin and looked as if he ought to be in bed. And what she was to make out of his loss of memory she did not know.

'You are sure he is not an impostor?' her husband asked her when she related her tale in the kitchen. Cook and the kitchen wench stared at her in amazement, for everyone had believed the marquis must be dead.

'Take the brandy in yourself. I would swear it was him, but much changed.'

'And no wonder if he has been ill all this time!' Cook said and crossed herself. 'It is quite shocking…shocking!'

'I shall decide this matter for myself.'

Warren picked up the tray and went out, leaving the women to exclaim and shake their heads over it again. He was shocked when he saw the change for himself, but he did not doubt his master's identity. He served the brandy to both gentlemen.

'Is there anything else, my lord? Would you like to retire? I will have a warming pan heated and passed between the sheets immediately.'

'Thank you, Warren, but I shall not retire just yet. I would like you to ask Miss Sommerton if she will join us please.'

'Miss Sommerton is not here.'

'Not here? I thought Mrs Warren spoke of her distress over my disappearance?'

'She was here until a few days ago, my lord. Lady Agatha took her back to Lytham Hall with her. Miss Sommerton was beside herself with grief. Mrs Warren thought she had lost her mind. We sent for your aunt and she took your young lady away.'

'My young lady?'

'Your fiancée, my lord. Lady Agatha told us you were to be married. And indeed, Miss Sommerton broke her heart over your disappearance. Like someone possessed she was. Walking along the beach at all hours and in the worst of weather, looking for you, refusing to give up when everyone else thought you lost. In the end she was ill herself, but she is better now.'

Lytham felt the pain smite him in his breast. Emma had become ill because she was so distressed over his disappearance. She must love him—but did he love her? He wished that he could remember.

'I see. Thank you, Warren. We shall dine at six. Please tell Mrs Warren that I shall want something light, but Mr Sommerton will expect a decent dinner.'

'Do not trouble overmuch for me. A baked ham and a capon or some such thing will do well enough if you have it.' Tom looked at the marquis as the door closed behind the butler. 'So you were engaged to Emma. Had I known, I would have risked being accused of complicity to save her pain. I had no idea she was in love with you. I had thought it might have been something else and this relieves my mind in that respect, though I feel terrible for letting her suffer as she did.'

Lytham's brows rose. 'Did you imagine I might make her my mistress? Alas, I have no memory of how things stand between us, but I could not have offered less than marriage to a young woman of good family.'

'There was some scandal, as I told you.'

'You did not tell me the whole. Perhaps you should.'

'Emma was seen helping you upstairs at an inn. The tale was that you were drunk and she by inference a whore—but it was the night that Pennington shot you the first time.'

'Yes, that would make sense of the rumour.'

Lytham was thoughtful as he sipped his brandy. This damnable loss of memory! It would seem likely that he had asked Miss Sommerton to marry him out of a desire to restore her reputation. It would be the action of a gentleman and he hoped he was that—but if that were so, why would Emma almost die of her grief?

And why did he feel this overwhelming sadness each time her name came into his mind? What had he done to her?

He was too weary to set out in search of her today. He would rest here for a day or so and then continue his journey.

'Do you think we should send word to Emma and Lady Agatha?' Tom asked, breaking into his thoughts. 'They must have been wretched over this business. I had not realised Emma would be so distressed or…' He looked contrite and anxious as he paused.

'You would have reported my whereabouts?' Lytham smiled. 'It was a terrifying risk, Tom, for had I not accepted your word you might have been hung as an accomplice. I can guess what your sister might feel about that!'

For a moment the curtain in his mind seemed to shift. He saw the picture of a woman's anxious face looking at him; they were in a wood and she had something in her hand.

'Emma is very beautiful.'

'Yes. I always thought she could be if she had the right clothes,' Tom remarked. 'Have you remembered her?'

'I saw a woman in my mind, a lovely woman. Is Emma dark-haired with wide clear eyes and a soft, generous mouth?'

'Yes, but don't be fooled by that calm manner of hers. She has a temper when roused,' Tom replied with a grin. 'You will remember that fast enough when you see her.'

'One must hope so,' Lytham said.

He finished his brandy. It had restored him a little, but he found it frustrating not to be able to remember. He should be able to recall the woman he was going to marry!

'No, we shall not send word,' he said at last. 'I understand that my estate is not far from here. We shall be there almost as soon as a letter. I would rather tell my aunt and Emma our story in person, Tom.'

He did not know why he was reluctant to let his family know of his survival. There was something regarding Emma lurking at the back of his mind, but he could not pull that curtain aside for long enough to discover it.

Emma had decided that she needed some air. Lady Agatha's cottage was very warm and she had been used to walking often at her own home. Besides, she was curious about the Hall. They had sent word up to the big house and Lytham's agent had called to discuss the situation.

'There are distant cousins,' Stephen Antrium told Emma. 'But I do not feel duty bound to inform them of the matter as yet. I shall wait for a few months and then discuss the way forward with his lordship's lawyers.'

'Lytham will be back long before it comes to that,' Lady Agatha said. 'You mark my words, Mr Antrium. I feel it in my bones.'

'I pray you are right, ma'am. His lordship has done won-

ders with this estate and I should not care to see it go to
rack and ruin once more. He is an excellent landlord, far
better than his father and brothers were, and there are other
good deeds of his that he would not allow me to speak of,
but there, I must say no more.' He smiled at Emma in a
friendly manner. 'Should you wish to be shown over the
estate, Miss Sommerton, you have only to send for me.'

'You are very good, sir,' Emma said, feeling like a fraud.
'It might be interesting to look over the house one day.'

'Mrs Williams will be delighted to show you. I shall tell
her to be ready for a visit from you.'

'Thank you, but it will be an informal visit. She must
not go to any trouble on my behalf.'

Emma had not intended to visit the Hall that morning,
merely to walk in the extensive gardens and look at the
house from outside. However, as she approached through
the rose garden, where the earth had been raked winter
clean and the bushes cut back to the stems to preserve them
through the worst of the weather, Mr Antrium came out of
the house to meet her.

'I chanced to see you walking this way from the window
of my office,' he said giving her a welcoming smile. 'Will
you come in and take some refreshment, Miss Sommerton?'

'Thank you. I am afraid I am taking you away from your
business. I meant only to walk and observe, not to intrude.
I hope I am not disturbing you, sir?'

'No, indeed, you are not hindering me,' he said. 'Mrs
Williams is excited at the prospect of your visit. If things
had been as they ought... You must know that we are all
devastated by his lordship's disappearance, as you must be,
Miss Sommerton.'

'Yes, I am,' Emma admitted truthfully. 'I loved him very
much.'

'Of course. We have heard how ill you were and that is why we all wish to make you welcome here, to make up as best we can for the terrible time you have suffered.'

Emma felt herself blush. How kind these people were and how guilty she felt for allowing the misconception to continue. Yet it had begun innocently enough and now she could do nothing. To confess the true situation would be too shaming.

She walked into the house with the young man at her side. He was not a handsome man, being snub-nosed, with sandy hair and pale eyes, but he was, she sensed, sincere and honest. She liked him and felt herself responding as he began to show her some of the main reception rooms.

It was a very fine house, though old; some repair and refurbishment had been done to the main wing in the last century, though it was in need of much more. The furniture consisted mainly of heavy oaken pieces, heavily carved and bought at the time the house was built, the silky surface of each piece polished to a brilliant shine over the years. The stone walls had at some time been panelled in oak, and that too had mellowed to a soft golden sheen, and there were huge paintings in many of the rooms of rather dour-looking men and women in period costume. Clearly Lytham's ancestors, Emma thought.

She looked for some resemblance to the present marquis and found none. One room, though, had been decorated in soft shades of green and the furniture here was of a more recent period, fashioned of mahogany and extremely elegant, though not new. There were pad-footed tables, comfortable wing chairs by the fireplace, a magnificent cabinet with a towering swan-necked pediment and a large writing bureau with its own elbow chair. On the far end wall as you entered, a portrait of a pretty woman dominated the room. Gazing up at it, Emma found what she had searched for elsewhere in vain and knew without being told that this was Lytham's mother.

'This is a lovely room,' she remarked. 'So different from the rest of the house.'

'It belonged to his lordship's mother. He has kept it exactly as it was, though I believe he seldom comes here. He prefers the library. My office is close by, which makes it convenient for business. His lordship does not care to stay in the country overlong.'

'Yes, Lady Agatha told me he prefers to stay in town.'

'His house there is beautiful,' Mr Antrium said. 'He had it done over recently and his lordship's taste is excellent— but you will perhaps have seen it for yourself?'

'No. I was staying in Bath before—' She broke off, unable to continue for the tightness at the back of her throat. 'I did not have the opportunity to visit.'

How terrible it was to keep up this deception. She felt as if she were committing a crime, but managed to regain her composure as the housekeeper came to greet her.

'Will you stay for nuncheon, Miss Sommerton? Then I could take you on a tour of the rest of the house this afternoon. You might like to see the bedrooms?'

Emma hesitated and was lost. She ought to refuse, of course, but this might be her only opportunity. 'Would it be a trouble to you? Could a message be sent to Lady Agatha so that she does not worry?'

'It would be a pleasure,' Mrs Williams assured her, beaming. 'I know we all want to tell you how happy we were to hear the news of your engagement.'

'Well, I am not sure that…'

'Oh, we know it hasn't been officially announced, miss,' Mrs Williams said. 'I suppose you were waiting to tell your mother as is right and proper, but Lady Agatha let the cat out of the bag, as it were. To tell the truth, it's what we've all been waiting for since his lordship came home from the wars. It's more than a body can do to keep such a thing secret. You wouldn't expect it, miss?'

'No, I suppose not.' Emma blushed. 'Thank you for being so kind.'

She allowed herself to be shown into a small parlour, where two places had been laid for nuncheon. Mr Antrium held out the chair at the head of the oval gate-legged table, and then took his place beside her. He engaged her in friendly conversation as the meal was served on delicate porcelain in a pretty turquoise blue pattern. It consisted of several courses, beginning with a delicious vegetable soup served with freshly baked bread, followed by cold capon, a pie of eels, which Mr Antrium clearly relished, a warm pork pie and side dishes of creamed potatoes, buttered parsnips and a quince tart.

'Goodness, does Mrs Williams always serve such a variety at midday?' Emma asked, feeling spoiled by the excellence of the meal and used to something lighter. 'Or was this in my honour?'

'I do believe she might have been planning to impress you,' Mr Antrium said with a smile. 'I have been eating rather more lavishly than I am used to of late.'

Emma smiled and nodded, making a special point of remarking on the quality of the fare served to them when Mrs Williams returned to show her over the house after their meal.

'Shall we begin with the main wing, Miss Sommerton?' Mrs Williams asked. 'The other wings are not much used and the furniture is kept under covers unless his lordship is in residence, though we have been used to keeping this part of the house in readiness. He sometimes pops in on us of a sudden. You never quite know with his lordship.'

'I see...' The housekeeper seemed to think like Lady

Agatha that the marquis would turn up in his own good time. Pray God that he did! She thought that she could bear anything if she could only see him again.

It took some time to tour the bedrooms on the first floor, for they were in better case than many of the reception rooms, because the marquis wanted his guests to be comfortable in their beds, according to the housekeeper.

'This is the master suite,' Mrs Williams said, stopping at the far end of the hall. 'Part of it is actually in the old wing, though it has been done up, as you might imagine. There are five rooms in all, Miss Sommerton. Perhaps you would like to explore on your own for a while? If you need help, please ring and I shall come at once.'

'Oh, I think I can find my way back,' Emma assured her. 'I have kept you too long from your duties already. I must thank you for your kindness and I shall not trouble you before I leave.'

'It was no trouble, miss. I hope we shall see you here as mistress very soon.'

Emma smiled, but made no answer. Her hand trembled as she opened the door and went into the first room, which was a pretty parlour, clearly a lady's room and decorated in shades of yellow, gold and cream. It led into a bedroom, also a lady's room, furnished in the style of perhaps twenty years earlier with pieces that must have come straight from Mr Chippendale's workshops.

Here there was little sign of the oak that filled most of the rest of the house; it had been replaced by smooth shining mahogany, wrought into tasteful designs: elegant elbow chairs, a pretty desk under the window, a cabinet with figurines set out on the shelves, little chests at the side of the bed, and a five-drawer chest at one end. On the dressing table there was a pretty mirror set on a stand and all manner of expensive trifles, including blue scent bottles with silver gilt clasps, silver boxes, silver buttonhooks, combs and brushes and an enamelled patch box.

Passing through the dressing room, Emma entered what was clearly the master bedroom, her heart catching as she caught the scent of cedar-wood. This was Lytham's own room! It was a scent she had noticed on his clothes on a couple of occasions.

The room was furnished in what was usually described as the Empire style, with imposing pieces of furniture that had obviously been commissioned to match. Everything was made of some dark wood that she did not immediately recognise and had stringing of a paler wood with some gilding and the Lytham coat of arms cut into the bed-head.

There was a dressing robe lying on a chair next to the bed. It was dark blue striped with a dusky gold. She approached it slowly, her heart racing as her hand moved towards it, then drew back. She had no right to touch his things, and yet the aching need to be near him was in her, making her eyes smart with the tears she had believed long cried out of her. How could she face the future without him?

'Oh, Lytham,' she whispered, allowing herself to touch the soft fabric at last. Her chest was tight as she fought the longing to pick up his robe and hold it to her face, to breathe in the remembered scent of him. 'Where are you, my love? Please come back to me. I need you so.'

So overcome by her emotions was she that she did not notice the door open behind her, and it was only when she heard a slight noise that she turned, expecting to see Mrs Williams. Her heart caught as she saw him standing there watching her, an odd expression on his face; for a moment she thought that she might faint. Had she conjured him up out of her need and longing? Was he flesh and blood or merely a figment of her fevered imagination?

'Lytham…' she whispered hoarsely, her throat so tight that she could scarcely speak. 'Is it truly you?'

'Emma?' he seemed to question, frowning as he hesitated. 'You really are beautiful. I had hardly believed my visions, but now I see you for myself.'

'My lord?' She was puzzled both by his words and his manner. He seemed unlike himself. And, indeed, there were marked changes in his appearance. 'Please, tell me I am not dreaming! I fear I must sit down or I may fall down.' She sat heavily on the edge of the bed as her legs almost gave way beneath her. 'Do you not know me? What is the matter? Are you truly alive and well?'

'Perhaps not truly well,' he answered, seeming to wake as from a trance. 'Forgive me if I frightened you. Williams told me these were my rooms and I had hoped that seeing them might bring back my memory, but it does not seem to have worked thus far.'

'You have been ill?' Emma caught at the only part of his speech that made sense to her. She gazed at his face, seeing the new-wrought lines of strain that illness had brought. 'Yes, I see a change in you. What happened, my lord? You must know that everyone has been very worried about you. We feared you might be dead.'

'Yes, I believe that was generally thought,' Lytham said. 'And I must apologise for it, Emma—but Tom thought it best until I was recovered lest another attempt was made on my life.'

'Another attempt—but surely Pennington was killed?' Her gaze narrowed as she looked at him. 'Are you speaking of my brother, sir? Was Tom involved in this?'

'He saved my life. Apparently I stumbled over the cliff when I was shot and though I fell on to a ledge, I might have died there if Tom had not carried me away and nursed me back to health.'

'How did Tom come to be there?' Emma demanded, feeling angry. If Tom had known…all this time! Surely he could have let her know?

'He had followed us from your home,' Lytham said, his eyes narrowing as he sensed her anger. 'He was not aware that my disappearance might cause you pain and distress, Emma. Tom had no knowledge of our engagement until we reached my house.'

'Our engagement…' Emma stared at him, her cheeks suddenly hot as she realised what he was saying. 'My lord, I should tell you at once—'

'No, please do not be angry with your brother,' he said with a smile of such sweetness it took her breath away, leaving her unable to continue. 'You must know that Tom had his reasons. He told you that he was afraid a man he had been riding with might try to murder me, I believe?' She nodded, unable to go on, though she knew she must speak out. 'And I believe you know the nature of their business? Had he been suspected of complicity in the attempt on my life, he might have been hung.' Emma nodded again, her heart pounding. 'Tom is finished with the life as you know, but it was fortunate that he decided to follow us that day or I might not be standing here today.'

'My lord.' Emma looked at him oddly. 'You mentioned a loss of memory just now—how complete is that?'

'I fear I can remember nothing before waking to find an old hag caring for me in some deserted shack. If it had not been for Tom, I might never have known who I was. I owe him so much, Emma, and I have decided that he shall manage the estate that was your father's for a year. I shall give him money to help him get it back into good heart and if he is successful, which I am certain he will be—it will be his own, as it ought always to have been.'

'Do you know how it came into your possession?'

'Tom told me everything. He was very honest. I like your brother, Emma. I should have liked him if we had met in other circumstances, but as it is I think he has become like a brother to me—which he will be soon enough in truth.'

'You mean our marriage?' She could not look at him for fear of betraying herself.

'Yes, of course. I do not know what we had spoken of in the matter of setting a date, but I think we must postpone it until the spring—if you do not object too much? By then I shall hope to recover all the parts of my life that are still eluding me.'

'Do you think that will happen, my lord?'

'Lytham. You should properly call me by my name, Emma.' His dark eyes dwelt on her thoughtfully. 'I am not perfectly sure of the depth of my feelings for you at this moment, though I believe I must have loved you very much. It must be best for our hopes of happiness if we spend some time together, getting to know one another.'

'Perhaps...' She could not go on for her heart was full.

'You are hurt by my speaking so plainly?' he asked. 'I thought it was best since there is no hiding the truth. To have pretended things were otherwise might have caused more hurt.'

'Yes, that is perfectly true.' Emma's heart was racing as she looked at him. She must speak out now, she must in all honesty! And yet she could not bring herself to say the words that would make him turn from her in disgust. She had allowed Lady Agatha to bring her here under false pretences and gained the friendship of his servants. He would be angry if he discovered her masquerade, accuse her of trying to force his hand, of duping him into some-thing he had never intended. Yet it was too difficult to speak, to watch the smiles of those people she had come to like turn to icy coldness, as they must. In time he would remember and then she would leave, but for a little longer she would linger and bask in the delight of a future that could never be hers. 'Yes, of course. I would say only this to you, Lytham. Should you discover that there has been a change in your feelings, for any reason, I release you from any promises you may have made me. If that happens, I shall go away and you may forget me.'

'Forget you, Emma?' He moved towards her, feeling an urgent need to take her in his arms and taste those lips. Her face had haunted his dreams since that first time of remembering and he wanted to make sure she was real, not just a figment of his imagination. She did not move away as he reached out for her, allowing him to draw her close, to kiss her softly on the lips. A great surge of desire flowed through him as he felt her instant response and he knew that he had done this before—that he had wanted her desperately once before—but something had stood in the way. He released her and drew back, seeing the way her mouth had softened with desire, her eyes smoky and languorous as though she too had wanted their lovemaking to continue. 'I do not think that once a man had held you, kissed you, he would ever willingly forget you, Emma.'

'I think we must see how you feel once you have come to know me,' Emma replied, finding it difficult to breathe. When he looked at her like that she felt close to swooning! She loved him so and to leave him would break her heart, though she must do it in the end. But he would regain his memory and then he would tell her to leave, his anger driving a wedge between them.

'I do not believe that I shall change my mind,' he said and for a moment he looked as he had before his illness had wrought a change in him, the old mocking expression there in his eyes once more. 'But perhaps we should go down. Mrs Williams will think I have seduced you if we stay here alone much longer. Besides, I know that Tom is anxious to make his peace with you.'

'I shall have some things to say to my brother,' Emma said, a gleam in her eye. 'I forgive you for not letting me know you were alive, Lytham—but Tom could have come to me. He must have known I would not betray him.'

'Apparently he was not sure that you truly believed it was not he who shot me the first time, Emma.'

She made no answer. The shock had made her forget everything but her pleasure in seeing him alive once more, but now she was remembering…the agony of believing him dead had almost killed her.

'Your aunt has been most distressed, Lytham. I think you must allow me to tell her that you are here—but she will want to see you at once, I know.'

'Then perhaps you will both dine with me this evening?' His smile set her heart racing again and she longed to be in his arms once more, to be truly his as she would have been if he had come to her that afternoon. 'And I shall have my carriage take you home.'

'It is not necessary, my lord,' she replied. 'I believe I shall walk. It is not far and I would have time to be alone with my thoughts for a while.'

'Of course. This has been a shock. I should not have come upon you unannounced, but I had not realised you were here.'

'I never intended…' Emma blushed. 'I was walking and Mr Antrium insisted I take some refreshment. That became lunch and a tour of the house. Mrs Williams left me here to explore these rooms alone.'

'I trust that you liked what you saw? Though truth to tell, I think there must be some changes made here. I had no idea it was such a mausoleum.'

'You have forgotten,' Emma said with a smile. 'Perhaps you always meant to change things but were too busy.'

'My man of business tells me that there is much to be done after my absence,' Lytham said and frowned. 'But this house must be a priority for I could not expect my wife to put up with it as it stands. You must advise me, Emma, tell me what you like and what you don't.'

'Yes, of course,' she said, though she could not meet his eyes. Oh, dear, this was becoming worse and worse. She had no right to oversee the refurbishing of a house in which she would never live. 'But now I must go or indeed Mrs Williams will think me lost to all propriety.'

'I shall see you this evening?' He caught her hand as she would have passed him, pressing it to his lips, his eyes meeting hers. 'You will not disappear into the mist like the myth I thought you must be when I first dreamed of you in my fever?'

'If I go, you will know why,' Emma said. 'I promise I shall not run off without your leave to go.'

'Then you will never leave me,' he said and smiled at her. 'At least only for a short time. As soon as we are truly comfortable with one another again I shall arrange the wedding.'

Chapter Eleven

'Did I not tell you it would be so?' Agatha Lynston gave a harsh cackle of laughter. Instead of being overset by the news, as Emma had feared, she was triumphant. 'I knew that scoundrel Pennington was no match for my nephew!'

'I can still scarcely believe it,' Emma confessed. The long walk home had helped her come to terms with Lytham's sudden arrival, the wind blowing some colour into her cheeks. Her eyes held a sparkle that had been missing of late. 'When I saw him first I thought I had imagined it, that he was but a dream.'

'A substantial ghost, Lytham.'

'He is much thinner than he was and he looks drawn. I think he is not truly recovered yet.'

'He is *alive,* gel. Give him time and he'll be back to his old ways, I dare say.' Lady Agatha frowned. 'You say he has lost his memory?'

'That was part of the reason Tom did not inform us of his whereabouts.' Emma hesitated and then decided to tell Lady Agatha the whole story.

'Damned young fool!' the old lady snorted. 'What would he have done if Lytham had died, as he might? He would have been a fugitive all his life. He might at least have told you the truth.'

'I scolded him roundly for it,' Emma replied. 'But, indeed, he was already contrite. He did not know how much it would mean to me to know that Lytham was safe.'

'Well, he has not heard the last of it for I mean to have my say!' Lady Agatha pulled the bell-rope and ordered tea from the maid who answered. 'So we are to dine with Lytham this evening. I hope he means to send his carriage. My servants are getting too old for jaunting here and there at night.'

Her grumbling disguised the relief she felt at knowing that Lytham was home. She had never let Emma guess how deep her doubts were, but she had been afraid that she might not see her great-nephew again. As her eyes swept over the younger woman she wondered what was troubling her. Emma was obviously happy that Lytham was alive, but something was on her mind.

'What is wrong, my dear?' she asked. 'He ain't called the wedding off, has he?'

'No.' Emma blushed as Lady Agatha's keen gaze dwelled on her face. 'It is merely delayed until the spring— so that we may get to know one another.'

'Are you afraid he won't feel the same as he did before his illness?'

'I suppose that is possible.'

'Rubbish! He cannot fail to love you, as I do myself. And so I shall tell him if he tries to cry off.'

'You must not,' Emma pleaded. 'I do not know what his feelings are. He could not remember me, other than as the woman to whom he had been told he was pledged in marriage.'

'Hadn't got round to giving you a ring, had he?' Lady Agatha's gaze narrowed and she looked thoughtful. 'Always was slow to make up his mind. Not that there was ever any doubt in my mind. He could not have done less after that damned young fool besmirched your name.'

Emma's heart lurched. Was that why Lady Agatha had believed that they were to marry? Of course it must be. She had told him it was his duty, but he had decided otherwise. If she had refused his offer of *carte blanche* perhaps…but she had not. She had been already so desperately in love with him that she was ready to cast aside everything for his sake. Therefore she was not entitled to wonder if he might have been thinking of asking her to marry him.

'Damn my idle tongue!' Lady Agatha said as she saw the doubts in Emma's eyes. 'I've made you think that was his reason for offering you his name, and of course it was never that. I knew as soon as he asked me to visit Bath that he was in love with you.'

If only she could believe it! Emma wished with all her heart that it were so. Yet would he have asked her to be his mistress if he truly loved her? Emma could not think it.

'Even if he loved me then, he may not do so now,' she replied. 'Who knows how his illness may have changed him? If I thought he had changed his mind, I should, of course release him.'

'Stuff and nonsense,' Lady Agatha said briskly. 'Go upstairs and rest before you change for the evening, Emma, as I intend to do. I hope Lytham has not forgotten that I keep early hours. My digestion will not stand town hours these days.'

'If he has forgotten, Mrs Williams will not,' Emma reassured her with a smile. It would be a wrench to part with her friend when the time came for her to leave, but at least Lady Agatha would not be alone. She would have the marquis to care for her and one day he would take a wife.

* * *

Lytham had spent almost an hour acquainting himself with the personal items in his room. He picked up combs and brushes, sniffed at pomade for grooming his hair and found it smelled pleasant, though he was not sure that he would use such a thing. Opening the huge armoire in the corner of the dressing room, he discovered that it was full of clothes, most of them comfortable plain garments for riding and country living, but there were also some fashionable coats that must have come from the best tailors. In fact, everything he discovered was of the finest quality, which seemed to indicate that he had fastidious taste.

He had hoped that something in the room might trigger his elusive memory, but even an exquisite miniature, which stated on the reverse that it was of the tenth marchioness and therefore his mother, brought no flicker of recognition. Damn it! He ought to remember his own mother. She was beautiful, but he thought she looked a little haughty, even cold—and he smiled as he considered the lady who would be his wife. Emma was flesh and blood, as warm as she was lovely.

Yet there was something that troubled him about her. It was a damned nuisance that he had no memory of his relationship with Emma! Especially as he suspected that she was hiding something from him.

There had been no doubt about her shock at seeing him alive, or the pleasure that had swept over her as she realised that he was actually there in the room with her. Nor could he doubt her response to that kiss. He had not meant to do that so soon, but the need to hold her had been so strong that he had not been able to resist.

The scent of her had lingered long after she had gone, arousing and frustrating him. He had wanted her so badly! Yet he could not remember anything that had passed between them.

From all he had been told and heard, and from the warmth of her lips beneath his, he believed that she cared for him, as he believed he had cared for her. No, surely she was in love with him? He had known other willing women, but none had been like her—how could he know that? He had no memory of those other women, but he knew that they had meant nothing to him.

Emma's face and name had been haunting him ever since Tom had spoken of her. Why? Why did he feel that he had done something to hurt her? She had not reproached him or given any indication that he had displeased her...but there was some reserve in her. Was it because he had changed physically or because he had requested that they wait until the spring to marry?

Yet how could he marry her until they had had time to know one another? She had not lost her memory, of course, but he was at a disadvantage. He did not know what would please her—and he wanted to please her. He knew that he had hurt her. She had not complained of the anguish she must have felt while he was missing—but he knew how she had suffered, for Mrs Warren had been forthright about it. He had been affected powerfully by the knowledge of Emma's grief, and it had made him even more determined never to hurt her again.

It would take a little time to break down this barrier between them, he thought, but he must not rush her. It was important for the future that they should be comfortable together. Yet when he recalled the urgent throbbing in his loins as he held her, he wondered how long he could wait to claim her as his own.

'So you've come back to us,' Agatha Lynston said, her questing eyes going over him. 'You look terrible, Lytham. No wonder Emma thought she had seen a ghost.'

Lytham laughed and kissed her cheek. 'Someone warned me that your tongue was sharp, Aunt.'

'It used to amuse you. You were always the only one of my relatives I cared for. Your father and brothers were bad, Lytham—bad blood. They did their best to ruin the family. It's as well they're gone, but I should be obliged if you would get yourself an heir before you disappear again.'

Her gruff tone held concern for him. He sensed it instinctively. He could not remember her, but knew that their relationship had been special.

'You must forgive her, Emma,' he said in a teasing tone. 'My aunt has always been one to call a spade a spade, I believe.'

'I ain't mealy-mouthed, never have been,' Lady Agatha said. 'Emma doesn't mind me. She knows what I mean.'

'I am sure Lady Agatha has your best interests at heart, my lord.'

'Lytham,' he said. 'Will you never learn to say it, Emma? Or is it only that I have displeased you again?'

His eyes widened as he spoke, for the words had come into his mind unbidden, and he had the strangest feeling that it was not the first time he had said something similar to her.

'You have not displeased me,' she said but her eyes would not meet his questing gaze. 'Forgive me, Lytham. I sometimes forget that we are engaged.'

He glanced at her hand. 'It seems I have been neglectful in buying you a ring. Perhaps I meant to have it made. No matter. Give me your hand if you will, Emma. This will suffice until I go up to town.'

Emma offered her left hand reluctantly. The ring he slid on to her finger was a small cluster of fine diamonds in the shape of a daisy and fitted well.

'Stephen reminded me that it was in the office strongbox,' he said with a little frown. 'It belonged to my mother. I understand it was her father's gift to her when she was wed. I am sure she would want you to have it.'

'It is beautiful, my...Lytham.'

'A trinket until something more suitable is arranged.'

'Thank you.' Emma's guilt rose up to haunt her. This was terrible! Why had she not spoken out long ago?

It was not easy to recover from the embarrassment of accepting a ring to which she had no right, but as they progressed into the dining room she felt the awkwardness alleviate. Lady Agatha was eager to hear everything Emma had told her from Lytham's own lips, and Mr Antrium put himself out to entertain his employer's fiancée, Tom joining in the conversation from time to time, but looking thoughtful.

'I am so relieved that I did nothing precipitate in the matter of his lordship's cousins,' Mr Antrium confessed. 'And I am sincerely happy to have him back home.'

'You will be invaluable to him in the coming weeks,' she said. 'It must be so awkward, so uncomfortable, to remember nothing of your past life. He will need good friends to help him.'

'I have heard of such cases,' the young man said with a serious expression. 'Sometimes the memory returns of a sudden, though there is apparently no certainty of it.'

'Then Lytham must learn his life all over again.'

'His lordship is a very intelligent man. I do not doubt that he will cope with a situation that others might find intolerable.'

It was clear to Emma that Mr Antrium was both fond of and an admirer of his employer. From the respect in the manner of his agent, and the happy smiles on the faces of his servants, Emma realised that all his people held him in affection.

* * *

Later, when it was time to leave, Mrs Williams brought Emma's cloak for her, fussing over her as she placed the soft velvet garment about her shoulders.

'Is it not the most wonderful news, Miss Sommerton?'

'Yes, wonderful,' Emma agreed. 'I think his lordship has had a marvellous escape.'

'And due to Mr Sommerton,' the housekeeper said with an approving beam at Tom as he came to take his farewell of his sister.

'I shall call to see you in the morning,' Tom said as he kissed Emma's cheek. 'I must hope that you will one day forgive me for keeping you in ignorance of the situation concerning Lytham?'

'Of course,' she said and smiled up at him. 'I was shocked when Lytham told me the story and cross with you, Tom, but I understand your dilemma. It was an awkward situation. Yet you ought to have known that I would support you.'

'I did not realise that Lytham meant so much to you. Had I done so, I would have taken the risk of coming to you.'

Emma blushed and shook her head. 'I was naturally distressed. Anyone would be.'

She felt that someone was staring at her, and looking up, met Lytham's dark gaze. His eyes seemed to express doubts and regret, but he smiled as he came to say goodnight and to escort them to the carriage, assisting first Lady Agatha and then Emma.

'I have things to discuss with Stephen, which I imagine must keep me busy for the morning, but perhaps we could ride together in the afternoon. Do you ride? Forgive me. I am not sure.'

'How could you be? I did not ride in London or Bath, though I enjoyed the pastime at home when it was possible.

Father had reduced the stables before he died and did not possess a horse suitable for my use, though Sir William allowed me to use something from his stables sometimes.'

'Stephen tells me I have one or two horses that might suit you, Emma. I beg you will use them whenever you wish.'

'Thank you. I shall ride with you tomorrow. At what time shall you be ready?'

'Why do you not come for nuncheon? I should have finished my business by then and shall be free to spend some time with you.'

'Thank you. I may walk back with Tom after his visit to me.'

Lytham kissed her hand, his thoughtful eyes dwelling on her face. Something was definitely troubling her, though she was trying to hide it.

'Goodnight, Emma. I shall look forward to our ride.'

'Goodnight, my lord.'

She turned away as he gave the order for the carriage to move off.

Emma was thoughtful as she undressed that night. What did she truly know of Lord Lynston? She had met him only a few times, but her defences had crumbled before the force of their mutual passion. In truth, she had learned more of his true nature from his servants than she had known of him previously.

It seemed that he was a better man than she might have expected from what was whispered about him, for he was certainly not the damnable rogue her friend Sir William Heathstone had believed him. Why then had he asked her to be his mistress? Thinking it through, she realised that it was not the behaviour of a gentleman. Although her name had been linked to scandal because of Bridget's indiscretion, and that night when he had been taken ill, she was respectable and of good family. He should properly have offered her marriage.

And she ought to have refused the offer he *had* made her!

Emma's cheeks were hot with shame as she recalled her own behaviour that afternoon. She had melted into his arms, offering herself and her love to him without reserve, like any wanton from the streets. What had she been thinking of?

It would shame her if Lytham recalled her unbridled passion and his own distaste for it. She had come to the conclusion that it must have been something in her that had sent him out to walk on the cliffs. What other reason could there be?

She ought to leave here as soon as possible, before she was exposed. Something in Lytham's gaze that evening had warned her that he had some doubts. She would not be able to bear it if his manner should become cold and distant, which it must if her deception were discovered.

Yet it was difficult to leave. For one thing she had very little money. She could ask Tom to lend her some but he would want to know why she needed it, and what could she tell him? He had the prospect of a secure future at the moment; if she told him the truth he might call Lytham out. And then there was the matter of her own future. If she was to leave she would have to find work somehow. There was no way out of this web into which she had walked of her own volition. For the moment she must go on as she was, and if Lytham should remember—then his natural disgust would make it easier to leave him.

Lytham paced the floor of his bedchamber, feeling much like a caged beast. Why would his wretched memory not return? He knew that something important was lurking behind that misty curtain in his mind, mocking him.

Several times that evening Emma had deliberately refused to meet his eyes. What in heaven's name had he done to her?

He must have done something to hurt her! Her eyes seemed almost to accuse him and she was holding back from him. He had had the leisure to observe her as she spoke to others and saw none of the reserve that she held towards him. Had he not been told of her desperation after his disappearance, he would have assumed that their engagement was merely a matter of convenience on both sides. For him it would be the obligation of providing an heir and for her…security?

He must have felt himself responsible for her welfare after her father's untimely death. Having talked at length with Tom and Stephen, he now understood the matter much better. Apparently, he had challenged Emma's father at the card table, goading him into gambling away his estate. He had no idea why he should have done so, but it seemed clear that he had, an unfortunate circumstance that had led to Sommerton's death. It would seem clear that he had an obligation to the family, made even more acute by the scandal caused by his illness at that inn.

Yet if that were all, why did his senses become inflamed at the mere mention of her name? That kiss had brought him almost to the point of no return, making him throb and burn for her, and only his fear of frightening her had made him draw back. Was it possible that they had been lovers? Would he have anticipated their wedding night?

It was not the behaviour of a gentleman, but was he a gentleman in the true sense of the word? Even Lady Agatha had admitted that there was bad blood in the family.

He could not know the truth and was frustrated again, cursing as he resumed his pacing.

What kind of a man was he?

'I meant to come earlier,' Tom said as they began their walk to the Hall that morning. 'But Lytham suggested I might like to talk to Stephen Antrium about Father's estate and I clean forgot the time.'

'It does not matter,' Emma assured him with a smile. 'I am glad to see you taking so much interest in the estate, Tom.'

'I want to make a success of it, prove that I'm not quite the fool Father thought me.'

She caught the note of defence in his voice, understanding how much the quarrel with their father had hurt him, and reached out to press his arm. 'I have never thought you a fool, Tom, just a little hot-tempered, as Father was himself.'

By this time they had reached the Hall and were welcomed by the housekeeper. She provided a warm drink to drive away the chill of their walk, and within ten minutes Lytham and his agent joined them. The two men were in close conversation when they arrived, but business was forgotten as they all went into nuncheon.

Once again several courses were served, though Emma refused to take more than cold meat and some bread and butter.

'You eat very little,' Lytham remarked, regarding her thoughtfully. 'You must order the menus as you wish them, Emma. Mrs Williams has consulted me, but I was not sure of what you would like.'

'I need only something simple in the middle of the day,' she told him. 'But you and Mr Antrium must not be deprived on my account. It is not for me to make changes to your arrangements.'

'I was thinking it might be easier if you and my aunt were to stay here at the hall—'

'Oh, no,' Emma said hastily and blushed as he raised his brows. 'Lady Agatha loves her home and we are quite comfortable there.'

'As you wish.' He frowned as if her refusal had displeased him, but said no more on the subject.

The meal was at an end. Tom and Mr Antrium took their leave and Emma was invited into the parlour next door to drink a dish of tea.

'I have asked for the horses in half an hour,' Lytham told her. 'I thought we might enjoy the opportunity to talk alone for a while.'

'Yes, of course,' Emma said. 'How are you feeling now? I believe you look a little better. Did you sleep well?'

'Tolerably well,' he agreed, though it had been hours before he had finally fallen asleep. 'Do you like to dance, Emma?'

She was surprised by the sudden change of topic and replied without thinking, 'Very much. Why do you ask?'

'I thought we might hold a small dance here to announce our engagement. Stephen is arranging for an advertisement in *The Times,* but I would like to give a dance to celebrate—and it would be a good way for me to get to know my neighbours again.'

'Yes, I am sure that it would.' Emma was hesitant. The trap seemed to be closing ever tighter. How could she let him tell everyone that they were to be married and then withdraw? If he announced it to the world, she would not be able to draw back then without causing a terrible scandal. She got to her feet and walked across to the window to look out at the park. 'I agree that you would find such an occasion a convenient way to rediscover friends—but are you sure you wish to announce our engagement just yet?'

'You are thinking that you may wish to withdraw if my memory does not return?'

'No, of course not...' She faltered and then turned to face him, her shoulders squaring as she decided that she must at least tell him a part of the truth. 'It is a little awkward, but there is something you should know.'

Lytham rose and came to stand before her, his eyes intent on her face, studying her, reading her discomfort. 'Have I upset you in some way, Emma? I really was ill for some time, you know. Once Tom told me who I was I could have sent word, but I was lost...alone in a world that made no sense. I did not know you were waiting for me or if anyone cared whether I lived. You cannot imagine how frustrating it is to have no knowledge of yourself other than what you have been told.'

'I do understand that this must be terrible for you,' Emma said, sensing his frustration and hurt. 'I am not angry with you, nor do I blame you for what happened.'

'Then what is bothering you? Please tell me, for I know something is—I can feel a reserve in you towards me and I think I have done something to harm you.'

'Oh, no, it is only that...you had not asked me to marry you,' Emma said, her cheeks pink. 'When Lady Agatha arrived at your mother's house she told everyone that I was your fiancée and insisted that I come here with her. I did not know what to do. I had been unwell and she was so kind—but then everyone believed we were engaged and I did not know how to tell them it was not so.'

Lytham smiled and experienced a sense of relief. 'You feel as if you are guilty of deceiving everyone, including me—is that it, Emma?'

'Yes.' She dropped her gaze as she felt his eyes intent upon her. 'It was very wrong of me. I should, of course, have made it clear at once that you had not spoken…but somehow I did not and then it was too difficult.'

'Emma, Emma,' Lytham chided and the look in his eyes caused her heart to miss a beat. 'Is that your terrible secret? Clearly I was at fault for being tardy. As I understand the situation, I must have confided my intention to my aunt. Indeed, I imagine that it was a matter of honour. After your reputation suffered because of my carelessness there was no other option open to me as a gentleman. Besides, I already feel deeply attracted to you and I believe you care something for me?'

She could not deny it when he looked at her that way, and it was now even more impossible to confess the shameful truth.

'Yet I think we should wait before we announce our intentions,' she said quietly. 'If by the spring you are sure of your feelings…'

'I shall not change my mind,' he said before she could finish. 'We shall marry next March and announce our engagement at Christmas. The dance may wait until then. Will that content you, Emma?'

It wanted no more than three weeks to Christmas, but she could not refuse. 'If you are of the same mind I—I am content.'

'It occurs to me that my proposal leaves something to be desired, Emma,' Lytham said and laughed. 'However, let us make it clear so that there may be no more doubts between us—I do most sincerely want and desire you as my wife, Miss Sommerton. Will you do me the honour of accepting my offer?'

Emma's heart caught, for the way he looked at her

seemed to show sincerity and a depth of feeling on his part that was all she could ask of the man she would marry.

'I am honoured by your proposal, my lord, and if you still wish it in the spring I shall marry you.'

'Then we are agreed,' he said and reached out to touch her cheek with his fingertips. 'Do not look so anxious, my love. I dare say my memory will return long before then.'

'Yes, we must hope so.'

He glanced at his pocket watch. 'I believe the stables are expecting us—shall we go? I thought you would like to choose your mount yourself since it is your first time.'

He held his hand out to her and she took it, her heart fluttering wildly. She had told him as much of the truth as she dare and he had dismissed her fears with laughter. He wanted to marry her, had asked her to be his wife, and God forgive her for the deception, but she wanted to marry him.

Alone in her room later that evening, Emma looked at herself in the mirror. Was what she was doing so very wrong? Lytham seemed to know what he wanted, and he *had* asked her to marry him—but would he have done so if he had remembered that afternoon when she had so very nearly become his mistress?

He had told her after their ride together that he was planning to take a short trip to town to visit his lawyers, and to consult a doctor that Stephen had told him about, to discover what the chances were of him ever remembering his past.

'You will not mind staying here with my aunt?' he asked, gazing down into her face, his dark eyes seeming as if they would pierce her very soul. 'I believe she is not always as well as she pretends and I must make some arrangement for her to have a companion. Otherwise it will be a wrench for her when we are in town or on some jaunt of our own.'

'Yes, I think it would be good for her to have a companion,' Emma agreed. 'Though she will have company when we are in residence at the Hall.'

'Do you enjoy living in the country, Emma?'

'I have been used to it,' she said with a smile. 'We lived very quietly at home, Mother and I, you know.'

'Where is your mother? May I fetch her to you? You will want her to be at the wedding?' He frowned. 'Forgive me. I had not realised until this moment that you had a parent living. No one had thought to tell me of Lady Sommerton's existence. Where is she and how is she managing to live?'

He looked upset at this lack, and she felt her heart go out to him. How terrible it must be not to be able to remember anything about yourself or the people you see every day.

'You did not know, how could you? And that is my fault for neglecting to tell you,' she said softly. 'My mother is in Italy for the winter with good friends. She will return in the spring.'

'Ah, then I must see if any letters have come for you. I dare say she will write care of the estate.'

'Tom will send them on,' she said. 'But letters take a long time to come from that distance and I dare say Mama will not write often. Indeed, I hope she is enjoying herself too much to think of it.'

'I shall be gone no more than a few days,' he said, his serious gaze dwelling thoughtfully on her face. 'But there are matters I must attend to, Emma. In the meantime, I ask you to make free of my home. Use it as you will—and perhaps you might make a friend of Maria.'

'Your late brother's wife?' Emma frowned. 'Lady Agatha sent a note when we first came here, asking her to dine

with us, but she declined. Do you think that I should call
on her?'

'It may be that she is embarrassed to meet you, because
of her involvement with Tom. I have not called to see her
thus far, but I shall certainly do so when I return from
town.'

'Then I shall call on her in the meantime,' Emma said.
'For we are bound to meet from time to time and I would
have no awkwardness between us.'

'Nor should there be any,' Lytham said. 'It is not for me
to say, Emma—but I believe that in another year or so Tom
may think of marrying and it is possible that he will ask
Maria to be his wife. I know that he intended to pay her a
visit before he left Lytham this afternoon.'

'You think that he cares for her?'

'Maria could have cleared him of all suspicion of my
brother's murder, but he would not let her speak,' Lytham
said. 'He was more concerned for her reputation than his
own, and that I think shows a certain feeling between them.
I shall do my best to re-establish Tom's reputation, for he
undoubtedly saved my life, and I owe him more than I can
ever repay.'

'Then I shall definitely call on Maria,' Emma said. 'I
must make a friend of her for my brother's sake.'

She would do so in the morning, she decided as she
finished dressing for dinner, glancing at her reflection in
the mirror. She was wearing one of the gowns Lytham had
had made for her and sent to the house by the sea, for the
maids had packed them with her own and she had not realised until they were at Lynston Cottage. The gown was
fashioned of heavy silk in a dark amber shade, very similar
to the one she had worn the afternoon that Lytham went
missing.

He was dining with them at the cottage that evening, and

she wondered if the gown she was wearing might help to trigger something in his memory. She could not wish him never to remember, though she knew that when he did he might turn from her in disgust. However, she had decided that she must risk that happening. To run away now would be cowardly. Besides, she loved him and it might be that he would never remember that he had meant her to be his mistress and not his wife.

Chapter Twelve

Emma saw a rather lovely woman picking yellow chrysanthemums in the garden of the Dower House as she approached the next morning. The weather was fine though chilly, and she was wearing a thick cloak over her gown, the hood pulled up over her head, but the woman picking flowers was wearing only a shawl as she placed them in her basket. She glanced up as Emma's shoes made a scrunching sound on the gravel, seeming startled at first and then resigned.

'Good morning, Miss Sommerton,' she said. 'I have been expecting you to call, though I was not sure you would want to meet me socially.'

'You are Lady Lynston?' Emma asked and received a nod in return. She knew instantly why her brother had fallen in love with this young woman, for she had large, soulful eyes that seemed to speak of an inner sadness, reminding Emma of a puppy Tom had once rescued from drowning and brought home. 'I am very pleased to meet you. Why should I not be?'

'You must know that I was the cause of your brother's disgrace?'

'I do not think that is quite the case,' Emma replied

gently. 'My brother is a man of some four and twenty years, and well able to choose for himself. Besides, it was some-one else who accused him of being a cheat—and as for the suspicion of murder, that never came to anything. My father was furious, of course, and it caused the split between them, but if had not been that it would have been something else. They were always out of sorts with one another, perhaps because they both have a temper when roused.'

Maria's dark brown eyes rested on Emma's face for a moment longer and then she smiled. 'Tom assured me I would like you,' she said. 'I should have come to see you before this, but I was afraid that you would be angry with me.'

Emma judged her to be two or three years older than Tom, perhaps a little more, but she had the kind of face that would be beautiful until the day she died, with high cheekbones and slanting eyes, the lashes long and silky against the cream and rose of her skin. Her hair was a reddish brown and pulled flat on the top of her head, curled into a large knot at the nape of her neck, as though she tried to hide her beauty by every means she could.

'I believe Tom cares for you,' Emma said. 'Therefore I could not be angry with you, Maria. I came to visit you in the hope that we shall be friends.'

'Yes, I think we may,' Maria said. 'I must admit I have been lonely here for the last year or two, though Lady Agatha invites me to dine from time to time, but it will be pleasant to have the company of a young woman.'

'Lytham is to give a dance to celebrate our engagement,' Emma said. 'I hope that you will come, Maria?'

'I have not been into company since…the accident,' she said and looked uncertain. 'Do you think I ought? I mean…there was a great deal of scandal after my husband was thrown from his horse.'

'I am certain you should,' Emma assured her. 'It would be a shame if you were to live in seclusion for the rest of your life. Indeed, I shall not allow it. If we are to be friends, I must insist that you come to my dance.'

Maria laughed softly. 'How refreshingly positive you are,' she said. 'I am not surprised Lytham is in love with you. I thought he would never marry. I am so glad that he has found you, Emma, and I shall be very happy to come to your dance. Now, will you come in and share a dish of tea with me?'

The morning spent with his lawyers had proved more than useful, Lytham thought as he walked down Bond Street towards the jewellers that he had been told he usually patronised. He was in a better position to understand his own affairs than he had been, and could now direct his attention towards the matter of a ring and a gift for Emma.

'You might have let me know you were alive!' An indignant voice accosted him, the gentleman's hand clasping his shoulder from behind. 'Damn it, Alex! I knew you were missing, but until I went to White's last night I had not heard that you had been found. Now I see you as large as life and still no word from you.'

Lytham turned, looking at the young man who was grinning at him, his words more accusing than his expression. He was blond, blue-eyed and extremely handsome and Lytham felt instinctively that he was fond of this man, who was perhaps five years his junior.

'Forgive me,' he said. 'I would have if…'

'If you had thought about it, I suppose,' Toby Edgerton said. 'It's as well that the wedding invitations have not gone out. I've a good mind not to send you one for your neglect.'

'I hope you won't cast me off. I am in need of friends,' Lytham said a trifle ruefully. 'Since you are about to be married and an expert on such things, tell me what I ought to buy as an engagement gift.'

'So you're going to marry the beauty,' Toby said his grin widening. 'I knew it when you asked me to invite her and the Merry Widow to my engagement dance. Mrs Flynn has married Howard, so I hear. They have taken the sister and gone off abroad for a while, but I dare say Miss Sommerton has already told you that?'

'I do not think Emma has had a letter from Mrs Flynn, though it may be waiting for her. I must hope that Tom will send her letters on when he reaches his estate.'

'Tom Sommerton? Given it back to him, have you? Of course I knew you would—you never wanted the damned thing in the first place. If Sommerton hadn't behaved so badly that evening you would never have allowed him to wager it, but we all knew he could never cover a half of what he had wagered. Anyone else would have had him thrown out of the club as a cheat. Still, all's well that ends well, what?'

'Yes, certainly,' Lytham said. 'I was thinking of visiting a jeweller's this morning, but that will keep—shall we go to the club together?'

'On my way there,' Toby agreed easily. 'I thought I might have a little work out later.' He gave Lytham a playful punch in the arm. 'You look as if it would do you no harm to go a few rounds in the ring.'

'Why not?' Lytham replied and smiled lazily.

'Morning, Lytham. Good to see you in town. Toby—I hope to see you and the lovely Miss Dawlish at my house next week.'

'Of course, Hattersly. Lucy is looking forward to it. In the country at the moment with her Mama but she'll be back next week.'

'I trust you are well, Hattersly,' Lytham said, thinking

that this chance meeting with Toby was a piece of good fortune. The young man must be Tobias Edgerton, for he had looked through his engagement book at his town house and recalled the name, also that Toby was engaged to a Miss Lucy Dawlish. He was learning much that he needed to know—and without telling his friend that he had lost his memory, something he was reluctant to do unless he was forced.

'You were remarkably polite to Hattersly,' Toby remarked as they moved on. 'First time I've known you to do more than nod to him in passing.'

'I must be mellowing,' Lytham said and raised his brows, his mouth curving in a mocking smile. 'I dare say it is because I almost died.'

'There was some talk of a shooting,' Toby said. 'Sounded rather suspicious to me—something about a court-martial while you were serving abroad?'

'We all thought Pennington had died in a bar brawl in Spain,' Lytham replied. 'The man carried a grudge against me—if it hadn't been for Tom Sommerton I might have been dead, if not of my wounds then of drowning.'

'Good grief,' Toby said looking amazed. 'That's a turn up—after the scandal with your brother.'

'Tom Sommerton was quite blameless in that,' Lytham replied. 'He has a cast-iron alibi for the afternoon John was thrown, and I do not for a moment believe he ever cheated at the card table. That tale was my brother's doing—and I dare say you may guess the reason behind it, though I am not at liberty to say.'

'Well, it just goes to show…' Toby said. 'We all thought Sommerton had gone for good after his father threw him out. What had he been doing?'

'I believe he went abroad,' Lytham replied vaguely. 'Now tell me—when is the wedding to be?'

Toby began to describe all the arrangements for his wedding in great detail as they walked. He was hailed by several gentlemen, and answered all of them by their names. As most of them also addressed Lytham he was able to add their faces to the growing list of his acquaintances. A very little persuasion brought more personal details from his companion, which helped him to form a picture of these men and the way they fitted into his former life.

It seemed that he was rather particular and had few close friendships. Most were no more than acquaintances, and he was able to merely nod in passing when addressed by strangers without causing undue offence.

At White's, where it seemed he was a member, and welcomed by the staff, who said they were glad to see him back, he was able to pick up the names of the gentlemen they met from the general conversation going on about him. He and Toby bespoke a light nuncheon, and then refused the offer of a game of cards, taking themselves off to the club run by a former professional pugilist. Here again, Lytham discovered that he was known and welcomed by the owner, who offered to spar with him for a few rounds.

'You look as if you need the exercise, my lord. You've lost some muscle and need to build your strength up again.'

'He would do better to spar with me, George,' Toby said. 'You'll be too much for him. He's been ill, you know.'

'You would hardly be a match for Lytham,' a voice drawled behind them. 'From what I've heard you are something of a pugilist, Lytham. I should be pleased to go a few rounds with you—if you want some real sport.'

'Good grief, Lindisfarne,' Toby said and looked sick. 'Don't take his challenge, Lytham. You're not up to his weight at the moment, he'll slaughter you.'

'Indeed?' Lytham was not sure why that name had put his hackles up, but he knew instinctively that he did not

like or trust this man, and also that he would never dream
of refusing a challenge from him. 'I think Toby is right and
I am a little out of form, sir—but if you care to indulge me
I shall accept your challenge.'

'Mistake…' Toby hissed. 'Man hates you.'

'Then I shall be on my guard,' Lytham replied in a similar whisper.

Stripped to the waist and eyeing his opponent minutes
later in the ring, Lytham knew immediately that this was
not to be a friendly bout. Lindisfarne was out for blood,
and he sensed that there was some quarrel between them,
though of course he did not remember it.

They began to spar equally enough, each man landing a
hit about the other's body to the encouraging praise of Gentleman George as the prize-fighter was generally known.
He had been a much-admired champion in his day and, like
others who had excelled in the sport, now earned his living
teaching gentlemen to fight.

'A little sharper, Lytham,' he commanded. 'You are giving your opponent too much time and space to come at
you. Lord Lindisfarne—you are aiming too low. Above the
belt, please, gentlemen.'

'Watch him, Alex,' warned Toby as Lindisfarne suddenly came at him with a flurry of blows. 'He's a sly hitter.
He'll catch you if you don't watch…' He groaned as the
blows found their mark, sending Lytham stumbling back
so that he lost his balance and fell on his back, his head
hitting the floor with a resounding crack that appeared to
knock him out. 'I warned you!'

Climbing into the ring as Gentleman George held Lindisfarne at bay, Toby bent over his friend anxiously, patting
his face and crying his name. Lytham's eyes flickered and
then opened. He grinned and put a hand to his cheek.

'That was a cracking facer,' he said. 'Not from you,

Toby? The last time I fought you—you couldn't swat a fly.'

'If you're going to insult me, I shan't warn you in future,' Toby said, greatly relieved by his friend's mockery. 'I told you—you aren't up to Lindisfarne's weight yet. You've lost a couple of stone by the looks of you while you were ill.'

'Lindisfarne…' Lytham looked beyond him to where Gentleman George was handing his opponent a towel to dry himself. 'Did he knock me down? I must have been in a daze, can't seem to remember.'

'I warned you not to fight him.' Toby gave him a mournful look. 'But naturally you wouldn't listen, but that's no more than usual, of course.'

'Naturally,' Lytham said and smiled. 'Give me a hand up, Toby. I must congratulate Lindisfarne on his win.'

He was feeling a little odd as he got to his feet, his memory seeming to have strange gaps in it. What on earth was he doing here—and why had he agreed to go a few rounds with Lindisfarne? The man was a disgrace and after his behaviour towards Mrs Flynn and Emma…

Emma! Good lord! What must she be thinking?

Lytham went through the motions of shaking hands with his opponent, his mind working frantically as he tried to make sense of his thoughts. Why was he here? Surely he had been with Emma at his mother's house…and then he was shot! He remembered turning as Pennington spoke and the gun had gone off almost immediately, giving him no chance to avoid the ball. The force of it in his shoulder had sent him staggering towards the edge of the cliffs and then he had known no more until he woke to find himself being tended by an old woman. He recalled his thoughts to the present with some difficulty.

'Splendid hit, Lindisfarne,' he said, his expression giving

nothing away. 'Perhaps you will allow me my chance of revenge another time?'

'Any time you like,' Lindisfarne sneered and went off towards the dressing rooms.

'You are out of condition, my lord,' Gentleman George said, giving Lytham a severe look. 'I believe you have been ill, my lord. You must begin a regimen to recover your muscle strength, and refrain from boxing over your weight until you are completely well again.'

'Thank you, George. I shall be pleased to follow the routine you set me when I first came to you—though I am planning on returning to the country soon.'

'Come to me when you can, my lord. If you were in peak condition, you would not have been such an easy target for the earl.'

'No…' Lytham moved his jaw gingerly. 'Yet I think I have learned something from him.'

He had left Emma to walk alone—why? Good grief! Now he remembered it all. What must she think of his behaviour? He shook his head as if to clear it, but the memory of those last moments remained to haunt him, not a hallucination then, but a product of his damnable humour!

'You can't be serious about going another round with Lindisfarne?' Toby asked after Lytham had taken a shower beneath the pump. 'I thought you despised the man?'

'Yes, I do, don't I?' Lytham said and grinned at him. The cold water had done its work, helping to refresh his mind and clear the last remnants of confusion. 'All the more reason to teach him a lesson, don't you think, my friend?'

He was feeling wonderful as the last gaps began to fill up in his memory, because now he could remember the man he had been before his illness and everything that had happened since.

He recalled Emma's embarrassed confession that he had not asked her to be his wife. What an intolerable position he had left her in! She must have been in torment since his disappearance. It was little wonder that she had been at her wit's end! Or that she had accepted his aunt's invitation to stay with her.

Because of his damnable behaviour she had been left without a home, and if the truth were known concerning her situation, a loss of reputation from which she could not hope to recover. She could not possibly have told his aunt what she believed to be her true situation, and must have suffered terribly at being forced to live what she thought was a lie. And it was his fault!

How alone and desperate she must have felt before his aunt took her home with her, and bless Agatha for acting so sensibly. He shuddered to think what might have happened to Emma had his great-aunt not taken her under her wing. And all because he had been enjoying a jest, amusing himself at Emma's expense! It would serve him right if she turned from him with the disgust she was entitled to feel.

Yet she had agreed to marry him. Was it because she loved him? Surely she must to have agreed to his outrageous offer in the first place?

What had possessed him to make it? If he had thought it a jest, it was in very poor taste. No, he seemed to recall that he had been testing her, to discover whether or not she truly cared for him. He might have married a score of respectable young ladies, some of them rather beautiful, but none of them had touched his heart, nor had they loved him. His position in Society and his fortune had made him a good catch—and Emma's manner had often been reserved towards him. The plain truth was that he had not been sure of her feelings towards him...until that afternoon.

He remembered kissing her, the way she had melted into

his embrace, giving herself up to him with such honesty and such loving trust that he had been horrified at what he had done. His passion had been such that he dare not confess his true intentions to her for fear that he would not be able to control his longing to make love to her. He had gone out to take the air and gain control of his feelings…and disappeared! Emma must have been distraught.

He ought to tell her at once that he had regained his memory, to explain and apologise, but if he did that she would be embarrassed—and he feared that her reaction would be to run away from him. He knew that he could not bear to lose her now, and must marry her even if she despised him for the wicked devil he was—had been. The prospect of life without her was intolerable, for he could never return to the aimless life he had known before meeting her. Something had changed in him, though he did not know whether it was his illness or the love he felt for Emma that had brought about this change.

He had never loved anyone as he did Emma. He had loved his mother as a child, but she had been a cold, reserved woman and he had soon learned not to run to her with a cut knee. His father's hatred had taught him never to expect a kind word, and his experience with the women he made his mistresses had been that he must pay for favours.

Emma had given so much of herself with little reason to trust him, and he could not risk losing her. Perhaps it would be better to keep the return of his memory a secret until after they were married.

'You look lovely, Emma,' said Lady Agatha, complimenting her on the new gown she was to wear that evening. Lytham had ordered it for her in town from a dressmaker she had used in the past and it fitted her perfectly. 'That colour becomes you, my dear. I like that shade of midnight blue on you, and the style is a little out of the ordinary.'

Emma smiled and thanked her. They were staying at the Hall for Christmas to make entertaining their guests more convenient. Lady Agatha had told her it was Lytham's habit to invite her for a few days at that time of year, and indeed Emma had not wanted to decline. She had found nothing but pleasure in her developing relationship with Lytham these past weeks, and had almost managed to quell any doubts. He was unfailingly courteous, always considerate, and she had already known that he could be a charming companion.

They had discovered many pastimes in which they shared a common interest, including poetry and literature, attending the theatre and listening to good music. They rode nearly every day when the weather permitted and dined together at least three times a week, either at Lady Agatha's home or the Hall.

Emma had been persuaded to make a list of all the changes she considered necessary to the main reception rooms and had found it a task she thoroughly enjoyed. There was much to do to make it a comfortable family home, and she looked forward to continuing her work over the coming months and years. Already new curtains ordered from an exclusive establishment in town had arrived for the drawing room and the rich shade of crimson, banded with gold braid, had given the huge chamber more warmth and colour.

Lytham had ordered a suite of furniture in the style of Mr Chippendale to replace the worn sofas that had begun to look sadly weary. Yet in many of the rooms Emma had decided that rearranging the existing pieces, but adding to them small comforts such as cushions and flowers, had made all the change necessary.

'Yes, I like this shade of blue,' Emma said in reply to Lady Agatha's earlier remark. 'I had something similar made when I was in town—but this certainly has more style. I dare say it was expensive.'

'What does that matter? You deserve a little spoiling, my dear.' Lady Agatha smiled at her benevolently. 'You must wear the pearls Lytham sent you, Emma. They are a family heirloom and given to brides on the day of their engagement. My nephew consulted me on what he ought to send for from the bank and I thought of the pearls—though I believe he intends to make a personal gift of some kind.'

'Oh, no,' Emma disclaimed. 'I have already been spoiled shamefully.'

'And why not?' Agatha Lynston demanded, her eyes bright and decidedly wicked. 'Lytham has far more than is strictly necessary. It will do him good to spend some of it on you.'

Emma laughed. 'Why are you so good to me, ma'am? I am sure I do not deserve it.'

'I never did hear such nonsense,' Lady Agatha replied. 'You are both lovely and good-natured, and my nephew is very fortunate to have secured you as his bride. Well, I shall go down now and leave you to finish your toilette— do not be long, my dear.'

Emma smiled, but said no more. She had almost stilled her doubts concerning her relationship with Lytham, or at least banished them to a far corner of her mind. Surely his manner towards her showed a deep tenderness? And, if he loved her, would it not simply spoil things if she told him the truth now? Her conscience pricked her from time to time, but she had decided it was something she must live with for the present.

She fastened the shorter length of pearls about her throat, choosing between the three strings of large, lustrous beads.

Each one had a diamond clasp, and all three could be linked together if so desired by a diamond pendent. However, she preferred the simple choker, which sat neatly at the base of her throat. She was just preparing to leave the room when Lytham knocked at the door and asked if he might be admitted. His eyes went over her appreciatively as she opened to him, resting on her face for a moment.

'You look beautiful,' he said. 'The Lytham pearls look well on you, Emma. They were Aunt Agatha's suggestion, but I thought this might improve upon tradition.'

He handed her a small box with an oval-humped lid, which she opened to discover a bangle of pearls and diamonds.

'Oh, that is lovely,' Emma said, slipping it over her hand so that it hung loosely on her wrist and holding it up for him to admire. 'Thank you. It is a wonderful surprise and goes well with the necklace.'

'And it is your own, never worn by any other Lytham bride,' he said. 'Now your hand please, my love.'

She offered him her hand and he removed the diamond cluster from her finger, replacing it with a large clear sapphire surrounded by fine diamonds.

'There, that is much better.'

The small diamond cluster lay abandoned on the dressing table, but Emma slipped it on to her right hand. 'Your ring is beautiful, Lytham, but I think this has become like a part of me. I shall continue to wear it, if you do not mind?'

'You may do as you wish, Emma.' He reached out to touch her cheek, moving a wisp of hair that curled in a tiny ringlet at her ear. 'You must know that I want only to make you happy?'

'Thank you.' She blushed at the tenderness in his eyes. 'I am very happy.' Her eyes gazed up at him, searching for any sign that he might have changed his mind and finding none. 'If you are still content?'

'How could I be otherwise, Emma? You are the woman I have waited for my whole life.'

Emma's hand trembled slightly as his strong fingers closed about it. She smiled and allowed him to lead her from the room.

'Tom brought me a letter from my mother when he came this morning,' she said. 'She is well and enjoying herself. She says that the Heathstones have invited her to make her home with them, but she may wish to go home when she knows that Tom is living there. I shall write at once and tell her.'

'And your own news, I trust? She may wish to return for the wedding. You know that your mother will always be welcome to stay with us for as long as she wishes?'

'You are very good.'

'Not at all. I think myself fortunate to have found you, Emma, and your family's happiness is my pleasure, not a duty.'

Her heart was full and she would have said more, but they had reached the drawing room where Tom, Lady Agatha and Maria were waiting for them. Tom was standing next to Maria and from his deferential manner as he listened to something she was saying, Emma thought it likely that Lytham was right concerning his intentions towards her. If Maria were his choice, she would not object, for she wanted him to be happy.

'Oh, you do look lovely,' Maria said as Emma went up to her and kissed her cheek.

'I'm so glad you came,' Emma said. 'Your dress is most attractive, Maria. Is it new?'

'No. I had it made some time ago, but I have not had the occasion to wear it.'

'Well, I think that shade of green is very much your colour.'

'Thank you. I like what you've done with the house. I was never allowed to make changes.' For a moment Maria's eyes were shadowed by unhappy memories. 'But I am delighted to see the changes you have made, Emma.'

'Lytham says I have not done half enough,' she replied and threw a laughing glance at him. 'But I have hardly started yet.'

Their guests had begun to arrive. Some were staying in the house and had waited to come down until their hosts were ready to receive them, some were at the houses of neighbours or other houses on the estate. One of the first to arrive was Toby Edgerton, his fiancée and her mother.

Watching Lytham's easy manner with his friend, Emma realised that he was very much more at ease than he had been in the first few days after his reappearance, but that was only natural. He was looking much better now, more like he had been before the illness that had almost ended his life.

She had noticed a slight difference in his manner when he returned from his visit to London, but had assumed that he was beginning to feel more at home with himself. He had told her that he had met several old friends in London, but she noticed that there was no awkwardness in his greeting to any of the guests. He was behaving exactly as if he had known them all his life.

He had known many of these people for a long time, of course, but he seemed so easy in his manner with them that Emma was slightly puzzled. She still found it difficult to recall everyone she had met since coming to Lytham Hall, and some of the guests were completely unknown to her. Yet Lytham seemed to have no difficulty in identifying them, or in finding some mutual topic of conversation.

'You look anxious, Miss Sommerton,' Stephen Antrium said to her and she turned to look at him. 'Is something bothering you?'

'Oh, it is nothing,' she said and smiled at him. 'I was merely wondering how Lytham is managing to remember everyone.'

'I believe he has spent many hours memorising names and facts,' Stephen replied. 'And he has visited every house in the district where we are on terms with the owners since his return.'

'Oh, I see,' Emma said and turned away as Toby Edgerton and Lucy Dawlish came up to her. 'Thank you, Stephen.'

'You look beautiful,' Toby said and he kissed Emma's cheek. 'You and Lucy will have much in common—our wedding next month, you know. I hope you and Lytham mean to come to it?'

'You must know that we could not possibly miss it,' Emma said and kissed Lucy on the cheek. 'That is a pretty dress, Lucy. You must tell me the name of your dressmaker.'

'Yes, of course,' Lucy replied and dimpled. 'That is if I can recall it—I have bought so many new dresses that I cannot remember exactly where every one came from.'

'Her papa swears she will ruin him,' Toby said. 'But I don't care if she spends a fortune on pretty things—she is worth every penny.'

'I am glad to hear it,' Emma said and laughed as they passed on and more guests came to greet her.

It was some time before she was released from greeting newcomers to mingle with the guests, who were drinking champagne and waiting for the dancing to begin. Card tables had been set up in another room, but most of the younger men had already been selecting their partners for the various dances.

Emma was to open the dancing with Lytham, of course, and they had selected a waltz as the first of the evening. Emma smiled as he bowed and asked her formally for the pleasure of taking her on the floor, enjoying the sensation of being held close to his heart as he gracefully whirled her about the room.

'We danced like this once before,' she told him. 'In Bath, I believe?'

'In my dreams I have held you in my arms many times, Emma.'

'Or was it in London—at Toby's engagement ball? I cannot perfectly remember.'

'Perhaps we danced then and in Bath,' Lytham said, gazing down at her face. 'What are you thinking, Emma?'

'Just that I like dancing with you,' she said and smiled up at him. It was foolish of her to test him like this. If he had recovered his memory, he would surely have told her. Why should he not?

'Then I shall dance with you all night and no one else.'

'You cannot do that,' she replied and shook her head at him. 'You have guests and you must ask the young ladies to dance, and Maria. Yes, you *must* dance with her, Lytham.'

'I shall certainly dance with Maria,' he said. 'It would not do to ignore her or to seem to slight her. I noticed that one or two ladies were a little distant with her when they arrived. I would not have her ostracised so I must do my utmost to show that I approve of her—and your brother, Emma. I have set certain rumours in circulation in London, and I hope to repair much of the damage to Tom's reputation very shortly.'

'That woman in the crimson gown,' Emma said. 'Lady

Leamington, I think…I noticed that she was very frosty towards Maria.'

'Lady Leamington is an old tabby,' Lytham replied. 'I understand she actually cut you in Bath, Emma, but I believe she had changed her tune this evening.'

'She was quite friendly,' Emma said. 'Yes, I remember now—she did cut me the evening that you took Lady Agatha home early.'

'My aunt reminded me of it,' he said. 'We were bound to invite her, because she is a distant cousin of sorts—but you need have little to do with her except at such affairs as these, Emma. She will not expect to be invited to weekends. We have never been on those terms.'

'I am glad to hear it. I cannot say I like her.' She supposed he could have learned these things from his aunt, but it gave her pause to wonder. Just how much of Lytham's memory had returned to him?

They completed the rest of their dance in silence, and then Emma was claimed by a succession of gentlemen who wished to dance with her. She danced with Lytham again just before supper and he took her into supper afterwards, where they were joined by Toby Edgerton, Lucy and several more of the younger guests.

Emma was talking to Lucy about her extensive shopping trips, some of which had been in Paris, and she was not immediately aware of the conversation between some of the gentlemen, until a burst of laughter caught her attention.

'Lytham was out of condition, of course, or Lindisfarne could never have landed him a facer,' Toby was saying. 'I look forward to the return bout. If I'm any judge, Lytham will teach him a lesson once he is fully fit again.'

'I believe I am almost that now,' Lytham replied. 'I shall not go out of my way to challenge Lindisfarne, but I must admit I do not much care for him.'

'You told me once you thought he was a blustering bully and a blaggard,' Toby said. 'It would do him good to be on the wrong side of a thrashing.'

'Personally, I would like to take a horsewhip to the man,' a gentleman who had his back towards Emma said harshly. 'I never could stand the fellow. I remember the time you went ten rounds with that black, Lytham. No one would take a bet on you—they all thought he must win because he was a professional—but you knocked him down in the end. How did you manage it? He was bigger and heavier than you.'

'It's all a matter of science,' Lytham replied and laughed. 'You have to watch your opponent, learn where his weakness is while keeping on your toes and out of reach—then when you are sure of him, you go in for the kill. The black was heavy and a bruising fighter but he had one fault. He had a habit of dropping his guard every so often. I waited and then I went straight in and it took only the one punch to lay him out.'

The colour drained from Emma's cheeks as she heard the general laughter. It was an amusing story, more suited to a gentleman's club perhaps, but she did not object to a little sporting talk—but how could Lytham have remembered in such detail?

And why had he not told her about the sparring bout he had taken part in with Lindisfarne? Was it over her? Had Lindisfarne insulted her?

'Is something the matter?' Lucy Dawlish inquired. 'You look quite pale, Emma.'

'I believe I am a little warm,' Emma replied, turning hot now as a tide of embarrassment washed over her. If Lytham had regained his memory, he must remember that afternoon at his mother's house! 'Would you excuse me, Lucy? I think I shall go upstairs and tidy myself.'

'Yes, it is warm at these affairs, isn't it?' Lucy said. 'I think I shall follow your example, Emma. My cheeks feel quite pink.'

Emma was forced to accompany Lucy upstairs, but at the top they parted and Emma hurried to her own bedchamber, where she splashed water on her heated cheeks and looked at herself in the mirror. Was it true—had Lytham's memory finally returned? And when had it happened? He had said nothing to her...made no mention of that afternoon.

When she thought about it, she had noticed an increase of confidence on his return from London, yet she had not really taken so much notice until this evening. It was his manner towards Toby that had alerted her. She had always known that they were very good friends and the warmth between them was apparent. Could their relationship have reached such ease if Lytham was not able to remember him?

Somehow she did not think that was possible. So that meant he remembered Toby well enough to feel at ease with him. She knew that some things had come back to him from time to time—but to remember so much of a boxing match? No, she did not think that held true. Did that mean that Lytham had remembered all his past life? If that was indeed the case, why had he not spoken to her of the afternoon when she had so nearly become his mistress? Was he waiting for her to confess it to him?

She pressed her hands against her cheeks, feeling the shame wash over her. What must he be thinking of her? Her first wild thought was to flee from the house so that she need not face him, but then in an instant she knew it was impossible. She could not make the situation worse by causing a dreadful scandal on the evening of their engagement. She must wait a little longer and then...she did not know what the outcome must be, but she must obviously ask him for the truth and be prepared for his scorn when he told her that he knew her terrible secret.

She finished tidying herself and left her bedchamber, going back down to the ballroom, where everyone was assembling for the dancing again. She was engaged for the next several dances and it was not until the guests were beginning to take their leave that Lytham came to her.

'I believe everyone enjoyed themselves,' he said, looking down at her. 'I hope you found the evening pleasant, Emma? It is good to have friends to visit sometimes, is it not?'

'Yes, of course, my lord. Lucy and Toby seem very happy. She is excited about the wedding, of course.'

'Yes.' He frowned as he caught the note of reserve in her voice. 'Is something wrong, my love?'

'No, of course not. Why should something be wrong? The evening went extremely well.'

'I meant with you—you seem not quite as happy as you were. Has something upset you?'

It was her chance to have it out with him, but now was not the time. 'You are quite wrong, Lytham,' she said. 'It is merely that I am a little tired and shall be glad to seek my bed.'

'I see.' He took her hand and kissed it. 'Then I wish you goodnight, Emma, and may your dreams be sweet.'

'Thank you—and yours also,' she said, but as she walked away from him she knew that her dreams would be anything but sweet. It would be a wonder if she could sleep at all!

Chapter Thirteen

After some considerable persuasion Maria had agreed to go with Emma to London for the wedding of Toby Edgerton and Lucy Dawlish. She had been reluctant at first, but when Emma explained that Lady Agatha had cried off she had agreed.

'Then I cannot refuse you,' she said and laughed. 'How can I? For otherwise you would have no chaperon, Emma. How shocking that would be. And my consequence can do so much for you.'

She was teasing, of course, and they laughed together. For Maria suspected that Emma's pleading was as much for her sake as her own. She and Lytham had clearly hit upon the plan of reintroducing her into the broader society of London and she could not deny their kindness: especially if she did not wish to spend the rest of her life in seclusion at Lytham.

Emma laughed at her friend's teasing, but was reminded of what had gone before and a faint blush came to her cheeks. Maria would not think it so very funny if she knew the truth!

As yet Emma had had no opportunity of speaking to Lytham about the recovery of his memory. Some of their guests had stayed on over Christmas, and afterwards Lytham had had business that had taken him elsewhere for some days, making it impossible for her to see him alone. Now they were here in London to attend the wedding of his particular friend and it was certain that Emma could not make a fuss until that was over and they returned to the country. She was not sure what she ought to do then—unless she confessed her shame to Lytham and took the consequences.

She had almost settled it in her mind that she would do so at the first opportunity and because of that she had withdrawn from him slightly. It would not do to show her feelings too plainly, for there might be painful decisions to be made in the near future.

She was dressing for a ball given by friends of Lord and Lady Dawlish two nights before the wedding when Lytham sent up a note to tell her that he would not be able to escort her and Maria.

Forgive me, but something has come to my attention, he had written. *I shall hope to join you later in the evening. I am sorry to inconvenience you, but there is no reason why you and Maria should not attend alone.*

'How provoking,' Maria said when Emma told her. 'It is always so much more comfortable to have a gentleman with one, is it not?'

'Yes—but Bridget and I went to parties without an escort, Maria. It is perfectly proper for you to do so and I am scarcely a green girl. I was Bridget Flynn's companion.'

'Yes, I know.' Maria refrained from saying more, but Emma understood how she felt.

'I believe it must have been important or Lytham would not have cried off at the last moment,' Emma said. 'Shall we stay home?'

Maria hesitated, then lifted her head, a martial light in her eyes.

'No, we shall not,' she said. 'We have neither of us done anything wrong and I do not see why we should cower at home and hide our heads just because Lytham is not there to lend us his consequence.'

'Bravo,' Emma said and smiled. 'That is exactly my own feeling, but I would not have forced it on you.'

'I must make an effort,' Maria said, her eyes dark with remembered sadness. 'There was so much scandal after John died and I felt responsible—but I refuse to hide away for the rest of my life. We shall go and be damned to the gossips!'

The ballroom was hot and crowded. Emma had been aware of some curious stares from certain of the dowagers as she and Maria entered alone, but although one or two had given them rather frosty looks, most people had been friendly.

Toby had named his friend a very scoundrel for not having sent him word. 'For I could easily have called for you. Lucy would not have minded coming with her mama,' he said. 'But now that you are here you will naturally join our party.'

His care of them had made it very much easier for he had danced with them both, and other gentlemen had not been long in seeking to add their names to both cards, once it was seen that Maria was willing to dance.

Emma had been dancing for most of the evening, but she had kept the supper dance free on purpose in case Lytham arrived. However, he had not done so by the time the music struck up and she decided that she would go out on to the balcony for a few minutes to cool herself before supper.

It was provoking of Lytham to stay away so long, almost

the whole evening was over and she missed him. She realised that if she were forced to leave him eventually it would
break her heart.

The balcony overlooked a very pretty garden with some
exciting statuary and what would be magnificent rose beds
in the summer. One thing she had not yet started to improve
at Lytham was the garden, but she would begin that in the
spring…if she was still there.

'So you are alone,' a voice said behind her, startling her.
She spun round to find herself staring at a man she had
hoped never to see again. 'Has he deserted you for his
mistress already? Or is a whisper I heard the truth—that
you were his mistress?'

Emma's face drained of colour as she looked at Lindisfarne. 'You have no right to speak to me like this,' she said
and tried to go past him and back into the ballroom. He
moved to prevent her, a sneer on his lips. 'Please allow me
to pass, sir.'

'When I am ready,' he said and the menace in his voice
sent a shiver through her. 'You were always a proud bitch,
Emma Sommerton, but undoubtedly a beauty. If you had
had Bridget's money, I might have married you.'

'I do not wish to listen to this,' Emma said. 'I prefer to
have nothing to do with you. Now allow me to pass. I
refuse to listen to any more of—'

'You will do as you're told, damn you,' he hissed, his
hand snaking out to grasp her wrist in a viselike grip. 'We
have some unfinished business, you and I, Emma Sommerton.' He was pushing her backwards, away from the
light to a dark corner of the balcony. She struggled, but his
hold on her was too strong and she felt herself knocked
against the wall, a cry of protest breaking from her as his
mouth came down on hers.

Emma gagged in disgust as he tried to invade her mouth

with his tongue, pushing at him and struggling for all she was worth as his hands clawed at the neck of her gown.

'Scream if you want to,' he suggested. 'It will make a fine scandal—especially when I tell everyone that you were my mistress before you became Lytham's.'

'That is a lie!' Emma cried and clawed at his face. He pulled back from her, putting a hand to the wound and looking at the blood on his fingers in disbelief. 'No one would believe you.'

'I'll make you pay for that...'

Lindisfarne raised his fist to strike her, but even as he did so Emma heard a growling noise and then someone grabbed Lindisfarne's arm and spun him round. In the next instant that same person threw a punch that floored the earl, splitting his lip.

'Damn you, Lytham,' he muttered as he lay sprawled at Emma's feet. 'You will meet me for this!'

'Willingly,' Lytham replied, eyes glittering in the light of the moon which had that moment sailed out from behind the clouds, giving a ghostly yellow backdrop to the scene Emma found so terrifying. 'In the ring, with swords or pistols, at your convenience.'

'No...' Emma cried, covering her face with her hands. 'You must not fight over me.' But she was not truly aware of what they were saying, feeling too embarrassed and ashamed to listen to what passed between them.

'This swine deserves to be taught a lesson he will not forget,' Lytham said, his face white with anger. Emma had never seen him look like this and she trembled. 'Well, Lindisfarne—name your pleasure.'

The earl had struggled to his feet, though it was clear he was still suffering from the effects of the blow that had made his lip bleed profusely.

'They tell me you are a better shot than a swordsman—

so I'll take the swords,' he sneered. 'That was a lucky blow, Lytham, I was not expecting it. But a thrashing in the ring is not satisfactory. Because of you and your whore, I lost the chance of a fortune.'

'You will do me the honour of asking your seconds to call upon me,' Lytham said in a voice that would have cut glass. 'Let me assure you that it will give me great pleasure to instruct you in the art of swordplay, Lindisfarne. Someone ought to have taught you to mind your manners years ago.' He gripped Emma's arm, propelling her towards the door that led back inside. 'I think we should leave. The stench out here is appalling.'

Emma allowed him to take her back inside. She was feeling bemused and confused over what had gone on out there—all that talk of a thrashing in the ring and fencing lessons. She had been so shocked that she was not really sure what the two men had said to one another. All she could think about was the tear at the neck of her gown and was praying that it would not be noticed. She held her fan in front of her in an effort to hide it.

'What on earth possessed you to go out there with him?' Lytham growled next to her ear.

'Nothing would have persuade me to do so,' Emma replied in a shocked whisper. 'How can you think it? I went out for some air and he must have followed me. Until he accosted me I did not even know he was here this evening.'

Lytham said no more, but a nerve was working in his throat as he led her through the ballroom to a small chamber near by that was for the moment deserted.

'Did he hurt you?' he asked in a softer tone.

'No, not very much. My gown is a little torn, but I have a pin in my reticule.'

'I shall send for your cloak. If Maria is not ready to leave, I dare say Toby will escort her home.'

'I am sure she will be ready.' Emma was upset and beginning to be angry now. 'She was not sure whether we ought to come alone, and now I think she was right. I am sure Lindisfarne would not have dared to act so badly if you had escorted us.'

'Perhaps not.' He saw the proud tilt of her head and understood her feelings. 'You are angry with me, Emma. Forgive me. My business was important or I would not have cried off.'

'It is not that alone.' She felt close to tears, but would not let him see it. 'How could you accuse me of having gone to the balcony with that man? After the way he behaved in Bath I would not have spoken to him unless forced. Indeed, I dislike him intensely.'

'I was angry. I spoke without thinking. Forgive me.'

She turned her face aside, feeling the sting of humiliation. How could he have thought such a thing? Yet she had agreed to be his mistress and a moral woman would have refused. Clearly she had forfeited all right to his respect. She felt the sting of humiliation and could not bear to look at him.

'I should like to leave now please. My head has begun to ache.'

'Yes, of course.' He looked at her anxiously, but she kept her face averted, not wishing him to see her distress. 'I shall send for your cloak and ask Maria to join us here.'

Emma gave him no answer. She was unbearably hurt. If Lytham thought so little of her he could not love her. She had agreed to become his mistress because she loved him, but his behaviour had shown her that he had no respect for her.

Maria joined her a few moments later. Emma had used the opportunity to put a pin in her gown and she was able to greet the other woman naturally.

'Is something wrong, Emma?'

'I have a little headache, nothing more,' Emma replied. 'I am sorry to spoil your evening, Maria.'

'There is nothing to spoil,' Maria assured her. 'It has been pleasant enough, but I am ready to leave. I am sorry you are unwell, Emma. You look rather pale.'

'I shall be better soon.'

They were prevented from saying more by the arrival of servants with their cloaks, closely followed by Lytham. Emma accepted his help, but she did not smile at him as he placed it about her shoulders or when he handed her into the carriage.

The journey to his house in Hanover Square was accomplished in near silence. Maria refrained from chattering because she believed Emma unwell. Emma and Lytham both had their own reasons for remaining silent.

'Emma,' Lytham said as they went into the spacious front hall. It was furnished in the style of Adam; its floor tiled with Italian marble and serviced by a magnificent curving staircase of gilded wood and ironwork. 'May I speak with you for a few moments in private, please?'

'May it wait until the morning?' she asked. 'My head is aching quite badly.'

'Yes, of course, if you wish.' He took her hand and kissed it. 'Please believe me when I say I never wished to cause you pain—not ever. I have always loved you, Emma.'

Emma's heart caught. For a moment she wished that she had agreed to speak with him. Why was he looking at her so oddly?

'We shall talk tomorrow,' she said. 'Goodnight, Lytham.'

'Goodnight, my love.'

Emma ran on up the stairs. Tears were burning behind her eyelids and it was not until she had undressed and sent her maid away that she was able to think properly and to remember. There had been some mention of a fist fight and fencing lessons—but she had been too overcome with shame at Lindisfarne's attack on her to take much notice. What exactly had Lytham said? She had been trying not to listen, but now it was suddenly important that she remember. Lindisfarne had mentioned pistols…Lytham was surely not going to fight a duel?

No, it was impossible! Duels were frowned upon these days. She had heard that the Regent had forbidden them. It would merely be a sporting contest, much like the one that had taken place in the boxing ring. Yet there had been an odd look in his eyes when he bade her goodnight…the way he had told her that he had always loved her… He was going to fight a duel!

Why had she not realised it immediately? But she had been in such distress. She had been so shamed by his apparent lack of respect for her, but that was no longer important. He was going to fight a duel over her. It must not happen. It was so foolish. He had arrived in time to stop the earl really harming her.

She must speak to him at once! She must make him see that this duel was too dangerous. He might be injured. He could die of his wounds. Emma could not bear to contemplate such an eventuality.

She pulled a heavy silk dressing robe over her nightgown and went out into the hall. Candelabra were still burning as her bare feet pattered softly over the thick carpet. She hurried to the room she knew was Lytham's. The door opened almost instantly to her knock and she saw that he had removed his coat, but was still wearing his breeches

and shirt, though it was opened down the front as if he had
been about to remove it.

'Emma—why have you come?'

'I did not realise,' she said. 'Tell me the truth, Lytham.
Are you going to fight a duel with Lindisfarne?'

'Of course. You did not think I would refuse his challenge?'

'I was confused, distressed, and I did not hear perfectly.
I thought it was merely a contest—like the sparring match
you spoke of at our engagement dance.'

'You heard me speak of that?' he asked and frowned.
'You should not be here dressed like that, Emma. Someone
may see you.'

'Do you think I care for that when you may be badly
wounded or killed? I have not forgotten that I was to have
been your mistress, if you have—' She broke off as he
grabbed her arm, pulling her inside and locking the door.

'No, Emma, I am not about to ravish you, though dressed
like that you tempt me sorely. I am making sure that no
one walks in on us. Servants like nothing better than to
gossip. I would not have them hear or see anything they
ought not.'

'You do not deny that what I said was true?'

'Only in that it does not go far enough.' His expression
was grave. 'I must beg your pardon for my despicable behaviour, Emma. I always meant you to be my wife, of
course. It was a jest—no, not even that. I was not sure how
you felt until that afternoon. I suppose I doubted that you
could love me, as I loved you. I wanted to see how far you
would go before you drew back.'

'You had given me no sign that I meant any more to you
than any other woman you had taken as your mistress,' she
replied indignantly.

'Did I not? I must have missed my vocation in life. I should clearly have been an actor.'

'Lytham! You mock me.'

'Only myself, dearest Emma.' He reached out to touch her cheek. 'You must know I love you?'

'Why did you not tell me you had recovered your memory?'

'Because…for the same reason as you did not tell me what a rogue I was. When I realised that you would not withdraw, that you really meant to be my mistress, I was overcome with shame. I am a very rogue for putting you through such torment, Emma. If I had come to you then, I could not have held my self-control. I wanted you so badly that I was afraid of losing my control.'

'I thought I had disgusted you by responding too freely.'

'Oh, my sweet, foolish Emma.'

Lytham reached out and drew her into his arms, kissing her tenderly but with such hunger that she trembled and clung to him, feeling as if she would melt for sheer pleasure.

'How you must have felt when I vanished! You had no home, no money to speak of—and I had put you in an impossible position, which must have led to a loss of respectability if it had been known. It is a wonder that you did not hate me for it.'

'I searched for you every day for as long as there was light,' she said, reaching up to touch his beloved face. 'My life meant nothing to me without you. If your aunt had not come, I think I should have died.'

'And then I would not have wanted to live.'

'You must not fight Lindisfarne! If you should be hurt or killed, I could not bear it.'

'I am reputed to be one of the best swordsmen in London, Emma. I shall not be killed, I promise. Besides, I cannot draw back. It is a matter of honour.'

'Honour be damned,' Emma cried and he laughed huskily, drawing her close to him once more so that she could feel the throbbing heat of his arousal and sensed his need. 'I care nothing for honour, Lytham, and everything for you. That is why I would have been your mistress and counted the world well lost for a little time of love.'

'My sweet, darling Emma,' he murmured, caressing the side of her face with his hand. 'Go to your bed and sleep peacefully, my dear one. The duel cannot take place until after Toby's wedding. I assure you that it will be no more than a fencing lesson to me. I shall bring Lindisfarne to his knees and make him write an abject apology to you.'

'You are so sure?' She gazed into his eyes.

'Return to your bed before I take you to mine, Emma.' He smiled and let her go. 'I think we must bring the day of our wedding forward or I shall go entirely mad.'

Emma laughed. Perhaps she was making too much of it. She had been right the first time—it was merely a contest of skill and honour, which would be satisfied at the first blood.

'You promise me that nothing terrible is going to happen if I leave you?'

'You may sleep and dream of our wedding night,' he said. 'Go now, my love—or I shall not be able to keep from making love to you. And I am determined you shall be my wife before that, Emma.'

She left him then, feeling reassured. Whether she would have slept so peacefully if she had known that Lytham's friends were to wait on him at six the next morning was another matter.

Emma did not wake until the maid brought in her breakfast tray the next morning. She yawned and smiled at the girl, feeling surprised that she had rested so well. Then she realised that things had been settled between her and Lytham and she had no more need to wonder how she would leave him. She would never leave him!

'Thank you, Betsy. You are spoiling me. I had intended to get up and come down for breakfast.'

'It was his lordship's orders, miss. He said you were to be allowed to sleep in—and that I should bring breakfast to you this morning.'

'Well, it is pleasant to be spoiled sometimes. Is Lady Lynston awake yet?'

'Yes, miss. She had her breakfast an hour ago. I think she is writing some letters in the small parlour.'

'Thank you. Please tell her that I shall be down shortly.'

Emma nibbled a sweet roll, glanced through a small pile of notes that had been sent to her, drank her chocolate and then rang for her maid to help her dress. She chose a walking gown of dark green velvet and a hat with a jaunty feather.

'Have you seen his lordship, Betsy? Do you know if he is down yet?'

'I'm not sure, miss. I could ask his man, if you like?'

'No, do not disturb Brunnings. It does not matter,' Emma replied. 'I had promised to go shopping with Lady Lynston. I shall write a note for Lytham and you can give it to Brunnings to deliver.'

'Yes, miss.'

Emma did not notice the look of relief in the girl's eyes. She was feeling much too happy to notice a slight hesitancy in Betsy's manner that morning. At last she had discussed *that* afternoon with Lytham and *he* had apologised. After all her soul searching and fear that he might despise her, it was a relief to know that he had been ashamed of his own behaviour and did not despise her for hers.

She would take him to task for it once all this other silly business was over. How could he have played such a trick on her? Yet she admitted to herself that she had not given him much idea of her true feelings for him until that afternoon. Aspiring mothers and their daughters must have relentlessly pursued him since he had inherited the title and it was little wonder he had doubted her love. Her reckless behaviour that afternoon must have convinced him that it was he she wanted, rather than his fortune.

Her mouth curved in a little smile as she recalled the way he had kissed her the previous night. He was wicked to have kept his recovered memory a secret from her and yet she understood his reasons for they were much the same as her own.

She was still smiling as she went downstairs to join Maria in the parlour. She was staring out of the window and seemed startled as Emma asked if she was ready to go shopping.

'You still mean to go?' she asked.

'Why not?' Emma's blood ran cold as she saw her friend's expression. Had Lytham lied to her about the duel? Her hand crept to her breast as if to still her racing heart. 'He told me the duel would not take place until after Toby's wedding—'

'Of course he did,' Maria said. 'He was afraid of your tears, Emma. It took place at eight this morning. I could not sleep and came down to fetch a book. I heard them talking in the library before they left. Toby was with him and Mr Charlton.'

'But it is already past ten!' Emma cried, her eyes flying to the pretty gilt mantle clock. 'Surely they should be back before now?'

'Yes, I would have expected to hear something by now. Unless…' Maria stopped speaking as she saw Emma's distress. 'But we would have heard if—'

'What is that?' Emma's head went up as she heard voices in the hall. 'Someone has come!' She ran to the door, her heart stopping as she saw Toby and another gentleman supporting Lytham. 'He has been wounded!'

'It is a flesh wound,' Lytham said and straightened up. 'I have lost a little blood, but I shall be better in a day or so.'

She moved towards him, feeling as if she were back in the nightmare of his disappearance. She could not bear this! It was too much. His right arm was in a sling, his shirtsleeve shredded where the blade had torn through it. His coat had been placed over his shoulders to protect him from the cold, but he could not have worn it because his arm was padded and bound with thick bandages.

'You promised me it would not happen,' she said in a voice thick with emotion. 'You said the duel was not until after Toby's wedding.'

'Forgive me, Emma. I did not want you to be awake all night worrying.'

'He needs to rest,' Toby said in an apologetic tone. 'We must get him to his bed.'

'Yes, of course. All this can wait.'

Several servants had come to assist their master and Emma went back into the parlour to join Maria.

'He has been wounded—' she said and broke off on a sob.

'I feared as much, but at least they have brought him home. You need not wonder if he is alive or dead.'

'He looks so pale,' Emma said and Maria came to put an arm about her, holding her until the brief storm of tears was over.

'Lytham has suffered worse and survived,' Toby said, coming into the room as she was drying her tears on Maria's kerchief. 'He served with Wellington, you know. I just wanted to tell you not to worry. I must leave you now. Much to do, you know—wedding tomorrow.'

'Yes, of course. I must thank you for taking care of him.'

'Doctor patched him up. He ain't too bad. Lindisfarne is in a worse case. Touch and go whether he survives, I dare say—not but that he didn't deserve it. Lytham would have retired after pricking him the first time, but he pressed the fight.'

'We must pray that he does survive,' Maria said. 'Lytham might otherwise be in some trouble.'

'We kept it all right and tight, plenty of witnesses to prove that Lindisfarne was at fault. It ain't as easy as it used to be, but Lytham's a favourite with the Regent. Brush through it, I dare say.'

'Providing they both recover,' Emma said with feeling.

'Just so,' Toby agreed and took himself off before she could add to this. 'Hope to see you both tomorrow.'

'Men!' Maria exclaimed as he went out. 'Why must they do these foolish things?'

'Lytham said it was a matter of honour.' Emma's voice broke on a sob. 'I do not know what I shall do if—'

'Begging your pardon, miss,' Betsy said as she came into the parlour at that moment. 'His lordship has asked if you would be so kind as to go up to him.'

'Yes, of course. I shall come at once.'

Emma almost ran from the room, her heart pounding. Had he taken a turn for the worse? She was out of breath when she arrived to discover that he was lying on top of the bed, propped up against a pile of pillows.

'Are you feeling worse?'

'Stop looking so terrified,' he said and smiled at her. 'I

am a little drunk, Emma. They gave me brandy to kill the pain while the surgeon patched me up. I was unable to walk by myself, but once I have had time to rest and drunk some strong coffee, which Brunnings is fetching for me now, I shall be fine. Believe me, Emma, it is no more than a scratch.'

'You wretch!' Emma cried as the relief swept over her. 'I thought you were dying.'

'I know.' The amusement danced in his eyes. 'That's why I asked for you to come as soon as I was settled. I might not be able to stand straight, my love—but I am not so far gone that I did not realise how upset you were.'

'Once we are married I shall not let you out of my sight. You cannot be trusted not to get into trouble!'

'I hope that nothing like this will happen again. I assure you that I do not make a habit of duelling. If Lindisfarne recovers, which I pray he may, I do not think he will be a danger to anyone again.'

'Oh, Lytham,' Emma said, tears trickling down her cheeks. 'Why do I love you so much?'

'Perhaps because you cannot help yourself,' he said softly. 'It is very much the same for me. I think I fell in love with you the day you came home with your hair wind-blown about your face and looked as if you wanted to throw me out of your house. If it was not then, it must have been when you took out that knife and prepared to patch me up after I was shot in the woods. My only regret is that I did not ask you to marry me then and there.'

'I should probably have refused,' Emma said with a rue-ful laugh. 'I was fighting my feelings for you then, and it was not until some time later that I knew I loved you.'

'You were adept at hiding your feelings and caused me much heartache, Emma Sommerton.'

'I am sure I have never caused you the least trouble,' she replied.

'That, my love,' he murmured as he held out his hand to her, 'is palpably not the case…'

Chapter Fourteen

'You are surely not intending to accompany us?' Emma asked as she saw Lytham come down the stairs the next morning. 'I am sure Toby would understand your reasons for not attending his wedding.'

'I dare say he might,' Lytham replied. 'But I have no intention of missing it. This coat is not the one I had intended to wear, but it will suffice. At least I was able to get it on, which did not please Brunnings for he has always disliked it. It has no style, you see.'

'You look well enough,' Emma said, her eyes moving over him with love as she recognised that mocking smile in his eyes. He was certainly himself again! 'But I think you foolish when you might be resting.'

'I believe you had a letter from Italy today, my love,' he said, changing the subject. 'Tom told me had sent it on to you—from your mother, one would suppose.'

'Provoking creature!' Emma cried, her eyes flashing at him. 'But, yes, the letter was from my mother—she writes to tell me she thinks she will stay in Italy for a year or two. She has made some friends there—the Count Grattini and his sister Maria. I believe there is a possibility that she may marry again.'

'Then she will not return for our wedding,' Lytham said, looking thoughtful. 'We must write and let her know when it is, of course, but perhaps we might take a trip to Italy ourselves—if you would like that?'

'Could we really?' Emma said, looking at him excitedly. 'I think I should like that very much.'

'It could be a part of our honeymoon trip,' he said. 'And it may be a good idea if we were to marry as soon as possible, quietly, and then leave the country for some months.'

Emma looked at him anxiously. 'What have you heard? Has Lindisfarne…?'

'I do not think so. However, I have been advised by a letter, which comes from the Regent's secretary, that it might be better if I were to remove myself from town for a few months. I do not think that I shall be charged with any offence, but to save making more scandal it might be better to comply with Prinny's request. He has made quite a thing of stamping out the practice of duelling and he cannot be seen to take sides in this. The newspapers delight in scurrilous attacks on him, without my making things worse. In a few months we may return and it will all be forgotten. Especially if Lindisfarne recovers, which I trust he will.'

'Yes, I see.' Emma gazed up at him. 'You know that I am ready to marry you whenever you wish, my love—and I would prefer a small private ceremony in any event.'

'Then we shall arrange it for next week by special licence at Lytham,' he said. 'A few of our closest friends may care to come; as for the others, we shall not mind if they prefer not to know us for the moment.'

'That is just what I want,' Emma said. 'I shall enjoy being a guest at Toby's and Lucy's wedding, but I would not want to have such an affair for myself.'

'Then if we are agreed I think we should leave before Maria grows tired of waiting for us.' Lytham said and offered her his good arm.

'You look wonderful,' Lady Agatha said, her eyes misty as she saw Emma dressed in her wedding gown. 'That pearly grey looks so well on you, my dear, and just a touch of midnight blue on the bonnet—charming.'

'Lytham saw this bonnet in town and bought it for me,' Emma said. 'I thought it would look well with the dress. He is forever buying me things.'

'It is very dashing,' Maria said and came to kiss her. 'And just right for a quiet country wedding.'

'Thank you,' Emma replied and smiled. Maria had promised to keep a friendly but unobtrusive eye on Lady Agatha while they were away, and a new companion had been hired who was to travel to Lytham after the wedding to take up her post. 'I think we should go down now, don't you? I do not wish to keep Lytham waiting.'

'Pooh!' Agatha Lynston said. 'It will not do him the slightest harm to wait a few minutes for his bride. He has kept me waiting for this day far too long.' She smiled and patted Emma's cheek with her gloved hand. 'But I have no fault to find with his chosen bride.'

Emma gave her a quick hug, which made her maid exclaim and fuss round her, repairing the damage to her toilette. Then they all trooped downstairs to where the carriages were waiting.

Lytham Church was small, hardly big enough to hold the sixty guests that had been invited—none had refused—and a crowd of well-wishers from the estate had gathered outside to cheer the bride as she arrived.

Tom was with her and he smiled cheerily at her. His future brother-in-law, who had managed to secure a confession from the man who had once accused him of cheating, had solved his most pressing problem.

'That is where I went the night I cried off taking you to the dance,' Lytham had confided to her when they returned from attending Toby and Lucy's wedding. 'I was asked to meet someone, who I may say was in hiding from his creditors. Apparently, it was not the first time he had been in Queer Street and he told me that my brother John had paid him to accuse Tom of cheating.'

'I suppose you paid him to sign his confession?' Emma asked, but received only an enigmatic smile.

'Provoking creature!' Emma cried, but she had not been cross with him. How could she when he had managed to secure the proof of Tom's innocence?

It was all she needed to complete her happiness and she suspected that it might not be too long before there was another wedding in the family.

Entering the church on her brother's arm, Emma saw Lytham waiting for her with Stephen Antrium at his side. It was another proof of his loyalty, she thought, for there must have been a dozen gentlemen he could have asked to stand up with him, but since he could not have Toby (who was, of course, on his honeymoon) as his best man, he had chosen his agent. Something that she knew had pleased Stephen Antrium very much indeed.

As she began to walk down the aisle towards him, Lytham turned his head to watch for her and the look of love he gave her made Emma's heart beat wildly. She had never believed that she could ever be so happy or that she would be loved this much.

Even the sun managed to break through the clouds, penetrating the gloom of the old church and sending showers of colour from the stained-glass windows onto the flagstones.

And then the bells were ringing out joyfully as she walked out of the church on her husband's arms, to be met by a shower of dried rose petals. A little girl came forward shyly to present her with a token tied up with blue ribbons, and several had posies of winter flowers.

Emma's own flowers had been grown at Lytham and were Christmas roses and some fragile fern from the hothouses, tied up with trailing lace. When all the villagers had paid their tributes, Lytham handed Emma into the carriage and scattered coins for the children. Emma waved as the horses moved off, and then turned to her husband with a smile.

'Well, my love,' he said and reached across to touch her cheek. 'Are you happy?'

'You know that I am,' she replied. 'This is the happiest day of my life.'

'There will be others equally as happy,' he promised and laughed ruefully. 'If I kissed you as I would like, I should ruin your gown. So I shall wait until we are alone.' He took her hand, turning it up to drop a kiss within the palm. 'Hold that until later.'

'I shall give it back to you,' Emma promised. 'You ask if I am happy—what of you, my husband? Are you content with your bride?'

'Do you need to ask?' he murmured huskily. 'Look at me like that, Emma, and you will not see much of your guests.'

'Behave yourself,' she warned, tapping his knee in mock reprimand. 'We have the rest of our lives to indulge ourselves, Lytham. We must not disappoint our friends, for some of them have travelled a considerable distance to be with us.'

'Indeed, you do right to chide me,' he said, a wicked glint in his eyes. 'For I am sorely tempted, my lady.'

Emma shook her head at him, but her heart was racing. If truth were told, she could hardly wait to be alone with him.

'At last,' Lytham said as the carriage taking them to the house where they were to stay for a few days before beginning their journey to Italy. 'I quite thought we should never be able to escape!'

'My impatient love,' Emma said and leaned over to brush her lips against his. He seized her, pressing her close and kissing her hungrily. 'But I must admit that I almost lost my patience with Aunt Agatha at the end. She kept remembering things she thought I ought to know about you, Lytham.'

'I hope she did not tell you what a terrible rogue I was?'

'Oh, yes,' Emma assured him naughtily. 'She has told me that many times, but I am well aware of your faults, my lord.'

He put a finger to her lips. 'Lytham,' he commanded. 'Or Alex if you wish. Anything but "my lord"!'

'I shall know exactly how to punish you if you displease me,' Emma teased and reached up to stroke his cheek.

'I hope that I shall never displease you,' Lytham said. 'I trust that you do not mind returning to my mother's house for our wedding night? It is but a short journey and I did not want to share you with others.'

'I think I shall like the house, if only we can exorcise the dreadful memories of that time,' Emma said. 'Besides, it is convenient for our ship and, as long as you do not decide to go walking alone, I shall be content.'

'If you think that anything will keep me from your bed this time,' Lytham said, 'you are sadly mistaken, madam.'

And nothing did keep him. He came to her with love in his eyes, pulling her hard against him to kiss her tenderly, his hands caressing the nape of her neck, then travelling down, pressing her against him. The passion flamed between them and Lytham swept her up in his arms, carrying her to the bed. The ghosts of the past were exorcised as he made love to her, tenderly at first but then with a hunger that consumed them both, carrying them to a far shore.

Afterwards, they lay in each other's arms, touching and kissing, whispering their secrets until the desire flamed once more.

'You are so beautiful,' he whispered as he bent his head, his tongue flicking at the rosy peaks of her breasts, sending thrills of pleasure through her entire body. She arched sensuously, feeling the burn of his arousal against her thigh, knowing that he wanted her again, and that she wanted him as urgently. Her hands moved down the firm contours of his back, tracing the scars that bore witness to earlier injuries that she had never guessed were there, her lips pressing against his shoulder as her breath came faster. 'I never lived until I met you, Emma. You are the mistress of my heart, my world, and my heaven.'

'You are everything to me,' she said. 'I had no hope of finding happiness until you began to take an interest in me. When you asked me to be your mistress I knew that even a few weeks or months of being with you meant more than a lifetime without you. To be your wife is more happiness than I could ever imagine.'

He pulled her against him, his hands moving down the silken arch of her back, cupping her buttocks so that she was conscious of his throbbing arousal, hot and hard as she curled into his body. There was no need for words, because the tenderness and love between them was saying all that they would ever want to hear.

Giving herself up to his loving, Emma smiled in the

darkness. She wanted nothing more than this man, to be with him like this, to be his wife and, if God blessed them, to bear his children.

*   *   *   *   *

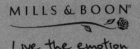

MILLS & BOON®

Live the emotion

Historical Romance™

THE VISCOUNT'S BRIDE
by Ann Elizabeth Cree

Faced with her guardian's unsavoury choice of husband or the
comfortable love of a sensible man, Lady Chloe determines on a
sensible match. But she hasn't counted on Brandt, Lord
Salcombe, thwarting her plans. It's not as if the wild and
passionate Brandt is ideal husband material himself!

Regency

HER GUARDIAN KNIGHT
by Joanna Makepeace

Medieval England

Rosamund Kinnersley first met Sir Simon Cauldwell on a
battlefield – and, though she fought for her honour, could not
deny one mad moment of longing to give in to his passion. Now
Rosamund and her brother are orphaned, and Simon is the
enemy knight appointed to act as their guardian!

THE HEART'S WAGER by Gayle Wilson

Colonel Devon Burke was determined to find the man to whom he
owed his life – and the mysterious, beautiful Julie de Valme seemed
his only hope for success. Julie's life had been destroyed the night
of her father's death – and now the one man she had come to trust
was blind to the woman she was beneath her disguise…

Regency

On sale 6th February 2004

*Available at most branches of WHSmith, Tesco, Martins, Borders,
Eason, Sainsbury's and all good paperback bookshops.*

0104/04